THE MOCKERY BIRD

GERALD DURRELL

THE MOCKERY BIRD

COLLINS
St James's Place, London
1981

William Collins Sons & Co Ltd
London · Glasgow · Sydney · Auckland
Toronto · Johannesburg

British Library Cataloguing in Publication Data
Durrell, Gerald.
The mockery bird.
I. Title
823′.914[F]   PR6054.U/

ISBN 0-00-222603-0

First published 1981
© Gerald Durrell 1981

Photoset in Imprint
Made and Printed in Great Britain by
William Collins Sons & Co Ltd, Glasgow

This book is for Lee

Chapter One

ZENKALI REVEALED

At the uttermost rim of the sea, on the imaginary line where the waters of the Indian and Pacific Oceans meet and merge, lies the island of Zenkali, a green and pleasant place, so remote that you would think that it could neither affect the outside world nor be influenced by it. Yet once, for two months in its history, Zenkali kept the whole of the civilised world enthralled, and a good deal of the uncivilised world in the shape of newspaper men, television commentators and the like. Needless to say, the price for thus flamboyantly occupying the world stage was a stiff one, and even today (though most of the wounds have healed over, the scars are still tender) you may acquire a black eye – or worse – down in the Mother Carey's Chickens, if you mention the matter, and in the newly built English Club people will start moving pointedly away from you if you have the bad taste to mention the Mockery Bird.

It all started in January. The islanders as usual had overeaten and overdrunk during the Christmas festivities and were now suffering the liver pangs associated with the patriotic gesture of eating roast turkey and plum pudding in a temperature slightly above ninety in the shade. The island lay dreaming in white sunlight, guarded by the cones of its two volcanoes, Timbalu and Matakama. Not one of the islanders (all busy with Alka-Seltzer and bicarbonate of soda) dreamt that fate was propelling across the vast ocean towards them something more deadly than a hurricane, more dampening than a tidal wave and more rearranging than an earthquake. It was twice as deadly for being so innocent in appearance, like a Pekinese puppy with hydrophobia. It was embodied in the tall, charming, blond Peter Foxglove, Esq., the new Assistant to H.M. Political Advisor.

On arrival in Djakarta, Peter had been alarmed to find that the vessel that was to take him to Zenkali was a converted French sardine boat of uncertain age and seaworthiness, run by a rotund, unshaven Greek called Aristotle Pappayatocopoulous, assisted in a gay but totally unseamanlike way by a crew of Zenkalis, who seemed to treat the whole idea of setting off across the ocean in a highly suspect craft with all the unprofessional enthusiasm of a group of Boy Scouts setting off across a pond in a leaking canoe. Everyone shouted instructions to everyone else, none of which anyone obeyed, and the whole thing was made all the more worrying by the fact that the good ship *Andromada III* had such a heavy list to starboard that a marble or any other circular object placed on the deck would at once have trickled to the rails and plopped into the greasy waters of the harbour. Peter's collection of pale cream calf-skin suitcases, chosen with such care at Assinders and Grope, tropical outfitters in London, obviously failed to impress the Zenkali crew; they were picked up, thrown to and fro between brown hands, scraped along the rail or any other handy protuberance, and finally dropped unceremoniously on the foredeck on top of a gently steaming pile of guano. Peter realised for the first time the drawbacks of not having a grasp of pidgin English, the lingua franca of Zenkali.

'I say, you there,' he said in what he hoped was a firm tone of voice, addressing a Zenkali who appeared to be slightly more intelligent than the others, 'are you the Mate?'

The Zenkali was a stalwart young man wearing battered trousers, a disintegrating straw hat and a handful of Coca-Cola bottle tops strung round his neck as a necklace. He removed his hat with an exquisitely polite gesture and held it clasped to his chest, while exposing a superb set of teeth which flashed in an enormous smile of good will.

'Are you the Mate?' Peter enquired again.

'Sah?' asked the boy, contriving to smile while at the same time frowning worriedly.

'Are you the Mate of this ship?' queried Peter for the third time, speaking very slowly and clearly.

'Ship!' said the boy, beaming, 'Yes, sah.'

'*You're* the Mate?'

'Yes, sah . . . ship,' said the boy, patting his hat.

The sweat was pouring down Peter's face and back. His handsome white ducks were now a dirty grey and the creases that had been in them when he had put them on some two hours previously had vanished. The cloth now hung limp and creased about him, looking as though it had been slept in by a dinosaur suffering from insomnia. Above all things, Peter wanted to get out of the sun, change into something dry and have a cool drink.

'What's your name?' he asked, trying another tack.

'Andromada Tree,' said the boy, unhesitatingly.

'Andromada? But that's a girl's name . . . oh, I see, you mean the *ship*'s called Andromada?'

'Yes, sah, ship,' said the boy happily, thus bringing the conversation full circle.

Peter wiped his face and throat on a sodden handkerchief and tried again.

'Me passenger,' he said, pointing at himself and feeling extremely silly. 'Me want cabin . . . me want hand luggage taken to cabin . . . me want cool drink . . . me passenger, savvy?'

'Me Andromada Tree,' the boy repeated, obviously feeling worried that Peter had not grasped this important point.

However, before Peter could call upon the Almighty to strike the boy dead, the Captain suddenly materialised at his elbow, exuding such a strong aroma of garlic that it made itself felt even above the combined odours of copra, guano and the six extremely reluctant cows that the Zenkali deck hands were now trying to chivvy on board with loud and melodious cries.

'Sir,' said the Captain, in a voice so deep and rich that it seemed to reverberate up from the engine room, 'I am the Captain, Aristotle Pappayatocopoulous. Me, I am at your service. People they call me Captain Pappas because they have exceeding difficulty in mispronouncing my name.'

'*Mispronouncing* your name?' asked Peter, thinking he had misheard.

'Yes, sir,' said the Captain, 'always they are having difficulty because they are mispronouncing my name.'

Peter began to feel that conversation with Captain Pappas was going to be as rewarding as the one he had just had with the supposed Mate.

'I am very pleased to meet you, Captain,' he said, 'my name is . . .'

'Rumba, Tango, Waltz,' interrupted the Captain, his face screwed up in thought, 'Polka, Faststep . . . no, no, . . . *Quickstep* . . . Palais Gliding, Lancers, Minuet, Foxtrot!'

'I beg your pardon?' said Peter.

'Do not be sorry, Mr. Foxtrot,' said the Captain, 'I am remembering your name with mnemonics . . . is Greek, you understand . . . mnemonics for remembering.'

'But my name is not Foxtrot,' said Peter, puzzled.

'Is not?' said the Captain, screwing up his eyes in astonishment. 'What is then, Veleta, maybe, eh? Maybe is Paso Doble, eh?'

'No,' said Peter firmly, 'my name is not Paso Doble, it is Foxglove.'

'Foxglove . . . *Foxglove*?' Captain Pappas stared at him in disbelief. 'Where they dance this Foxglove?'

'You don't dance it . . . it's a sort of . . . well, it's a kind of flower,' explained Peter, feeling the inadequacies of his name for the first time in his life.

'Flower . . . you mean flower like in gardens?' asked the Captain.

'Yes,' said Peter.

The Captain leaned his bulk up against the rails and closed his eyes.

'Foxglove,' he intoned in a deep authoritative voice, 'Foxglove, Rose, Hibiscus, Dahlia, Golden Rods, Pansy, *Foxglove*.'

'I wonder if . . .' began Peter.

'Bougainvillaea, Tulip, Sunflower, Bluebell,' the Captain continued, oblivious, displaying a breadth of botanical knowledge that seemed likely to keep him there indefinitely. 'Begonia, Sweetest Williams, Buttercup, Foxglove.'

He opened his tiny black eyes and beamed at Peter.

'Now I am remembering your name always,' he said triumphantly, 'always she is in my memory. This is an excellent way to remember, no? It Greek way . . . excellent . . . the best, eh?'

'Excellent,' said Peter, heartily, 'and now I wonder if it would be too much trouble to show me to my cabin, have my luggage taken to it and then get me a cold drink?'

'Of course, of course,' said the Captain, 'I get Kalaki to show you cabin . . . I fix everything . . . don't you worry about a damn thing.'

He shouted a string of instructions in what Peter took to be rapid pidgin English which seemed to be understood by the boy that presumably was the Mate. He immediately got two companions and between them they picked up the baggage and disappeared into the bowels of the ship with it.

'Follow them, kind sir,' said the Captain with a grandiloquent gesture, 'they will show you your cabin . . . best cabin on the ship . . . best cabin for new Assisting Officer.'

'You know who I am?' asked Peter in surprise.

The Captain laughed loudly, throwing back his head and displaying in all its glory a sort of dental Fort Knox flashing between his full lips. He laid a fat finger along his pockmarked nose, pointing at his glittering little eye.

'I know everything that happens in Zenkali. I knows everythings and everyone. Like the good Lord my eyes is everywhere, and not a camel falleth to the ground without someone she tells me. Anything you want in Zenkali, you just let me know.'

'Thank you very much,' said Peter. Then, with the Captain's fat hand propelling him gently, he found himself stumbling down a greasy companionway, into the dark and noisy depths of the little ship, which smelt strongly of bilge water, paint and, for some obscure reason, Parma Violets.

The three-day voyage on the *Andromada III* gave Peter ample time to bitterly regret the fact that he had not waited to travel to Zenkali on the *Empress of Asia*, a larger passenger boat that visited the island once a month. As *Andromada III* lurched and shuddered her way across the ocean he also began to regret that he had been so eager to agree to taking this post in the first place. Lying in his coffin-like bunk, he remembered how flattered he had been when his uncle had given him the news.

'We're sending you to Zenkali,' Sir Osbert had said, surveying his only living relative with a cold blue eye through his monocle, 'and I don't want you to get into any trouble there.'

'Good Lord, Uncle, that's marvellous,' Peter had said, enthusiastically. He had a friend, one Hugo Charteris, who had spent a month in Zenkali and had come back raving about its charms like a demented travel agent.

'We are not sending you out there on holiday,' said Sir Osbert, acidly, 'you are to assist that fool Oliphant.'

He started to pace up and down his office. Outside, snow was falling and London rumbled and roared through veils of lace-like flakes.

'The situation in Zenkali is . . . er . . . um . . . difficult,' confessed Sir Osbert. 'As you know, they have been promised self-government . . . or, to be more accurate, power is going to fall into the hands of that ridiculous monarch of theirs, King Tamalawala the Third.'

'I thought he was supposed to be rather good news as far as kings go,' said Peter, 'progressive and so forth.'

'The man is a clown,' snapped Sir Osbert, 'a perfect example of what you get when you send a cannibal to Eton. He is – not to put too fine a point on it – a bounder. And when you get a wog who is a bounder, believe me you get a bounder and a half. When we ruled Zenkali, we could keep him under some control, but now . . . but now . . .'

He picked up an ebony ruler from his desk and beat the palm of his hand with it in suppressed fury.

'The quack says I'm not to get excited . . . the old ticker, d'you see? But I said to him "How d'you expect me to remain calm when the government is chuckin' away the Empire piecemeal?" '

He paused for a moment, breathing deeply. Peter said nothing. His views were diametrically opposed to his uncle's and had caused dissension in the past. He did not want to scotch his chances of going to Zenkali.

'The Empire, I would remind you, for which we Foxgloves fought and died,' his uncle went on. 'Now, with your flippant modern ideas you might think this unimportant, but I assure you it is not. Do you realise that at every important event in English history and the formation of the Empire a Foxglove has been present?'

'Yes, Uncle,' said Peter, 'but you shouldn't get excited.'

'Agincourt had a Foxglove, Battle of Trafalgar had a Foxglove . . . Waterloo had a Foxglove; Australia, New Zealand, riddled with Foxgloves . . . India full of 'em . . . North West Frontier practically held single-handed by Foxgloves . . . Africa overflowing with them. Then we got that damned Labour Government into power and they started giving away the Empire like a . . . like a lot of old clothes. It's enough to give one a heart attack, watching these inept grocers' sons, trade unionists and other prinked-up peasantry, wandering about Whitehall, dropping aspirates like snowflakes, dishing out the Empire to a lot of people who haven't even stopped eating their own grandmothers yet.'

He sat down at his desk and mopped his face with his handkerchief.

'Well,' he went on when he was calmer, 'the tricky part of the situation is this: just as we're about to give these people self-government the Chiefs of Staff decide that Zenkali is of military importance. Want to keep the Russians out of the Indian Ocean, or some such thing. Damned ridiculous; place is just a fly-dropping on the map. Anyway, there's a great to-do. They want to build an airstrip and then blow a hole in the reef so they can get a destroyer into the bay. But this means they have to flood some valleys and create a hydro-electric scheme. They tried to get Aldabra for it, but they were prevented by a lot of fluffy minded animal lovers. The world's gone *mad* . . . imagine it, the British Armed Forces not getting what they want because of a lot of bloody Giant Tortoises! I ask you, whatever next? Would a lot of Giant Tortoises have helped us on the Somme? Or in the Battle of Britain? Would they have helped at Trafalgar, or lumbering about at Jutland? I tell you, people have no sense of proportion nowadays.'

'So what's going to happen?' asked Peter, fascinated.

'Well, negotiations are going on, but the King is a wily black, I can tell you; they teach them that sort of thing at Eton,' said Sir Osbert, who was a Rugby man. 'He'll drive a hard bargain, mark my words. He knows he's got us where he wants us because of a lot of blasted reptiles. I ask you, the British Government being blackmailed because of a lot of tortoises, bah!'

'Would the airstrip be a good thing for Zenkali?' asked Peter.

'Of course it would. Just what they need . . . a lot of sailors and airmen, fine upstanding lads, spending their money on souvenirs and . . . er . . . er . . . well, all the things sailors and airmen spend money on. Then there's the hydro-electric scheme . . . that'll provide employment. The whole thing will be excellent for the island, mark my words, in spite of what that imbecile Oliphant says. But the situation is ticklish. King hasn't agreed yet. Big names involved, you know. Lord Hammer . . . Hammersteins and Gallop . . . they're going to do the dam and so forth . . . at least, it's got to go out to tender, of course, but it's just a formality, really. Anyway, the situation, as I say, is delicate in the extreme and so I don't want you rockin' the boat, d'you hear?'

'Yes, sir,' said Peter, dutifully.

'I just want you to keep your eyes and ears open and report back to me if there is anything untoward going on, d'you see. You simply can't be too careful when dealing with a bunch of wogs.'

So now Peter was on the high seas, on his way to Zenkali and wondering dismally whether he would be buried at sea by a mourning Captain Pappas. Presently, since his stomach had nothing left in it to bring up, he fell into a fitful sleep.

He awoke next morning to find that the storm had blown itself out, and that the ship was now chugging across an azure sea as smooth as a mirror. The sky was delphinium blue, little flocks of Flying Fish leapt from the glittering sea and glided before the bows and, at the stern, two albatrosses hung motionless in the air, but keeping pace with the ship effortlessly, as if anchored to the stern by invisible cords. Feeling much better and cheered by the weather, Peter made his way to the tiny saloon in search of breakfast. He found Captain Pappas already ensconced, avidly devouring an enormous and exceptionally greasy plate of bacon, eggs, sausages, beans and fried bread.

'Good morning, good morning,' cried the Captain jovially, his mouth full, 'you sleep well, eh?'

'Yes, thank you,' Peter lied, averting his eyes from the Captain's plate with a shudder.

'Good, good,' said the Captain, 'now you have good breakfast, eh? Plenty bacon and eggs, no? I got damn good cook on my ship, he cook anything.'

'Thank you, but I don't eat breakfast,' said Peter hastily, 'I'll just have some coffee and toast, if I may.'

The Captain roared an order and coffee and toast appeared. The Captain, picking his goldmine of teeth with a split matchstick, watched Peter with a fatherly eye.

'So,' he said at last, 'you never been Zenkali before?'

'No, never. I understand it's a lovely island.'

'She is beautiful; very, very beautiful. She is so beautiful that almost she is like a Greek island. But, of course, not like Greece . . . no, no . . . she is full of this niggers, you understand? They all right, but they very primitive. Not civilised like Greeks, you understand?'

'Yes,' said Peter, wondering how the local Zenkalis took to being called niggers on the eve of self-determination. 'I understand they're getting self-government soon?'

'Self-government . . . *self-government*?' roared Captain Pappas. 'Is not self-government for the Zenkalis. No, no, Mr. Foxtrot, is only self-government for Kingy.'

'Kingy? What's Kingy?' asked Peter, giving up any attempt to get the Captain to memorise his name.

'Kingy is the King,' said the Captain, astonished by Peter's ignorance.

'And you call him Kingy? Isn't that rather like . . . well . . . lèse-majesté?'

'What?' asked the Captain, never having come across this phrase before.

'Well, isn't it rather rude to call him Kingy?'

'No, is not rude. He call himself Kingy. Is . . . how you say . . . a nuckname.'

'A nickname?'

'Maybe that too,' said the Captain doubtfully, 'everyone, she call him Kingy. You see, Mr. Foxtrot,' Captain Pappas went on, 'there are two tribes on Zenkali, the Fangouas and the Ginkas, eh? Fangouas are the biggest tribe . . . maybe fifty thousand people. Kingy is King for the Fangouas, you understand. Ginka tribe very small . . . maybe five . . . six thousand people. They got Chief Gowsa Manalowoba. Fangouas being biggest tribe they rule Zenkali. Fangouas no like Ginkas and Ginkas no like Fangouas. When Zenkali gets self-government, the government will be Kingy, you see? Kingy very, very clever man. He want to rule all of the people all of the time, like Abraham Lincoln, you understand?'

'But don't they have a Parliament . . . a sort of Legislative Assembly in which they are all represented?' asked Peter.

'Oh, yes, they have Parliament, but the Parliament, she do what Kingy say.'

'That sounds very undemocratic.'

The Captain beamed like a gold searchlight. 'Yes, in Zenkali we have democracy of one; is Kingy.'

'Do you know anything about this airstrip?' asked Peter, cautiously.

'Yes. Is big swindle,' said Captain Pappas with the faintest tinge of Greek envy in his voice, 'is swindle by that black bastard, Looja. He Minister of Development. He biggest crook on Zenkali. Nobody like Looja. Everybody hate his guts. Even his own mother hate his guts because he swindled her, too.'

'But why is he Minister of Development if he's a crook?'

'I don't know, Kingy made him Minister.'

'And what's the swindle?' Peter asked.

'To have airstrip there must be more electricity. Now Zenkali only got small generator, enough for town. But always she is breaking down, eh? Well, so they need more electricity so they are going to make a dam up on Matakama . . . she volcano. They build dam in valley, eh? And which bastard you think own valley? Looja.'

'But if he owns the valley and they put the dam there, that's not a swindle,' said Peter, puzzled.

'Looja did not have valley last years,' said the Captain, 'only when they start talk about airstrip he buy valley. He buy valley very cheap because no one want valley. Now they must have valley, Looja will sell valley to Government for plenty. This for Minister of Development is swindle.'

'Yes, I see what you mean,' said Peter, thoughtfully.

'Now,' said Captain Pappas, closing one eye and holding up a fat finger, 'swindle number twos. If they are making dam they must get many different firms to give them prices, you understand?'

'It has to go out to tender?'

'Something like that. Then the Government choose cheapest firm, no? But Looja has already promised a firm they get the job. So Looja will pretend that they ask all these other firms, and Looja will say that this firm is cheapest. Is not cheapest. I know. I got friends in Djakarta tells me this. Looja get paid plenty, plenty by this big company in England. So he get money for valley *and* money for dam. He is damn bloody bastard swindler.'

The Captain sat back and gazed at Peter mournfully, trying to look – rather unsuccessfully – like a man who would never try and perpetrate such a swindle.

'But if you have proof, why doesn't someone tell Kingy?' asked Peter. 'After all, the man is Minister of Development and, if this is true, all he is developing is his own bank balance.'

'Har!' said the Captain, moodily picking his teeth, 'no use to tell Kingy. Maybe Kingy get money from Looja.'

'Will the airstrip be good for Zenkali?' Peter enquired.

'She is good thing for *me*,' said the Captain. 'I bring cement, bricks, all sorts of things for building; I am bringing all sorts of tins for food; I am bringing all sorts of juke boxes for sailors. I buy, very cheap, fifty juke boxes in Djakarta. I sell them to Mother Carey's Chickens.'

'Mother Carey's Chickens?' queried Peter, 'what on earth's that?'

'She a bar, how you say in England . . . a pub, no? She on docks at Zenkali. All sailors go there to drink and have nice girls, you understand?'

Peter said he understood.

'So when Zenkali get airstrip and British Fleet and Airforce come to Zenkali, plenty of sailors and airmen go to Mother Carey's Chickens, and they listen to my juke boxes, they drink plenty beer I bring from Djakarta, they have plenty girls and so I bring penicillin for the Doctor. Airstrip is good for my business, you understand?'

Peter said he had no idea that an airstrip could have so many ramifications.

'Well,' said the Captain, stretching and yawning, 'I go

on bridge now. Later we drink together, before lunch, eh?'

'Thank you,' said Peter, 'I shall enjoy that.'

After the Captain had left him, Peter made his way up on to the deck, found a dilapidated deckchair and stretched out in the sun. He started to read a book he had acquired just before he left England. It had been privately printed on flimsy rice paper in Singapore, and it was entitled *ZENKALI – A Fragmentary Guide for the Casual Visitor.* The author had concealed his true name under the sobriquet 'Capricorn'. It rapidly became apparent why the writer had taken this precaution. If Peter had expected an ordinary sort of guide book, his fears were set at rest by the opening sentence of the Introduction.

'Zenkali,' vouchsafed Capricorn, *'is one of the most charming, idiotic, frustrating, stupid and delicious islands it has ever been my delight to visit. In a lifetime spent collecting idiotic islands, I confess I have never come across one with so many ingredients of lunacy mixed together in one small spot. Suffice it to say that, upon my arrival in Zenkali, I was entranced to find almost the entire population of the capital assembled in the main square. They were not assembled for any religious or political motives, but were merely gazing with deep interest at a group of firemen, in the most resplendent uniforms and helmets, who were endeavouring (in a rather desultory way) to put out their fire-engine which had, by some mysterious means, caught fire and was blazing away. Since then I have resided in Zenkali for over twenty years and, though it has never quite risen again to the heights of the fire-engine conflagration, it has provided me with many surprising insights into human nature and many thought-provoking incidents.'*

After this introduction, the guide itself should turn out to be something of a novelty, Peter thought.

'The Island of Zenkali lies on the Tropic of Capricorn athwart the entirely spurious borderline between the

Indian and Pacific Oceans, Long.77 Lat.20. It fortunately lies outside the cyclone and hurricane areas and so enjoys a tranquil existence compared to other islands in these waters. There are, roughly speaking, two seasons; hot and very hot. They tend to merge into each other, depending on the strength of the trade winds, but generally, it is hot from January to June and very hot for the other months. The island is a hundred miles long by twenty-five broad at its widest point. Shaped roughly like a capital C lying face downwards, its carunculated topography is dominated by the defunct volcanoes, Timbalu and Matakama, the latter being the larger and having a fair sized crater lake in its cone. Owing to the universally sex-starved condition of all mariners in the early days of world exploration these two prominent peaks prompted the Arabs (first to discover the island in 1224) to call it "Isle of Houris' Breasts". The Portuguese who followed them (1464) were less poetic and called it "Isle of Two Breasts". The Dutch, taking the island in 1670, displayed little imagination and called the place "Hausfrau Klingle". This did show, however, that they too recognised the biological configuration of the landscape. When the Dutch abandoned the island in 1700 it was taken over by the French who, presumably finding that they could not improve on the mammary nomenclature that had gone before, called it simply "Isle de Poitrine". Finally, when the British took the island from the French (1818) they rechristened it "Welcome Island". Now the island has reverted to the original name given to it by its original owners, Zenkali, which simply means "Pleasant Island" which indeed it is.'

The writer went on to deal with the various occupations of the island caustically and concisely.

'The succeeding waves of foreigners that occupied the island left practically nothing behind that was of any use to the indigenous inhabitants. The Arabs introduced the Abacus, which, for a people who could neither read, write or count beyond five, was a gift of dubious value.

The Portuguese left two coastal forts, which rapidly disintegrated, and a method of making wine (now called Zenkali Nectar) from a species of local plum. This is almost undrinkable and if imbibed in sufficient quantities, it is said to have a disastrous effect on both one's eyesight and sexual prowess. The French left the docks, which are quite solid and good, and an endless series of recipes based on the local fauna, most of which they had exterminated by their culinary activities before they left. The Dutch left behind the fine solid buildings that now constitute Government House, the King's Palace, the Administrative Headquarters and the Parliament building. There are also one or two very nice Dutch planters' houses dotted about the island. They are, of course, no use to any but the European inhabitants, since the Zenkalis prefer to live (as they have for centuries) in their excellent palm thatch houses (resembling the Bornean Long Houses) or else in rather attractive clapboard houses neatly made from Amela wood. It is to be feared that when the English finally depart they will leave behind them, as usual, an abiding sense of confusion, a fanatical reverence for the game of cricket and a determination on the part of the Zenkalis to always celebrate the Queen's Birthday and Burns Night, since they have no such celebrations of their own and have, in the past, derived much innocent amusement from watching the solemnity with which their rulers indulged in these two curious functions.'

Peter wondered, not for the first time in his career, why it was that the Europeans would never leave well alone, why it was that they were so determined that other races should behave in exactly the same way as they behaved. Why inflict – of all dreary and incomprehensible celebrations – Burns Night on the unfortunate Zenkalis? He presumed that all other forms of activity, more liable to lead to licentiousness, had been stamped out by the missionaries. It was too much to hope that there had been no missionaries in Zenkali's history. He flipped to the section in the guide marked 'Religion' and found that the author shared his views on the inadvisability of letting missionaries loose in foreign climes.

'*It has always been the unhappy fate of the so-called Heathen to be badgered and bewildered by the religious convictions of his conquerors. In the case of Zenkali the occupying forces were, fortunately, too busy fighting wars or exploiting the island to worry overmuch about the immortal souls of its inhabitants. The Arabs obviously thought that the Zenkalis might be more of a liability than an asset to Mahomet and so (apart from taking some of the more attractive boys and girls with them when they left) they could not be said to have had a far-reaching effect. The Portuguese built a couple of churches. The Dutch built more churches but would not let the Zenkalis into them. This seemed to suit the Zenkalis very well. During this period the smaller tribe, the Ginkas, worshipped Tambaca, the Fish God, personified by the dolphin. This is, of course, a mammal, but worse flaws than this have been smoothed over in other religions. The Fangoua tribe – before the advent of the French – worshipped a curious endemic bird which they called Tio-Namala and which the French christened l'Oiseau Moquerie, loosely translated as the Mockery Bird. However, the French being Catholic and therefore of an impatient nature when it came to other peoples' beliefs, very soon discovered that the Mockery Bird was exceptionally good to eat and so, by the time they were vanquished by the British and gave up the island, they had, as it were, eaten the Mockery Bird to extinction in spite of protests from the Fangouas. Thus, for some time, this tribe was forced to curtail all religious activities. With the British came a change. European nations, when they invade small islands, bring with them noxious familiars in the shape of dogs, cats, rats, goats, pigs and so on, which harry and extirpate the local fauna, while their missionaries harass the local population. However, in this case, the missionaries proved to be (if I may use the phrase) a God-send as far as the Fangouas were concerned. Ever since they had lost the Mockery Bird, the Ginkas had been exceptionally unpleasant to the Fangouas (as only a minority group can be) and had boasted that they were the only people on the island with a true God. Naturally, this sort of brash boasting led to several unpleasant incidents and many a Ginka and Fangoua brave had ended, aromatically seasoned, on the dining table of his foes. But with the coming of the missionaries it gave the Fangouas a chance to embrace Christianity and thus prove themselves superior to the Ginkas. So, at the time of writing, the Fangoua tribe is roughly divided between Catholic and Church of England, with a handful of brave souls who have embraced a curious American religious faction called The Church of the Second Coming.'*

At this point, Captain Pappas appeared on deck followed by two of the Zenkali crew, one carrying a deckchair, and the other a portable bar containing a comprehensive array of drinks.

'Ha, Mr. Foxtrot,' said the Captain, carefully lowering his bulk into the chair. 'Now we have drink before lunch, eh? Just like they do on *Queen Elizabeth*, eh? What you drink? I have everything, do not be shy.'

'Er . . . thank you,' said Peter. 'It's a shade early for me . . . but I'll have a weak brandy and soda, please . . . no! no! . . . Captain!! Whoa! . . . I said a *weak* one.'

'Brandy is very good for the stomach,' confided the Captain, handing Peter a glass containing approximately five fingers of brandy, to which had been added a teaspoonful of soda. 'Brandy for the stomach, whisky for the lungs, ouzo for the brains and champagne for the seduction.'

'Champagne for what?' asked Peter, puzzled.

'Seduction,' said the Captain, frowning, 'you know . . . seduction of beautiful young girls . . . you drink champagne from their knickers like they do in books.'

'Don't you mean slippers?'

'Those too,' agreed the Captain, pouring himself out a brain-curdling slug of ouzo and adding just enough water to turn it opalescent. 'Here's to you and your new job.'

They drank in silence and Peter wondered if one could get cirrhosis of the liver in forty-eight hours.

'I think you will likes Zenkali,' continued the Captain, settling himself back in his creaking chair, 'is very good place to be . . . good climate . . . good people. You like fishing, eh? Plenty fishing in Zenkali . . . sharks, barracuda, even swordfish. You like hunting, eh? Plenty wild deers, wild goats, plenty wild pigs. Yes, you can hunts and fishes until the crows come home.'

'What about the volcanoes?' asked Peter. 'Are they worth climbing?'

'Climbing?' queried Captain Pappas, screwing up his face in puzzlement, 'what climbing?'

'You know, mountain climbing . . . it's one of my hobbies. I spend a lot of my holidays climbing mountains in Scotland and Wales. I wondered if the volcanoes were worth climbing.'

'No one climbs volcanoes. Very hard work,' said the Captain, quite patently appalled at the very idea. 'Very hot work. No, you just fishes and hunts like I tells you. You get nice Zenkali girl and she can cook all you fish and hunt, eh?'

'I'm not sure that I want a nice Zenkali girl.'

'A nice young Zenkali girl, eh? She cook for you, wash for you, keep your house clean, eh? Then you make lots of babies, no?' said the Captain, beaming at Peter in a fatherly way, obviously visualising him sitting in a great pool of squeaking, parti-coloured offspring. 'I know lots of good young Zenkali girls . . . some very pretty . . . some even virgins. If you want I get you nice young Zenkali girl of good family . . . good girl, not bad one, eh? One with big breasts so she have plenty milk for feeding babies, eh?'

'Thank you,' said Peter, slightly shaken by this kindly

offer. 'We'll see. I haven't even *got* there yet. Can't rush things, you know.'

'I fix you up, don't you worry,' said the Captain with massive confidence. 'I can fix anything in Zenkali. I knows everyone in Zenkali and everyone knows *me*. Whatever you want I fix.'

The warm sunshine and the warm air had a very soporific effect, and the glitter from the waves dazzled his eyes. Peter lay back in his chair, relaxed and closed his eyes as he listened to his new friend. The Captain's voice was rather soothing, rising and falling like the deep notes of a cello. Drenched in sunshine, full of brandy, Peter fell asleep. He woke with a start some twenty minutes later to find that the Captain was still in full voice.

'. . . so I says to him, you listen to me you bastard, no one calls me a crooks, you hear? So I picks him up and throws him into the sea . . . he have to swim half a mile to shore,' said the Captain with satisfaction, 'but there were no sharks that day so he made it.'

'What a pity,' said Peter, feeling he should make some contribution to the conversation.

'No one calls *me* a crook,' the Captain confided. 'Come . . . we go and have some lunch now.'

After a gigantic lunch, during which the Captain continued to extol the virtues of the Zenkali maidens and recounted various blood-curdling tales of what he had done to different people in Zenkali who had dared to try and get the better of him, Peter dragged himself down to his cabin. This was stifling, but it was the only place where he could escape the Captain. Like many before, he was discovering that the friendship and hospitality of a Greek can be an overwhelming thing. So in spite of the temperature in his cabin he flung himself on to his narrow bunk and tried to sleep, reflecting that it was better than spending the afternoon drinking wine and playing gin rummy, which is what the Captain had in mind.

Some hours later he awoke – more dead than alive – from a heavy sleep. He dressed and made his way shakily on deck and fell into his deckchair, gazing at the sunset for a while, collecting his thoughts.

The western sky was orange smudged with veins of red, and the sea was indigo with flecks of yellow, green and scarlet quivering on the surface where the evening breeze combed it. A smouldering sun like an apricot was just touching the horizon. In the distance a line of dolphins rose and fell on the placid sea in a crumple of foam, like the backs of a herd of polished black rocking horses. The two albatrosses were still attached to the stern, floating without wing beat. The Zenkali (whom Peter still mentally referred to as Andromada Tree) appeared, smiling his wide, good-natured smile and carrying the portable bar. His job appeared to include that of Chief Officer, bosun, helmsman and bartender. Peter helped himself to a modest brandy, added soda and ice, and lay back, sipping it gently and watching the changing colours in the sky, like oil spreading across a sunlit puddle, and the gleaming muscular backs of the dolphins which had now moved so close to the ship that he could hear their snorts as they broke surface. Presently, he opened his newly acquired guide book to see if there was any more information on these graceful and beautiful animals. He turned to the section dealing with Natural History.

'*Before the advent of the Arabs,*' the guide book stated, '*the two tribes on Zenkali existed in an uneasy peace with each other. The chief reason for this was that the island was blessed with a particularly rich fauna so that no man's cooking pot was ever empty. The population of the two tribes was small compared to today's numbers, and while one tribe confined itself to the East of the island, the other lived contentedly in the West. In between was a sort of no man's land in which the fauna was allowed to flourish more or less unmolested. There was, for example, a superfluity of Giant Tortoises, whose numbers must have ranged into the tens of thousands. That excellent and observant French naturalist, Le Comte d'Armadeau, states that one could "progress in places for nearly a league upon the backs of these monstrous turtles without setting one's foot to the ground". That this was no exaggeration is borne out by the log books of the early sailing ships which called in at Zenkali to water and victual and take on board the Giant Tortoise as living provender, much as modern ships take on tinned hams. So it was that between December 1759 and December 1761, no less than 21,600 tortoises were taken by ships. With these sort of unthinking depredations, it is not to be wondered at that this interesting reptile became extinct during the middle of the French occupation.*

'As soon as the Arabs and the Europeans started to appear, it was inevitable that most of the other interesting indigenous species (mainly harmless, ground-living and defenceless) should disappear, being slaughtered for food or sport by the invaders, harried and killed by their imported predators – dogs, pigs and the like – and affected by the alteration to their habitat brought about by the destruction of the natural forest to make way for sugar plantations, which, mercifully, did not succeed. These plantations now grow the Amela tree, the biological mainstay of the island (see Economics) and the only tree species which has the distinction of having survived the European invasion with its concomitant host of new plants and trees, all inimical to the native flora.

'So, joining the Giant Tortoises in oblivion, went a large and spectacular ground living crepuscular Parrot bigger than the largest known Macaw, five species of Rail, a small, flightless Cormorant (related to the Galapagos species), and a group of ten species of highly coloured and curiously adapted honey eating birds resembling the Huias of New Zealand. From an anthropological point of view the most grievous loss was that of the Mockery Bird, which, as mentioned earlier, formed the basis for the religion of the Fangouas. They

believed that the Bird God, Tio-Namala, resided in this curious species, and therefore the bird, its nest and eggs were all considered tabu. They were not, however, considered tabu by the French, and, naturally, to the Fangoua, the sight of their overlords hunting the Mockery Bird and serving it up in a wide variety of delicious disguises filled them with despondency, particularly as the God Tio-Namala did not seem able to vent his wrath on the French in the way a good god should. However, after several efforts to reason with the French only resulted in a wide selection of headmen being hung for insubordination, the Fangouas gave up all attempts to argue, and within a very short time the Mockery Bird joined the Giant Tortoise as a thing of the past, and left the Fangouas inconsolable.

'In appearance the Mockery Bird was probably the most curious avian species to exist on Zenkali. Related, some think to the Solitaire of Rodrigues Island in the Mascarenes, it was a bird about the size of a goose, standing high on long, strong legs. It had an elongated, slightly curved beak (not unlike that of a Hornbill) with a large casque on top. In the female, this was represented by a mere plate on the forehead. Its wings were minuscule and of no use for flying, and the bird was apparently of an extraordinarily confiding disposition so that it naturally formed the ideal quarry for the French since it could not fly and it did not run away. In its heyday it was almost as numerous as the Giant Tortoise, but in island faunas there is no safety in numbers. The Fangouas called the bird Tio-Namala, which means Bird of God Tiomala. The French called it Oiseau Moquerie, the Mockery Bird, because of its cry which is said to resemble a wild, mocking laugh. All that remains of this fascinating bird is a pair of stuffed specimens in Paris, another pair in Antwerp, five or six stuffed cock birds in various other world museums and half a dozen skeletons and a handful of bones. There is one nicely mounted cock bird in the museum at Dzamandzar.

'It is curious that at the same time that the Mockery Bird became extinct the Ombu tree vanished. This was a peculiar tree that, at uncertain intervals, produced a fruit that apparently formed an important part of the Mockery Bird's diet. At the time of writing there is only one Ombu tree in existence, a specimen reputed to be well over three hundred years old, in the Botanical Gardens outside Dzamandzar. Although it has produced fruit fairly frequently the seeds never germinate. It seems that this tree – surely the rarest tree in the world – will eventually die without issue.'

Peter put the book down and, sipping his drink, he watched the sunset, now green and purple above an almost black sea, and thought about the Ombu tree. He had known about animals becoming extinct and, until quite recently, like many people, had concluded that this was a natural process, like the vanishing of dinosaurs, and nothing whatsoever to do with man. Now he knew this to be untrue. But, in a curious way, he had never thought of trees and plants as being things that could suffer the same fate as animals. For the first time he saw the thing as a whole; if you destroyed the forests you, by the same token, destroyed the creatures that lived in, around and on the forest. Destroy the creatures and you destroyed the forest which in many ways was dependent upon them. He poured himself out another drink and went on with his reading.

'From the human beings' point of view the single most important species on Zenkali must assuredly be the Amela Moth. This singular member of the Hawk Moth family resembles in many ways the European Hummingbird Hawk Moth. It is a large insect with a four-inch wing span and a heavy body. Like its European counterpart, it flies with incredible swiftness and, like the bird after which it is named, it can fly backwards as well as forwards. In flight its wings become a mere blur and this, combined with a series of feather-like scales on the blunt of its body do make it look, at first

glance, much more birdlike than mothlike. Its resem-
blance to the hummingbirds or the sunbirds is further
enhanced by its inordinately long proboscis (four inches
long when fully stretched) which looks curiously like a
curved beak. The upper wings are ash grey, heavily
blotched with black and gold. The lower wings are a
bright magenta with a broad black border. This moth is
the only insect on Zenkali with a proboscis long enough to
penetrate and thus fertilise the trumpet shaped flower of
the Amela tree and is therefore of vital economic
importance to the island (see Economics). As soon as its
link with the Amela tree was realised a total ban on the
use of insecticides was put into force on the island. This
means, of course, that the rest of the insect world benefits
as well, and Zenkali is now overrun by a wide range of
insects, some more noxious than others.'

As instructed, Peter turned to Economics, not because
he had any love or understanding of the topic but he
wanted to learn as much about the island as possible. He
was delighted to find that the economy of Zenkali was so
limited and straightforward that even an economist would
have had difficulty in complicating it. It rested squarely
upon a tree; the Amela tree.

'In view of what has happened to the rest of the world,
Zenkali can think itself lucky that it has no minerals of
any worth, neither has it any oil. In consequence there is
no industry, that is if you discount the minor light
industries which are few and small. Instead, Zenkali
could be described as a one crop island. In the past, there
have been many attempts to make the island self
supporting with crops like sugar, bananas, pineapples
and so on. They all failed. Then the extraordinary
properties of the Amela tree came to light and
immediately this became the one thing that the whole
economy of the island rested upon and, indeed, still rests
upon.

'Zenkali is lucky in that it lies outside the cyclone and
hurricane area and, in consequence, has a very stable

climate. Thus the all-important Amela tree can flourish. As mentioned before, it is the only endemic tree to survive the European onslaught, and it is found nowhere else in the world (indeed it refuses, in a most recalcitrant manner, to grow anywhere else in the world, lacking the Amela Moth to fertilise it) and so Zenkali has a monopoly of this most remarkable tree, probably now outranking the palm tree as the vegetable growth with the maximum amount of talents. The tree itself is twenty to twenty-five feet high with a trunk some twelve inches in diameter. The trunk is straight and smooth, and the wood is fine and hard, of a pleasant honey-yellow with a beautiful grain. Like the red Cedar, it is impervious to all insect attack, even that of the powerful termite. So the wood is of great value for both building and furniture making. In addition, the tree is incredibly fast-growing for such a dense wood and achieves its maximum height in five years, though it is believed that a seven-year-old tree gives better quality timber. The attributes of this tree do not end here. The flowers – long, scarlet, trumpet-shaped blooms growing in clusters – provide a heavy, rich and unique scent (midway, some say, between a rose and a carnation) much in demand as an additive in the scent trade. The fruit, somewhat resembling strawberries of a deep purple colour and growing in clusters, when crushed and the juice refined, provide an oil which is recognised as one of the finest and best procurable, and is therefore widely used in various industries, ranging from the manufacture of precision instruments to cosmetics. As if this were not enough, it has recently been discovered that the heart-shaped, rather fleshy leaf when dried and chemically treated yields Amineaphrone, a drug used in a wide range of medicaments. So this unique tree yields four separate and very important products, all of which bring in a very high revenue (indeed, the only revenue) to Zenkali, and thus give it a financially secure future, a thing generally lacking in small tropical islands of this sort.'

Deep breathing in the fading light, accompanied by a strong odour of garlic, announced to Peter the arrival of the Captain, who eased himself into a chair and poured out a substantial drink.

'We have special dinner tonight, Mr. Foxtrot,' he announced with satisfaction, 'we have Greek dinner, eh? We celebrate last night before Zenkali, eh? We drink and then we dance.'

'Dance?' said Peter in some alarm, visualising himself locked in the bear-like hug of Captain Pappas, being waltzed around the deck.

'Dance,' repeated Captain Pappas firmly, 'Greek dance, eh? I teach you Greek dance . . . best kind dance in the world.'

'Thank you,' said Peter, resigning himself to an alcoholic and athletic evening.

He was not disappointed. The dinner, though he had to admit to its excellence, was of mammoth proportions and accompanied by an apparently endless quantity of white and red wine, depending on the delicacy they were eating. At the end of this, three of the young Zenkalis got up and started some very creditable Greek dancing to the accompaniment of the strains of a bazouki, played with great verve and feeling by Captain Pappas. It seemed amazing that his sausage-like fingers should be able to coax such sweet melodies out of the instrument. Presently, hazy with good wine and fellowship, Peter found himself, his arms draped around the bronzed, sweating necks of the grinning Zenkalis, treading a not altogether stately measure across the deck, while the bazouki whined and trembled and the Captain's deep bass voice rang out across the moonlit sea. At length, having sworn eternal friendship with all the Zenkalis and Captain Pappas, Peter staggered off to bed, singing lustily. As he undressed and got into his bunk he suddenly thought of the Ombu tree and was immediately grief-stricken that he should be enjoying himself so much while the tree, the sole survivor of its race, had no one of its kind to keep it company.

'No one to sing with,' reflected Peter sorrowfully, 'no one to dance with. It's cruel.'

He took off his clothes, dropped them on the floor and fell back, naked, on his bunk.

'Be of good cheer, dear old Ombu tree,' he murmured as he fell asleep, 'Peter Foxglove, Esq., is coming to your rescue.' He had no idea at the time, of course, that he was not talking nonsense.

Chapter Two

———◄ ❋ ►———

ZENKALI INSPECTED

He awoke, to his amazement, at five o'clock and without a discernible hangover. Since he was sure that Zenkali must now be in sight, he washed and dressed and hurried into the bows of the ship. The air was still and cool; the sea, deep blue and smooth as an opal, with small flocks of sea birds drifting across it. The sky was a faint powder blue smudged with orange where the sun was rising. Slightly to starboard and still a few miles away lay Zenkali. Its crescent shape, with the twin volcanoes on each arm, was very distinctive. In this early light the whole island looked dark green, with purple-black shadows cast by the volcanoes and mountains. The island was hedged with a rim of white surf where the swell broke upon the partially submerged coral reef, and each volcano was wearing a jaunty early morning headgear of cloud. Peter watched fascinated as the rising sun made the colours of the island more solid and brilliant, and the surface of the sea broke up into a million fish-like glitters of silver.

Captain Pappas appeared on the bridge yawning vastly, scratching himself through his open shirt. His chest and stomach were covered with a bear-like pelt of thick black hair, and the hair on his head was dishevelled and standing on end.

'Good morning,' he roared down to Peter, 'how you feeling?'

'Fine,' said Peter, 'never better.'

'Is good, Greek dancing,' proclaimed the Captain, as one vouchsafing a sovereign remedy, 'is good for the body. You

34

see Zenkali, eh? She's fine island, no? We reach port in maybe two – three hours.'

'Three hours?' said Peter in surprise, 'but it looks so close.'

'No, she is not close. She much bigger when you get close,' said the Captain. 'You want some breakfast, Mr. Foxtrot? You hungry, eh?'

Peter suddenly discovered that he had developed a prodigious appetite.

'I'd love some breakfast,' he shouted to the Captain, 'I'm so hungry I could eat a Clydesdale, hooves and all.'

'I dunno if we got,' said the Captain, scowling at the thought that maybe his ship could be found defective in some way, 'I think you ask cook, eh?'

An hour later Peter had done his packing and was up in the bows once more to witness their passage through the reef, which, to someone not familiar with the art of reef running was at once exciting, frightening and exhilarating. The island now loomed large, bathed in sunlight that picked out all the shimmering foliage that covered the land from beach to mountain top. Greens, golds, scarlets, pinks, blues and yellows in a multicoloured tapestry that only the tropics can produce. Crescent beaches gleamed as white as elephants' tusks along the shore, and the waters inside the reef were the palest, and most transparent of blue, so that one could clearly see the seascape of coral beds lying beneath the surface. The reef itself was between twenty and fifty feet in width, and lay some two feet beneath the surface of the sea. On this great step the sea surged and then crumpled into hissing, dissolving foam as it ran over the lip of razor-sharp coral. Rocking on this gigantic swell, swung to and fro by the long, smooth rollers, the *Andromada III* chugged cheerfully along, parallel with the foaming, snarling reef but keeping a distance of some eighty feet from what looked like certain shipwreck. Whatever Captain Pappas' other failings might be, he certainly knew the Zenkali reef. He urged his boat along the edge of it until they came to a break in the long, undulating carpet of foam. The break was not more than a hundred feet wide, through which the huge rollers jostled their way with a frightening roaring noise and then dissolved into a tumbled bed of foam and broken wavelets within the reef. The Captain turned the *Andromada III* sharply and took the gap at a run. They rocked and shook briefly in the tangled blue muscles of waves, then shook free and slid out on to the smooth, diamond bright waters of the lagoon.

'You see, I am one damn fine sailor,' shouted Captain Pappas from the bridge, his face split by a great grin of triumph.

'Too right,' Peter shouted back.

'All Greek are good sailors . . . best in world. We anchor in maybe five minutes, eh?' He waved a hand like a ham at Peter and disappeared inside the diminutive wheelhouse on the bridge.

Andromada III chugged across the limpid waters of the lagoon and presently entered Mocquerie Bay in which lay the port and capital of Zenkali, Dzamandzar. They rounded a headland on top of which was an imposing building in pinkish stone, which Peter took to be the Palace. Then the bay opened up and he could see the stone bulwarks of the harbour and behind it, sprawling over gently undulating hills with the two distant volcanoes as a backdrop, the multicoloured houses that made up the town. The houses were neat little clapboard dwellings with thatched roofs, with here and there a more solid building of coral blocks. Each of the houses was painted a different primary colour, and so the whole effect was as if a box of coloured bricks had been thrown down among the magenta cumulus clouds of Bougainvillaea bushes, and the startling blue of the jacaranda trees, with here and there a group of blood-red flame-of-the-forest in full bloom.

Peter was enchanted. It exceeded all his wildest dreams. Here, he thought, was a town you could really call a town, one to be proud of, a town so distinctive that it could not possibly be confused with any other community anywhere else in the world. He already felt a passionate attachment to it and he had not even *smelt* it yet, and he knew how important smell was when it came to judging a town or city. But he was not even disappointed by the smell, for the *Andromada III* dropped anchor with a rattle and a splash and then, guided by her chain, came around and was soon securely docked alongside the wharf. The warm air brought the scent of Zenkali to Peter. It was an intoxicating mixture, as complex as smelling the colours in a Persian rug. There was palm oil, coconut oil, a million flower scents, the smell of sunshine on dried leaves, the heady smell of woodsmoke, pineapples, pawpaws, mangoes and lemons, the smell of sea salt and fresh fish, bread and drains and donkeys and blue sky and early morning dew, and a million other scents that he had not the time to unravel at that moment, for he was interrupted by a very large, glossy Zenkali who materialised on the deck in front of him. The man was obviously of some official standing, for he wore a scarlet tarboosh, a dark blue uniform coat with white frogging, white shorts and blue, knee-length stockings and brown boots as polished as his face. In his hand he carried, somewhat incongruously, a long, slender cleft stick and sticking in the cleft, a folded paper.

'Sah, Mr. Foxglove, sah, welcome, sah,' said the messenger, saluting smartly.

'Thank you,' said Peter fascinated, sketching a salute in return. The messenger presented the end of the cleft stick to him.

'Dis na book for you, sah, from Masa Hannibal, sah,' the messenger explained.

Gingerly, Peter extracted the message from the end of the cleft stick and opened it. It was a single sheet written in elegant copperplate handwriting on thick ivory coloured paper.

'Dear Foxglove,' he read. 'Welcome. Do not worry about anything. Just follow the man with the cleft stick. H.'

The messenger grinned broadly at Peter.

'Masa go come with me,' he said. 'We go for Masa

Hannibal's house in Kingy Cart. By 'n' by they send Masa's bags.'

In a daze, Peter followed the man with the cleft stick off the *Andromada III* and on to the docks where two capacious basketwork rickshaws – looking not unlike bamboo bathchairs – were waiting with large Zenkalis between the shafts. Peter entered one and the messenger occupied the other and they were soon bowling through the streets of the town. When they reached the outskirts, the rickshaws turned up a broad gravel drive and eventually stopped outside a long, low house set among a forest of giant banyan trees whose trunks looked like groups of massive black candles that had melted and half fused together. The messenger led Peter up the front stairs and across the wide, gleaming verandah, heavy with the scent of a myriad flowers in clay tubs the size of baths or in hanging baskets that decorated its length. At the front door, which consisted of two huge, intricately carved Javanese screens, the messenger paused and took a silver whistle from his pocket. He blew a short but complicated fanfare. While they waited Peter admired the dipping flight of some twenty or so giant blue butterflies that, like bits of lost sky, were maypoling round the flowers, occasionally pausing to refresh themselves from the blooms.

The door was opened at last by a Zenkali steward in a crisp, white uniform and a scarlet sash. He beamed at Peter and gave a tiny bow.

'Good morning, sah, Mr. Foxglove,' he said. 'You go come, please, dis way . . . Masa go wait for you.'

He turned and led Peter down a wide hallway, the walls of which were decorated by long Chinese paintings on silk that coiled gently in the breeze. Beneath them a set of big Chinese bowls contained magnificent orchids whose subtle colours matched the paintings. The steward paused at a door, knocked deferentially and then cocked his head, listening.

'Go away!' roared a fearsome voice from inside, 'go away, you unalphabetic heathen . . . take your pagan carcase away from this house of pain and suffering and never let me set eyes upon your miserable, black, pithecanthropic features again.'

'Dat Masa Hannibal,' said the steward with some pride. Undeterred by both the belligerence of the voice and its instructions, he opened the door a crack and stuck his head in.

'Get out, . . . *get out!*' snarled the voice. 'Get out, you snivelling missing link. Don't come cringing round me, trying to extirpate your guilt. If I were not a kind and gentle man, I would deem it my duty to get you twenty years' hard labour for attempted murder, you wog to end all wogs.'

Was this, Peter wondered in astonishment, the voice of Hannibal Oliphant?

The steward waited patiently until the man inside the room had paused for breath and then he said:

'Please, sah, Mr. Foxglove, he done come.'

There was a short pause, and then the voice bellowed, 'Well don't just stand there, you murdering illiterate, send the new Masa in one time, d'you hear?'

The steward threw open the door and ushered Peter into a vast and magnificent room about sixty feet long by thirty wide, with tremendously high ceilings in which broad-bladed fans turned like black windmills against the white? The polished wood floor was covered with a scattering of many-coloured Persian carpets that must have been worth a king's ransom. The furniture was mostly dark, heavily carved wood from Kashmir and consisted of deep sofas and chairs, each piled high with cushions in multicoloured Thai silks. The walls were covered with a collection of strange masks, beautiful Impressionist paintings, more Chinese scrolls on silk, Tibetan prayer wheels, antique blunderbusses, spears, shields and several glass-fronted cupboards full of ivory carvings and delicate ceramics. Everywhere there were bookcases with rainbows of books in them, spilling out into piles on the floor. At one end of the room was a large desk, its top covered with tottering piles of papers and magazines and scientific reprints. Along one wall five tall french windows led out on to a verandah, and beyond that stretched green lawns and a tapestry of flowering shrubs that led down to an oval swimming pool decked out in terracotta tiles. In the centre of the pool, a fountain some eighteen feet high curved up like a silver fleur-de-lis in the sunshine.

Near one of the open French windows was a beautifully ornate rocking-chair in pale amber wood. The arms were two delicately carved peacocks and their raised tails came together to make the huge fan-shaped back. Sitting in this breathtaking chair, leaning back against a cumulus of multicoloured silken cushions, sat Hannibal Hubert Hildebrand Oliphant, Political Advisor to the King of Zenkali and his Government, wearing a white cotton shirt with wide sleeves, a brilliant batik cloth round his loins and Javanese slippers in red and gold with turned up toes. He was short and very broad with a massive head crowned by a mane of iron grey hair. A large, mobile mouth, sensuous and sardonic, drooped beneath an eagle-beak of a nose. Under bushy eyebrows, sparkling black gypsy's eyes gazed out with humorous arrogance. The man's personality hit you as forcefully as the heat from a great fire on a cold night. By his side was a table on which were arranged a number of bottles and a large silver ice bucket. Around his chair lay a bulldog, a Dalmatian, an Irish Wolfhound, two Pekinese, four King Charles spaniels and a colossal Tibetan mastiff so big that for some time Peter was under the impression that it was a tame bear.

Sitting among the dogs, on a large apricot-coloured cushion, hugging her knees, was one of the most beautiful girls Peter had ever seen. At twenty-eight, being handsome and with considerable natural charm, Peter had not been without his fair share of female acquaintances. The girl he was now looking at took his breath away. She was slender with a peach-like skin burnt by the sun to the colour of polished bronze. Her dark hair, held in a simple gold clasp, fell to her waist, with ripples in it like the eddies in a moonlit river. Her nose was small and slightly *retroussé* with a fine dusting of freckles, and her mouth was generous and shaped for laughter. But it was her large almond shaped eyes that were most remarkable. Above slightly high cheekbones and under dark, graceful brows, they were an intense smokey blue, almost violet, with tiny black flecks that enhanced their size. All he had to do now, he reflected, was to discover that either she was married to some sweaty, retarded male totally unworthy of her, or else that she had a voice like a fishwife and bad breath. He was suddenly jolted out of his trance by Hannibal Oliphant's derisive voice.

'When you have finished standing there like a mentally defective jobbernowl drinking in Miss Damien's undoubted charms, perhaps you might spare me a cursory glance,' he suggested. 'Why not come over here, if you have not lost all power of movement, so that I don't rupture my vocal chords shouting at you?'

Peter pulled himself together with an effort and walked across the room to where the rocking-chair moved slowly to and fro.

'So,' said Hannibal Oliphant, holding out his left hand to be shaken since his right one was encased in bandages, 'so, you're Foxglove, eh? Nephew of Sir Osbert?'

There was something in the way Hannibal drawled out the name that warned Peter. He remembered his uncle's scornful description – 'that fool Oliphant' – and he decided to tread warily.

'Yes, sir,' he said, 'but I hope you won't hold it against me.'

Hannibal gave him a sharp look, then his eyes twinkled.

'Call me Hannibal,' he commanded, 'everyone else does.'

'Thank you,' said Peter.

'Sit down, sit down. Audrey, get the lad a drink,' said Hannibal, settling himself more comfortably on his cushions.

The girl rose and mixed Peter a rum and coke. She

handed it to him with such a ravishing smile that he almost dropped the glass. Hannibal watched this with a sardonic grin, rocking gently to and fro in his great chair.

'Well now,' he said, sipping his drink, 'what did Sir Osbert, bless him, send you out for?'

Peter looked surprised.

'Why, to assist you,' he said, puzzled, 'I assumed that you had asked for an assistant.'

Hannibal raised eyebrows like tattered white banners.

'Do I,' he enquired of Audrey, 'do I look like a man in need of assistance?'

'Well, you needed assistance just now,' Audrey pointed out, and Peter was delighted to discover that she had a faint Irish accent. Hannibal waved his bandaged hand at Peter.

'Owing to a ridiculous edict that prevents the use of insecticides here, we are beset on all sides by hordes of malignant insects that, sensing their immunity, spare no effort to try and dominate us. It is a situation that Mr. H. G. Wells would have revelled in, dear boy. Only this morning, a hornet, striped like a member of some chain gang and approximately twice the size of the Spirit of St. Louis, came zooming in here, bent on murder. I called for my Neanderthal steward to come and protect his master's person and the fool, with the aid of a tennis racket, knocks this ravening insect straight on to my chest. Fearing it would stab me to the heart, I made wild efforts to dislodge it, with the result that it sank a sting like a harpoon into my hand. It is only because this girl arrived and has some slight knowledge of first aid that amputation at the elbow was averted.'

'Disregard Hannibal,' said the girl, picking up one of the Pekinese and cuddling it in her arms so that it snorted with pleasure. 'He is, without doubt, one of the most obnoxious people on the island, and his powers of exaggeration are unlimited.'

'The Irish peasantry were always recalcitrant,' said Hannibal, gazing mournfully at the girl; then he turned to Peter.

'Well, tell me, if your obnoxious uncle did not send you to spy on us . . .'

'Look here,' Peter interrupted, 'I am *not* a spy. If my uncle had asked me to do that I wouldn't be here.'

'No offence, no offence,' said Hannibal soothingly, 'but we've had three of them sent out by your uncle to be "my assistant" and I've had to send them all packing when I found out what they had been sent out for.'

There was a pause.

'It's true,' said Audrey softly. Peter looked at her and sighed.

'All right, I know my uncle's an old bastard, but I assure you that I am not his man, neither do I share his views.' Hannibal grinned at him.

'Don't get it wrong, my boy. Your uncle is a wog hater. *I* am a wog lover.'

Peter remembered the flood of vituperation that Hannibal had poured on his steward's head and the imperturbable way the Zenkali had treated it. Obviously Hannibal had his own curious method of being a wog lover, as he termed it.

'Well,' said Hannibal, comfortably, 'now we've got *that* out of the way, we can talk. Tell me, had you any particular reason for wanting to come to this God-forsaken, evilly-governed, nigger-infested hole?'

'Yes,' said Peter, 'I had a friend called Hugo Charteris. He spent a month here and came back raving about it. It sounded like the sort of tropical paradise which you generally discover is just a myth. But this one is real.'

'Ah yes, dear me,' said Hannibal mournfully. 'I know exactly what you mean. I, too, have spent my life searching for the ideal spot, the Eden on earth, and so, what happens? I end up in this God-forsaken backwater, enshrined for more years than I care to remember, like a butterfly in amber.'

'That's all codswallop, and you know it,' said Audrey.

'*Codswallop?*' asked Hannibal. 'Where do you get these expressions . . .what d'you mean, codswallop?'

'I get the expressions from you,' said Audrey, smiling, 'and what I mean is that you simply dote on this place and all who dwell in it, and you wouldn't live anywhere else in the world if they paid you.'

'Would that they did pay me. As it is, I have to eke out a pauper-like existence, trying desperately to make ends meet,' said Hannibal, glaring round the vast room.

'But what is wrong with it here?' asked Peter, interested, since Hannibal seemed serious.

'Everything,' said Hannibal spaciously.

'Rubbish! Don't listen to him,' said Audrey. 'He's as rich as Croesus and he doesn't have to work, so he just dabbles in all the intrigues and manipulation that goes on. He's got all the instincts for intrigue of a Levantine moneylender. Also, he loves to complain. The only time to start worrying is when he *stops* complaining.'

'You see what I have to put up with from the local ingrates?' Hannibal said to Peter. 'I assure you, my dear boy, you have come to the very end of the earth, a section of Hades undreamt of by Dante. The natives are positively Stone Age, and what Europeans there are here have a mental level only just a fraction higher than that of the average cretin. Don't, I beg of you, look for any culture *here*. It is as intellectually stimulating as Highgate cemetery and twice as well populated.'

'Well,' said Peter, 'if I'm going to work here, I'd better hear the worst. First, what d'you want me to do?'

'Nothing very much,' said Hannibal moodily, and he got up, refilled his glass and then paced up and down, pausing now and then to scratch a dozing dog with his toe.

'In a moment, I'll take you to see Kingy and then pop in to Government House to make a leg at H.E. Just politesse, really; they just want to know whether you've got four eyes or something, so they'll recognise you again. All harmless stuff. But the situation here is far from harmless.'

He sat down again and rocked in his chair, scowling. Presently he went on.

'Zenkali is going to get self-government, there are no two

ways about that. Much as some people would like to, there is no way of stopping it, nor indeed should it be stopped. To all intents and purposes, up to a few months ago, they had self-government: it was all over bar the shouting, and I was merely sitting about with my feet up offering a bit of advice here and there when asked and waiting for the great day to dawn. Then some damn fool in Whitehall goes and thinks up this airfield caper. Have you heard about it?'

'Only from Captain Pappas,' said Peter, 'and that was a somewhat garbled account.'

'It would be,' snorted Hannibal, 'well, in a nutshell, they suddenly decided – after years of considering Zenkali of absolutely no use, militarily speaking – that this was the ideal place to put a damn great airfield in a belated attempt to keep the Russians out of the Indian Ocean. Leaving aside the fact that the military boys are trying to perform that time honoured task of closing the stable door after the horse has gone, I personally don't think that the airfield and all the things that inevitably go with it, would be beneficial to the island.

'You keep saying that, but you never explain *why*,' said Audrey.

'It is difficult to explain without being thought a terrible old die-hard, a sort of Colonel Blimp, defying all progress and all change. I assure you it is not that. I grant you that I feel there is too much cant talked in the world about "progress" without very many people actually sitting down and finding out whether or not in most cases progress isn't retrogression. However, for the sake of this argument, let us let the rest of the world go hang for a moment and concentrate entirely on Zenkali's unique position in the world – and make no mistake Zenkali *is* unique. Tell me where else you would find a country with the following attributes: one, it's so remote that, even nowadays, everyone leaves it alone; two, it has no racial strife to speak of, if you overlook the occasional spear-flourishing that the Fangouas and the Ginkas indulge in, more as a salve to their manly pride than anything and to a large extent brought about by boredom. Three, mercifully, no minerals or oil so no big power is interested in "mothering" us. Four, full employment, if you discount those chronic drunks and geriatrics who can't work. Five, no heavy industry and very little light industry so that your people have not been tempted away from the land, and we are still basically an agricultural society producing not only enough foods for ourselves (with one or two minor exceptions) but even enough for a modest export quota. Six, and most important of all, the Good Lord has seen fit to give us and us alone the Amela tree from which stems the entire wealth of this island.'

Hannibal got out of his chair again and started to pace up and down restlessly. Then he paused and drank deeply, one foot resting on the massive back of the Tibetan mastiff.

'Make no mistake, my boy, on this island there is only one thing of any importance at all, and that is the Amela. It provides us with our most valuable export, it allows us to balance our books and it makes sure that every Zenkali has – to quote Louis XIV – a chicken in his cooking pot. Thanks to this remarkable tree, income tax is practically unknown and taxation on imported goods is so small as to be negligible. Every year this tree allows our budget to be balanced in such a way that we can maintain the island to the best possible advantage of the islanders.'

'But that's all very well,' said Peter, emboldened by his second drink, 'but do you think it's very wise for the whole future of the island to be dependent on one crop?'

'Why not?' asked Hannibal. 'Look at Mauritius, almost entirely reliant on sugar. One decent cyclone and the whole economy of that island is undermined. Here we have no cyclones and, short of the earth starting to spin in a different way, we *can* have no cyclones. That is why I say this island is unique. And, if it is left alone, it can go on and prosper. But if we allow this stupid airstrip thing to go through I can see nothing but disaster looming ahead.'

'But why?' asked Audrey again. 'You still haven't told us why.'

'My dear,' said Hannibal, 'it is not, as you seem to imagine, a simple airstrip which will allow you to go weekend shopping in Djakarta. No, it is a military installation. In order to produce the damn airfield at all, you've got to have a fairly massive hydro-electric scheme, for a start. As soon as we have a supply of electricity that can be relied on, you will get an immediate clamour for industry, with all its attendant miseries. The airfield itself will have to be, as it were, fed and watered, and how do you think they are going to do that? By blowing a bloody great hole in the reef which will allow quite sizeable naval vessels to come in and anchor. So overnight we become Plymouth dockyard with a large airstrip covered with fighters, and therefore, in the event of any trouble, an immediate target for the enemy. Quite apart from anything else, imagine the effect of five or six thousand bored and virile young sailors and airmen confined here. The mind boggles at the prospect. No, I am against the whole thing, lock, stock and barrel, but I fear that no-one will listen to me. And, of course, now that unpleasant tyke Looja has got his oily fingers in the pie I dread to think what the consequences will be.'

'Is it true that he snapped up the only valley that you can put the hydro-electric scheme in?' asked Peter.

'I'm afraid so,' said Hannibal dismally, 'and it was all my fault. I was so busy trying to persuade Kingy that the whole airfield idea was a bad thing that I did not look to my defences. I should have got Kingy to slap an embargo on the sale of land, at least until the matter was decided one way or the other. As it is, that unmitigated suppurating sore, Looja, went and did some smart speculation on his own. Of course he picked up the area dirt cheap. No-one wanted the damn valleys. You couldn't do anything with them; they were too hard to get into, for a start. So Looja bought them up cheap. But, mark my words, there will be trouble over that.'

'Why?' asked Peter. 'I mean, apart from obvious reasons?'

'Well, as you may know, there is a certain amount of jealous friction between the Ginkas and the Fangouas. Well, friend Looja is a Fangoua and he bought the damned valleys off the chief of the Ginkas, Gowsa Manalowoba. Naturally, when old Gowsa – who's a nice old rogue in his way – finds that he has been swindled out of several hundred thousand pounds by Looja he will not take kindly to it. He wouldn't like it if anyone did it, but for it to be Looja will be the last straw. I mean, if we held a public opinion poll as to who was the most unpopular person on Zenkali, both Ginkas and Fangouas would unhesitatingly vote for Looja. The vote would be unanimous. He has a certain repulsive quality about him which would get him turned out of a leper colony. He is the best living argument for infanticide that I know, and most if not all of Zenkali shares my view.'

'Captain Pappas said something about him getting bribes from the firm that's going to do the hydro-electric scheme,' said Peter. 'Is there any truth in that?'

'More than likely,' said Hannibal, 'but it's a fairly recent rumour that no one has actually tracked to its lair as yet. But I would put nothing past Looja. He makes Judas Iscariot look like St. Francis of Assisi.'

'Why is he Minister of Development if he is so untrustworthy?' said Peter.

'One of Kingy's ideas,' said Hannibal, gloomily. 'As a monarch he has an extraordinary grasp on political manipulation, but just occasionally he does things that make my frontal lobes throb. When he appointed Looja, to everyone's horror I might say, I asked him why and he said that he preferred to keep his rogues where he could see them, and to give them enough power so that it was not worth their while to lose the job by too much double dealing. I must confess up until now Looja has toed the line, but I suppose the chance of becoming a millionaire was too much of a temptation for him. Anyway, I foresee stormy times ahead and I have warned Kingy, but I don't think he will listen. For some obscure reason, he seems to think that this airstrip and all its attendant miseries will be good for the island and that he owes it to his people. Occasionally he takes his role seriously, and it's always then that he makes a mistake.'

'But it's worse when he starts indulging in his sense of humour,' said Audrey. 'Look how many noses he put out of joint when he started the Book Boys.'

'Book Boys . . . what are they?' asked Peter, intrigued.

'You were brought here by one this morning,' said Hannibal, 'sort of King's messenger. It all came about because Kingy had been reading some book on early African exploration, you know, Stanley and Johnstone and so on. Well they apparently spent a lot of time sending messages in cleft sticks, and this tickled Kingy so much that he invented the messengers, each armed, as you may have noticed, with a cleft stick, for carrying messages and for guiding people. They're called Kingy's Book Boys, because book in pidgin English means anything that's written. It created an uproar among the more educated Zenkalis, who said it was taking things back to the Stone Age and the whole thing was a blot on every civilised Zenkali and so on. You know the song. Kingy's reply was, I think, nothing short of masterly. He said that the Europeans were always holding it against coloured races for not having invented the wheel and as they had invented the cleft stick he felt they ought to be proud of their heritage, not ashamed of it.

'However, fascinating and mischievous though his sense of humour is, it can produce difficult results. Only the other day, the Ginkas got a little out of hand about a land tax problem. Well, I was suddenly galvanised into activity when I heard that Kingy was suggesting bringing back cannibalism as a punishment for tax evasion.'

Audrey threw back her head and laughed immoderately.

'What on earth did you do?' asked Peter.

'Well, it wasn't easy,' Hannibal said, picking up a King Charles spaniel and kissing it on the nose, 'I had to give Kingy some of his own medicine. You see, I knew it was a joke but everyone else thought it was serious . . . you should have seen Government House . . . turmoil wasn't in it . . . H.E. almost had kittens. Anyway, I went down to the palace and gave my famous Colonial Office imitation.'

He stuck his thumb into an imaginary waistcoat, adjusted an imaginary *pince-nez* and modulated his voice to that high-pitched, querulous bleat that only an upbringing in the Home Counties of England, coupled with an education at an impeccable Public School and University can produce.

'Things,' he bleated, 'were gettin' out of hand, blacka-moors gettin' restive. Meantersay, for this part of the world, dashed ugly, what? Blackamoors throwing stones and so forth . . . one jolly old nig-nog cut himself quite severely on a sickle he was waving about. I meantersay, for Zenkali it was almost another Indian Mutiny. So Kingy pretended to lash himself into a fury . . . as much of a fury as one of his size *can* lash themselves into . . . and threatened to bring back cannibalism. Well now, meantersay, this is where yours truly had to step in smartish, dontcherknow. Had to explain the ethics to old King Coon. Told him it's all right to shoot a chappie in a fair fight, or even slip a little hemlock into his noggin if you get the chance, what? But *eating* your adversary . . . dear me, no . . . *totally* unethical . . . not British, I meantersay.'

Hannibal threw back his head and laughed joyously at his own imitation and so infectious was his mirth and so child-like his pride in his performance that Peter found he was laughing too, as much at Hannibal as with him. Peter found himself warming to this curious man. His person-ality was so mercurial that it was often difficult to know whether he was serious or just indulging in another flood of exaggerated rhetoric of which he seemed so fond.

'How did Kingy take that?' asked Audrey.

'He loved it, said it was the best imitation of an Empire-builder he had heard since he left Eton.'

'And what about the cannibalism thing?' asked Peter.

'Well, he reluctantly agreed to give up the idea. I really

think the only reason he wanted to do it was because he'd got a recipe handed down from his great-great-grand-mother, who, I believe was a sort of Mrs. Beeton of her day. It starts something like "take five fallen adversaries, still warm . . ." When I pointed out to him that it would be murder he said he didn't see why, since there would be no corpses as evidence. He can be very irritating sometimes.'

'So it all ended happily?' asked Audrey.

'Oh, yes,' said Hannibal, 'after the old rogue had had his laugh. But I wouldn't be surprised if he didn't bring it up again, he got such a kick out of it. Probably when they get self-government. It'll probably be one of his first edicts, just to set Government House a-tremble. Kingy loves the Governor, but he also likes to make him twitch. And, of course, the poor old boy's a perfect fall guy. I mean, as soon as you've met him you have only one desire in life and that is to pull his leg, so one can't altogether blame Kingy, I suppose.'

'Well, if you're going to the Palace you'd better go,' said Audrey.

'Yes, yes, don't fuss me, woman,' said Hannibal testily, 'Where's that blasted assassin? . . . Tomba! . . . Tomba! . . . TOMBA! Oh, there you are.'

Tomba, at the sound of his name, had appeared among the furniture with the startling suddenness of a genie out of a bottle.

'Masa call?' he asked.

'Of course I called,' said Hannibal, 'Masa Foxglove and I go go for Kingy's Palace, you hear? You go get Kingy Carts one time.'

'Yes, sah,' said Tomba and disappeared.

'Come, my dear boy,' said Hannibal, lighting a long thin cigar, 'we must away . . . where's my hat . . . why do people always hide my possessions? . . . Ah, here it is.'

He unearthed from a chair a large, battered Victorian pith helmet and set it upon his tangled mane of hair.

'Come along, little doggie-woggies,' he roared suddenly. 'Good Uncle Hannibal take you walkie-pawkies.'

The dogs rose in a body and surrounded him, a sea of waving tails, all barking vociferously.

'What are you doing tomorrow?' asked Hannibal raising his voice above the uproar.

'Me?' said Audrey, startled. 'Nothing, why?'

'Do me a favour,' said Hannibal, earnestly. 'I have an enormous workload. Take young Foxglove out for the day ... show him a bit of the island ... introduce him around ... you know the form ... new boy ... needs cosseting ... woman's touch and all that sort of thing.'

'Well, I don't know if Peter really wants ...' she began, doubtfully.

'I would simply love it,' said Peter, hastily, 'can't think of anything I should like better. And I promise not to ask too many silly questions.'

'Well, if you're sure you wouldn't rather explore on your own ...?' she said.

'No, no, nothing like a guided tour in a new place,' said Peter, smiling, 'and I'm sure you're the person best qualified to show me round and put me in the picture.'

'Well, I don't know about that,' said Audrey 'but will about eight tomorrow morning be all right?'

'Splendid,' said Peter.

The mass of excited dogs following, Hannibal stalked off along the hall and down the verandah steps, to where two rickshaws with powerful Zenkalis between the shafts awaited them.

'We go go for Kingy house,' Hannibal instructed the Zenkalis as he climbed into one rickshaw, 'you go run quick quick, you hear, or dis Masa 'e go kill you.'

'Yes, sah, we hear,' said the grinning boys.

Peter climbed into his rickshaw and the two vehicles set off, the dogs panting and yapping around the wheels, with the exception of the Dalmatian, who took up his position underneath Hannibal's rickshaw. The two stalwart Zenkalis were so well matched that the rickshaws moved along smoothly, side by side, as if lashed together.

'Why do you call these things Kingy Carts?' asked Peter.

'It's the only form of transport allowed within the city limits,' explained Hannibal. 'Sensible, really. Provides employment and they are cheap to run, more or less silent and they don't pollute.'

'Yes, I think they're a wonderful idea,' agreed Peter enthusiastically, 'so much better than a lot of damned cars.'

'Quite,' said Hannibal, 'and they have one other overriding advantage: they all belong to Kingy. He, as it were, invented them. He has the monopoly on their construction – he's got a rickshaw factory run by his uncle – and the boys that pull them have to pay Kingy a royalty, if you'll pardon the expression. They are called Kingy Carriers and like the Book Boys it's considered quite a distinguished job because it's connected with the King. These boys, for instance, have to pass a very stringent test before they can buy a Kingy Cart and set up in business. They have to run three miles in record time during the heat of the day, carrying a hundredweight of potatoes or similar vegetable, and at the end of it, wrestle a bull to its knees. I tell you, it makes the English driving test look anaemic by comparison.'

The Kingy Cart boys had settled down to a steady lope and the rickshaws, with a mere whisper of wheels on the red dust road, moved steadily through the countryside. On the left, through copses of flame-of-the-forest trees, standing root deep in scarlet pools of their own petals, Peter could see the blue, smooth waters of the lagoon and, in the distance, like a wind-moved garland of white flowers, the foam rim that marked the reef. To the right, the hillside rose in a series of gentle undulations, and was freckled with numerous small, multicoloured clapboard houses, each standing in its own garden, neatly fenced with bamboo. These little gardens were overflowing with sugar cane, coconut palms, feathery bushes of cassava, the great, gleaming leaves of sweet potato and everywhere the giant shade-generous breadfruit trees. Goats, tethered under the trees, gazed at them with pale, fierce eyes and bleated indignantly and hordes of chickens, ducks and turkeys left the comfort of their dust baths on the road's surface and ran squawking, fluttering and gobbling into the undergrowth.

'Pretty girl, that,' said Hannibal, musingly.

'Ravishing,' said Peter, enthusiastically. 'I'm surprised she's not married.'

'Too much sense and Irish stubbornness . . . and anyway, there's nobody here worth marrying, except me, and she very wisely won't have me,' Hannibal said with a chuckle. 'Her father's a mad Irishman in the old sense. He runs the *Zenkali Voice* – our local newspaper – famous for its trenchant leading articles and for containing more typographical errors per page than anything since the original *Canterbury Tales*. Only the other day there was a front-page picture of our noble King and a bedraggled brace of wild boar he'd shot, and the caption read: "Mrs. Amazooga, one hundred and five today, pictured with her two sons". Inside, there was a picture of the unfortunate lady and her sons over the caption: "A devil-may-care hunter who always gets his prey". The shock alone is enough to prevent her from reaching one hundred and six. Thank God our monarch has a sense of humour. But poor old Damien's always creating havoc like that. He threw the nursing fraternity into a rare state of confusion some time ago with his article on Florence Nightingale entitled "The Lady with the Lump".'

Peter laughed.

'Does Audrey help him?' he asked.

'Yes and no, tries to make him eat instead of drink, tries to make sure the errors in the paper are kept to a minimum. But with an Irish father and a Zenkali staff and typesetter, it's a work of supererogation,' said Hannibal and then, spotting another rickshaw that was approaching them, he groaned, 'Watch out, here comes the one black spot on the Zenkali horizon, friend Looja.'

As the rickshaws drew level and stopped, Peter looked curiously at the man who seemed capable of generating such animosity. Looja was tiny, scarcely five feet high and very slender, looking as though he had been put together out of chicken bones and fine brown parchment. The predominant features of his head were a large, hooked nose, an impressive and carefully coiffured head of snow white hair, and a pair of large and expressionless black eyes. He was dressed in an exquisite pale grey suit and a white silk shirt, showing a protective snowy battlement of two-inch cuffs around his slender wrists, on one of which crouched, blinking in the sun, a gold watch. His shoes, polished as sea shells, had obviously been made with the same loving care as his suit. The final touch was that he was wearing an Old Rugbeian tie. He leaned forward in his rickshaw, his eyes as flat and expressionless as a cobra's, and let his lips part the merest millimetre or two, displaying small, white teeth like a puppy's.

'Hannibal, my dear fellow,' he said with immense warmth, his eyes cold, 'my dear fellow, whither away?'

'Good morning, Looja,' said Hannibal, grinning sardonically. 'We're off to see Kingy. Aren't you going in the wrong direction? I understood there was a special meeting at twelve. How will they do without you?'

'No one, as you of all people should be aware, my dear Hannibal, is indispensable. But I shall be there. I'm just returning for some papers I forgot,' said Looja, and looked at Peter. 'You must be Mr. Foxglove, Hannibal's new assistant. I am Muramana Looja. I know your dear uncle well. I'm delighted to meet you. Forgive me, but the ridiculous restriction of these quaint vehicles – a product of our monarch's puckish sense of humour – prevents me from shaking your hand and greeting you properly. Next time, however, next time.' He waved a tiny hand at them and his rickshaw rolled away.

'Good God,' said Peter, in genuine awe, 'what a repulsive creature. Even if I hadn't known about him I would have found him repellent. He exudes a menacing, poisonous air; and he's so still – like turning over a rock and finding a small black scorpion crouched under it.'

'Well put,' said Hannibal. 'Now you have seen and

judged our cat among the pigeons, our fox in the hen run, our death-watch in the wainscot. Is it true that he knows your uncle?'

'Well, Uncle never mentioned him to me,' said Peter.

'H'm, curious. Very curious,' said Hannibal and, lying back, tilted his absurd hat over his eyes and appeared to fall asleep.

The road wound round and round, circumnavigating Dzamandzar, and eventually climbing up on to the headland that formed one arm of Mocquerie Bay Presently they came to a pair of impressive gate posts made out of blocks of coral and, hanging between them wrought-iron gates in which was worked the official emblem of Zenkali, a Dolphin and a Mockery Bird on each side of an Amela tree. Two sentry boxes guarded the gate and attached to them were two gigantic Zenkali soldiers, wearing yellow jackets frogged with gold braid, black trousers and large white pith helmets from which yellow ostrich plumes curved majestically. The whole military effect was somewhat marred, however, by the fact that one sentry was squatting down on his haunches, throwing dice, while the other watched the results thoughtfully, picking his nose. Their rifles, being of no immediate use, were propped up inside the sentry boxes. As the rickshaws rounded the corner, there was an undignified scramble on the part of the sentries to retrieve their guns before they could stand smartly to attention and shoulder arms, stamping their feet in the dust with great efficiency.

'We done come for see Kingy,' explained Hannibal, 'open up, boys.'

The sentries opened the gates and the rickshaws sped down the curving driveway, lined by huge mango and banyan trees. They came to the Palace, a large, low building, built out of massive coral blocks painted pale pink, so that the whole building looked like some strange and beautiful cake from a master confectioner. As the carriers came to a halt, breathing deeply and glossy with sweat, the front doors of the Palace opened and a major-domo appeared, dressed in a scarlet uniform and tarboosh, followed by three lesser mortals in white uniforms.

'Good morning, sah, Mr. Hannibal,' said the major-domo, grinning from ear to ear, 'you well, sah?'

'I'm well, Malapi,' said Hannibal, dismounting, 'be a good fellow and take these damn dogs round to the kitchen, will you? Don't give them too much to eat, mind, or they'll get sick all over my carpets. Where's Kingy? I've brought the new Masa, Mr. Foxglove, to see him.'

'Welcome, Masa, welcome,' said Malapi, bowing to Peter. 'Kingy in garden, sah, Mr. Hannibal, you go come dis way, please.'

He led them quickly into the great, dim hall of the Palace, full of strange, dusty-looking portraits, and then out into the sunlit garden in the hollow square formed by the building. Here lawns like velvet were nurtured by some twenty or thirty little fountains that threw up lace-like mists of droplets into the still air, which was rich with the scent of a hundred different flowers and shrubs that overflowed the beds on all sides. A confetti of white doves fed on the grass and at one corner of the lawn two peacocks shimmered their tails in an ecstasy of self-satisfaction. In the centre of the garden was a pagoda consisting of upright columns of coral blocks supporting a criss-cross of thick wooden beams. This edifice supported a giant eiderdown of magenta and red Bougainvillea, throbbing and glittering under the assault of a myriad butterflies, bees, beetles and other insects. In the shade beneath this creeper was slung a hammock, which could easily have contained four ordinary men. But it only just accommodated the person of King Tamalawala Umber the Third.

The King was six foot four when he stood up and, at eighteen stone, he was built like a huge, chocolate-coloured Shire horse. His big bland face looked more Polynesian than African, with wide but not fleshy lips and a straight nose. He had eyes as big as walnuts and their size was enhanced by the clear white that surrounded them. He was wearing a scarlet skull cap, embroidered with gold flowers and a long, flowing, white robe with a frill of lace round the neck and cuffs and a panel of broderie anglaise down the front, rather like a Victorian nightgown. He wore simple red leather sandals and his only ornaments were a thin gold bangle on one wrist and a plain gold ring embracing a sapphire the size of a sugar lump. He lay back in the broad bosom of the hammock, one leg dangling over the side. Horn-rimmed spectacles were perched on the end of his nose and he was reading a copy of *The Times*. All around him was a snowdrift of newspapers in a multitude of languages. On a small table near the hammock rested an atlas, five dictionaries, scissors, pens and a large scrapbook.

'What Ho! Kingy,' called Hannibal unceremoniously, as they made their way across the soft, damp lawns to the Bougainvillea bower, 'What Ho! What Ho!'

Kingy laid down his newspaper and pushed his horn-rimmed glasses up on to his forehead. His face split into a dazzling smile of welcome as he launched himself out of the hammock through a foam of newspapers.

'Hannibal, you rogue, you're late. I thought you weren't coming,' he called, and his voice was deep and rich. He engulfed one of Hannibal's hands tenderly in his own huge ones and shook it gently.

'Sorry we are a bit on the late side,' Hannibal apologised, 'blame Foxglove here . . . he was telling me all about his sex life.'

Kingy turned his blinding grin on to the embarrassed Peter.

'Mr. Foxglove,' he boomed, holding out his hand, 'welcome to Zenkali.'

'I'm very pleased to be here, your Majesty,' said Peter, 'and I am sure I will find your kingdom delightful.'

'I fear, however, from a purely sexual point of view,' Kingy went on, 'you might find us somewhat dull, eh, Hannibal?'

'I would like to point out, sir, that I do not – as Mr.

Oliphant would imply – spend all my days preoccupied with sex.'

'*What* a pity,' said Kingy earnestly, but with a twinkle in his brown eyes, 'I sometimes feel that is the missing ingredient in our tranquil lives here. But do come and sit down and have a drink.'

Kingy produced glasses and, from a Thermos flask, he filled them with a viscous white fluid.

'What do you think of it?' he asked anxiously, as Peter took a sip and then drew a deep, shuddering breath.

'Excellent,' said Peter hoarsely.

'It's a little invention of my own,' said Kingy proudly, 'a delicate mixture of white rum, kummel, coconut cream and milk. Taken in any quantity it has such a disastrous effect on me that I have been forced to christen it *Lèse-Majesté*.'

He sat back, pulled his glasses down on to his nose, took a sip from his glass and rolled it round his mouth.

'Now, Mr. Foxglove, you bring us, I hope, news from the outside world?'

'I'm afraid not, sir,' said Peter. 'You see, I was in Barbados just before being sent here, and that's not really the hub of the universe.'

'What a pity,' said Kingy with a sigh, 'as you can see, I try and keep abreast of world affairs with the aid of newspapers, but as they arrive a month late I am always the last to hear about the latest assassination or who deposed whom. It is very embarrassing, I can tell you, to dash off a cordial note to some head of state, only to have it returned marked "not known at this address". It makes people think that you're not taking a serious interest in world affairs.'

Hannibal gave a snort of laughter but remained silent.

'Mind you, I sometimes wonder about the world's press, Mr. Foxglove, don't you? One can't help feeling as one peruses these human documents that it is – if I may misquote Lincoln – information of the feeble, by the feeble and for the feeble. The only satisfaction the world press gives me now is when it provides a succulent morsel for my scrapbook. Only last month there was a lovely bit about a man in Surbiton where I had digs when I was a student at the London School of Economics. This fellow was walking along the road when he was hit on the head by a block of green ice and rendered unconscious. Now who would expect to be knocked unconscious by a block of ice in salubrious Surbiton, of all suburbs? But worse was to follow. The police, after their normal length of time being mystified, discovered that the ice was a solid block of urine, ejected by mistake from a passing high altitude jet. I ask you, what is the world coming to when you can be assassinated by human waste products in Surbiton? Then I read in the *Singapore Times* that it is rumoured that the Prince of Snails is to marry soon. Turning royalty into invertebrates should surely be punished by long terms of imprisonment, don't you think?' asked Kingy.

'If that was the case, poor Martin Damien would be permanently incarcerated,' said Hannibal. 'I trust you saw your portrait on the front page?'

'Yes, I did,' said Kingy, beaming, 'simply delicious. I sent poor Mrs. Amazooga a big basket of fruit and some flowers as compensation, and it gave me the perfect chance to write Martin one of my most savage letters. It was so encrusted with seals you could hardly read it. I even threatened him with deportation. I wonder why he never takes any notice of my letters?'

'Consider yourself lucky he doesn't print one,' said Hannibal.

'I wish he would,' said Kingy, wistfully, 'I've always wanted to appear in print.'

'He does enough damage with his misprints,' said Hannibal, gloomily.

'Oh, *no!*' cried Kingy, 'if it wasn't for the humour in the *Zenkali Voice* I would abdicate immediately. Some weeks ago for instance, I read that the "Guard of Honour was inspected by the King who wore a peach-coloured satin dress with a Brussels lace veil and carried a bouquet of cream coloured hibiscus. The bridesmaids were Corporal

Ammibo Allim and Colour Sergeant Goola Masufa, who also received a condemnation for courage".'

The King laughed uproariously, throwing back his head. His giant body shook with mirth.

'Take it from me, Mr. Foxglove,' he said, wiping his eyes, 'if you ever get into a position of power, have your press run by an Irishman with a Zenkali compositor. It makes life worth living.'

'What time's your council meeting?' asked Hannibal, glancing at his watch.

'Oh, Hannibal, Hannibal,' said Kingy testily, 'why do you have to remind me of business when I'm enjoying myself?'

'Are you taking a vote on the airstrip?'

'Yes, we are,' said Kingy and glanced at Hannibal uncomfortably. 'Damn it, Hannibal, I know you don't like the idea but everyone else does, so what can I do? When all's said and done, I have got to consider the future of Zenkali and everyone thinks this will be good for the island. Come now, admit that it might have advantages, my dear fellow. The idea can't be all bad.'

'To me the thing is ludicrous,' said Hannibal stubbornly. 'You don't want a bloody great airstrip here, you don't want thousands of uncouth servicemen lounging about eating their heads off, you don't want Mocquerie Bay full of naval vessels and, above all, you don't want a happy, self-supporting island turned into a place of military importance.'

'Well, I admit some of your arguments are valid, but whatever my private feelings may be, there is a very strong lobby for the scheme and I simply can't go against it, as you well know.'

'Yes, a lobby run by that creature Looja,' said Hannibal angrily. 'The fact that it has his support is enough to damn it in my eyes.'

'You have not met Looja, my Minister of Development, Mr. Foxglove?' Kingy enquired.

'Not really,' said Peter.

'No? Well, that is a treat in store for you. I'm afraid I must warn you that he is universally disliked and that he lacks both charm and trustworthiness, and if one must have a rogue it is essential that they have charm, at least. No, I'm afraid that Looja is not altogether a pleasant man. In fact, I would go further and say that, quite definitely, he is the sort of wog that gets us wogs a bad name.'

'Has he really got that damn valley?' asked Hannibal.

'Yes, I'm afraid so,' said Kingy sadly, 'right from under our noses, too. I'm afraid we're losing our grip, Hannibal. What do you think the little twister said when I tackled him about it? He said that he was quite unaware of the transaction, that it had been done without his knowledge by his wife. You have to give him full marks for audacity, if nothing else.'

'The whole thing is very depressing,' said Hannibal.

'I know, I know,' said Kingy, getting to his feet, 'but there is nothing much I can do about it, you know. After all, we can control the development, Hannibal, and if we're careful it won't ruin the island. You know I am just as anxious as you are that no harm should befall Zenkali.'

'Of course I know that,' said Hannibal, 'in fact, you're the only thing that gives me any hope.'

'Well, we do manage to have a certain amount of fun together in this dull business of ruling, don't we?' said Kingy, grinning. 'Goodbye, Mr. Foxglove. I hope you settle in well and that Hannibal does not ill-treat you. I must warn you that the last assistant he had left here to have a nervous breakdown. Come and see me again.'

'I'd be delighted to,' said Peter.

Kingy smiled and waved a massive hand in dismissal.

'Now,' said Hannibal, 'a quick visit to Government House and you will have done your duty and can relax. I think you'll find the Gov. and his missus charming, if a trifle other-worldly.'

His Excellency, Sir Adrian Blythe-Warick, was a small, stocky, rather stunted little man who looked as if he had been heavily starched early on in his career and had never quite succeeded in breaking loose. He wore a wide frozen grin.

'Foxglove . . . Foxglove . . . yes, yes,' he said, shaking Peter's hand. He cleared his throat several times. He had a faint, whispering voice like the mating cry of a very tiny shrew. 'Glad to have you aboard, m'boy . . . glad indeed . . . yes, yes, dashed ticklish yes . . . we need every shoulder to the . . . um . . . yes . . . diplomacy . . . tact . . . discretion and so forth called for . . . but I'm sure you have tact, m'boy . . . you look a fine, upstanding young . . . um . . . yes . . . just the sort we need . . . salt of the earth . . . and so forth . . . um . . . yes. Glad to have you aboard.'

'Thank you, sir,' said Peter.

'Yes, well, Hannibal, my dear fellow, get us all a drink . . . um . . . mainbrace . . . hair of . . . do you play bridge, Foxglove?'

'No, sir, I'm afraid not,' said Peter.

'Ah . . . yes . . . well . . . pity,' said Sir Adrian regretfully, 'But you must come to lunch, anyway.'

'Thank you, sir,' said Peter, and felt he needed the drink that Hannibal had prepared for him.

'Hope you like Zenkali . . .' whispered the Governor. 'Tropical paradise . . . getting self-government, d'you know . . . had to come, of course . . . old order changeth . . . um, yes . . . fine upstanding king . . . salt of the . . . even though . . . well, well, he can't help it, poor chap . . . Eton, you know . . . yes . . . still, salt of the earth . . . painful . . . but still . . . important thing . . . Queen and country, Commonwealth . . . yes, never say die, what?'

'Quite, Your Excellency,' said Hannibal smoothly, 'I have explained it all to Foxglove.'

'Good . . . good . . .' said Sir Adrian. 'You must bring him to lunch.'

At that moment, the door opened and in trotted, like a small, clockwork toy, Lady Emerald Blythe-Warick. At the first disbelieving glance, Peter thought she was in fancy dress, for she was dressed from head to toe in green. Not only were her clothes, stockings and shoes green, but even her hair had a greenish tinge, such as a sloth gets from the primitive algae that inhabits its pelt. She was bedecked with emeralds. Bracelets, necklaces, brooches and medallions. She clicked, chimed and tinkled as she moved. Birdlike, she looked about her with quick movements of the head. In one hand, she clasped a small and beautifully made tortoiseshell ear trumpet.

'Ah . . . Emmie . . . yes . . . this is young Foxglove, m'dear . . . fine, upstanding . . . salt of . . . my wife,' said Sir Adrian, making a vague gesture at her like a man trying to escape from a strait-jacket.

'Who's this, dear?' asked Lady Emerald, beaming and bobbing at Peter, plugging her ear trumpet into her ear, which she found with some difficulty, lurking behind an ornate emerald earring.

'Foxglove, m'dear, Foxglove,' said Sir Adrian, screwing his voice up to a muted squeak. 'Fine . . . upstanding . . . just joined . . . glad.'

'Poxdove, Poxdove? What an interesting name,' said Her Ladyship, delightedly. 'So curious – old English, I've no doubt. They say there was a lot of pox about in those days. Now if you had been called Poxchicken, I would not have found it so curious, since the derivation is more obvious. But I suppose since chickens can get it, doves can, too. Disease, as they say, knows no barriers of creed, class or colour. Although they do say Eskimos die of it, don't they? Or am I thinking of Amerindians? Anyway, one thing I am certain of and that's that Guinea Fowl don't get it. Do you like Guinea Fowl?'

'I'm devoted to them, Your Ladyship,' said Peter.

'Her Ladyship breeds Guinea Fowl,' explained Hannibal long-sufferingly.

'I have a lot of Guinea Fowl, Mr. Poxdove,' Her Ladyship went on. 'I breed them. I find them most intelligent birds, rather like dogs with feathers. You must come and help me feed them some time and you'll see – it's positively uncanny, the way they understand. You must ask this nice young man to lunch, Adrian,' announced

Lady Emerald. 'We don't see enough of him.'

'I have asked him, m'dear,' said Adrian, 'yes, yes ... but he doesn't play bridge ... still no matter ... he's welcome ... most welcome.'

With the combination of Sir Adrian and Lady Emerald the conversation ranged widely but inconclusively, and it was with relief that Peter saw Hannibal finish his drink.

'Must get Foxglove settled in, sir,' he said to the Governor, 'make sure he's all right.'

'Yes, yes, everthing shipshape and Bristol ... um,' said the Governor. 'Delighted to ... yes ... Hannibal knows the ... um ... um ... ropes, yes. You must come and have lunch when you've dropped anchor ... Yes.'

'You must come and have lunch, Mr. Poxdove,' said Her Ladyship, oblivious of her husband's invitation. 'I'll get my husband to ask you. And then you can feed my Guinea Fowl. And don't forget to bring that charming little wife of yours – we don't see nearly enough of her.'

They set off once more in their rickshaws with their entourage of dogs, and Hannibal lit one of his long cigars and seemed content to remain silent. Peter lay back in his rickshaw and relaxed. Soon they came on to the coast road that ran along the edge of Mocquerie Bay. The road passed through groves of fir-like Casuarina trees that threw a delicate fretted shade. Beyond them lay the wide white beach and the clear, inviting waters of the lagoon. Periodically the road crossed small bridges spanning shallow streams that ran, glittering and shimmering between rocks as black and shiny as tar. Here and there on the banks groups of women stood spreading their washing on the green grass in an explosion of colours like a great flower bed. They would straighten up as the rickshaws approached and wave languid brown arms, their white smiles flashing and their voices shrill as parakeets, as they called greetings. On the beach there were clusters of black canoes like beached porpoises and around them on the brilliant sands the fishermen crouched mending their nets. Green lizards with orange heads darted across the road in front of them and the cool Casuarina groves were full of the twitter and glint of bird life. Peter drank it all in and thought that he had never been to a place in which he had felt, instantly, so happy. The colours, the scents, the atmosphere, the people, all were somehow exactly right.

'This is going to be your house,' said Hannibal suddenly, pointing up the road with his cigar. 'It's small, but it's right on the beach and I thought you'd prefer that to the other one which is stuck up behind the town.'

Through the Casuarina trees, Peter could just make out the shape of a low, white bungalow lying practically on the beach.

'It looks marvellous,' he said, 'I never expected anything quite so Hollywood. I thought it would be a rough wooden shack in the middle of town with no running water and a smell of donkeys.'

'You've got running water, electricity of a sort, a telephone when it works, and a staff of three to minister to your wants. You should be pretty comfortable,' said Hannibal as the rickshaws drew up outside the bungalow. The three servants appeared on the deep shady verandah. A short, plump man, with a brown pudding face, a gigantic grin and merry eyes wore a red sash round his white uniform.

'Welcome, sah, welcome,' he said, bouncing up and down on his toes, like someone waiting to play a game of tennis. 'Me Amos, sah, me steward.'

He bowed eagerly over Peter's proffered hand.

'Dis, sah, na small boy. 'E called Tulip, sah,' he said, pointing to a fourteen-year-old boy with a cast in one eye and teeth that stuck out. The boy stood twiddling his toes in the dust shyly and merely bobbed his head to Peter's greeting, his eyes on the ground.

'Dis, sah, na cook man, sah,' Amos went on, 'him very good cook, sah. Dey de call um Samson. 'E bloody fine cook, sah.'

Samson, who was tall, excessively thin and lugubrious looking, rather like an emaciated bloodhound, stared fixedly at Peter, without any expression on his face.

'Hello, Samson,' said Peter, thinking as he said it that Samson was an extremely bad advertisement for his culinary art.

'Welcome, Mr. Foxglove, sah,' bellowed Samson in a muted roar like a professional sergeant-major with laryngitis. 'Me Samson, me cook.'

'Er . . . yes, well, it's nice to meet you all,' said Peter, 'and now, Amos, have we any drink in the house?'

'Yessah,' said Amos, grinning, 'Missy Audley done fetch um.'

'Missy Audley . . . does he mean Miss Damien?' Peter asked Hannibal.

'Yes,' said Hannibal, 'Audrey fixes up all the bachelor establishments. Woman's touch and all that sort of thing.'

'Well, come in and have a drink,' said Peter. 'You'll be my first guest.'

'I suppose a tiny noggin wouldn't do any harm,' said Hannibal, heaving himself out of the rickshaw, 'a sort of housewarming . . . my duty really.'

Amos led them across the wide, shady verandah and into a long, cool room. Tall french windows at one end led out on to the back verandah, the Casuarina whispered in the garden and the canna lilies stood in scarlet ranks like guardsmen. Beyond was the dazzling beach and the pale blue waters of the lagoon. Amos left them and then came bustling back with two frothing tankards.

'Well, here's luck,' said Hannibal.

'Cheers,' said Peter.

'Yes,' said Hannibal, wandering to the french windows and looking out, 'not a bad little shack, this . . . I expect you'll soon feel at home.'

At home? Peter already felt as though he had lived in this little house all his life.

Chapter Three

———◄ ❋ ►———

ZENKALI APPROVED

Tulip, his teeth protruding even more with concentration, woke him at dawn with a tray of tea and a mango. Amos, strutting behind, supervised every move with an eagle eye. Their quiet 'Good mornings' and the scuff of their bare feet on the tiles was soothing as they moved about, opening shutters and laying out clothes. Outside the sky was leaf-green and every bird in Zenkali was greeting the dawn. Peter ate and drank peacefully and then, half an hour later, lowered himself into the warm sea and lay face downwards watching the pageant of fish that moved in the gin-clear waters beneath his mask. So brilliant were the colours and shapes, so complex the web of life beneath him, that he lost all count of time. Suddenly, he became aware that someone was shouting his name and, sitting up saw Audrey at the sea's edge. He swam hastily back to the beach and waded ashore.

'I'm sorry,' he said, towelling himself rapidly. 'I lost all track of time . . . I've never seen anything so fabulous as that bit of reef.'

'It's remarkable, isn't it?' Audrey agreed, sitting down on the sand. 'And the incredible thing is that one never seems to get used to it. Every time you go out you see something new. I'm afraid it's like a drug for me. I have even been known to miss a lunch at Government House because I was snorkeling and forgot the time.'

'Hardly a crime, more self-defence, surely?' said Peter.

'Oh, no,' said Audrey. 'I love going to lunch at Gov.

House. I think H.E. and his Lady are enchanting and everything is so dotty. Lunch parties there can be hysterical. I wouldn't miss one for the world. Did Hannibal take you to make your mark with His Excellency?'

'Yes, yesterday afternoon. It was quite an experience. I'm used to much stuffier Government Houses and Governors than that. This was like visiting a couple of dormice in a doll's house.'

'Tell me,' said Audrey, smiling.

So he described his visit to Government House and when he came to Lady Emerald's final remark Audrey crowed with delighted laughter.

'Dear Lady Emerald,' she said, 'she really lives in another world. What did you say?'

'Nothing,' said Peter. 'I was about to explain my bachelor state when I caught Hannibal's eye and he shook his head.'

'But she really is so sweet and muddled that you can't help liking her,' said Audrey. 'Did you meet the A.D.C. Diggory? Hannibal calls him a primitive Australian instrument. He's almost as bad as H.E. and Mrs. They make a lovely trio.'

'No, I was spared Diggory,' said Peter, 'but I suppose I shall run into him during the course of my duties. Tell me, is there something weird lurking behind every bush in Zenkali?'

'You mean human?' asked Audrey.

'Yes,' said Peter, 'after all, you can hardly call Hannibal, Kingy or the contents of Government House usual.'

'Well,' she admitted, 'they are a bit eccentric by normal standards, I suppose. I think it's islands in general and Zenkali in particular. It's a sort of island disease people get where every quirk and foible of their characters is exaggerated and magnified. Zenkali, especially, seems to attract this sort of person and then it acts as a sort of hothouse and turns them into something rare and curious.'

Audrey got to her feet and brushed the sand from her hands.

'Today I want to introduce you to a few more of our home-grown eccentrics. They, after all, are the ones who make the island tick,' she said.

'I can't wait,' said Peter, 'as long as you promise to show me the Ombu tree as well.'

'Of course,' said Audrey.

She was driving a battered but serviceable Mini Moke and in the back Peter saw a basket of food and a small ice chest for drinks.

'I thought we'd picnic,' said Audrey, gesturing at them, 'there's a nice spot up on Matakama.'

'What, near evil Looja's valley?'

'Yes. It's a wonderful area, probably one of the prettiest in the island. But it won't be pretty for long with the valleys flooded, a huge dam and an airfield,' said Audrey, gloomily.

'I take it that you're really against the whole scheme?' he asked.

'Yes, I am. You know, everyone here is really very simple, very happy and by and large, very *good*.'

'Even Looja?'

'Every Eden has its snake. I'm not trying to pretend this is an island of saints. But basically they are gentle, mildly eccentric and – if you like, child-like. So this airstrip business is rather like putting a box of fireworks and some matches in a well-conducted nursery. I think Hannibal is right. The old devil generally is. Anyway, let's forget about the bloody airfield for the moment and enjoy the drive.'

They drove through the brilliant countryside and since it was the big market day in Dzamandzar, the road was thronged with Zenkalis bringing in their merchandise and livestock. There were fat old ladies waddling along, clad in brilliant batik cloths, huge baskets of mangoes, coco yams, pineapples or pawpaws so perfectly balanced on their heads that they looked as if they had been welded there. There were young men carrying lengths of golden sugar cane, or poles from which dangled – like some strange feathered fruit – rows of chickens slung by their legs. Wooden wagons drawn by humped, long-horned Zebus squeaked, rattled and lurched along, trailing clouds of pink dust. They were piled high with baskets, sweet potatoes, cane chairs, sacks of rice and sugar and red clay cooking pots. Elderly grizzled herdsmen, wrapped in scarlet blankets, prodded herds of cattle and goats into activity with their spears, while the herds were kept from spilling off the road into the lush countryside by fleet-footed little boys with sticks and small packs of smooth-coated, amber-coloured swift and vociferous dogs. Everyone shouted and gossiped and joked. Groups sang as they walked along and, if their brown hands were not otherwise occupied, played slender bamboo pipes or twanged twelve-stringed valihas or beat on tiny, pot-bellied drums. Fat old ladies exchanged saucy badinage with each other and doubtless ribald stories which made them laugh until their fat shook. Slender girls, walking as gracefully as colts under their heavy loads, seemed to drift along the road, exchanging parrot-sharp repartee with the young bloods and gazed about them with bold, mulberry-bright eyes. The glitter of colour and the music of voice and instrument flowed down the red road towards Dzamandzar in a haze of rose-coloured dust.

'This is the monthly market in the town,' explained Audrey, driving skilfully with one hand while she waved the other one in greeting. Everyone waved, everyone smiled, everyone called out 'I see ya, Missy Audley . . . walka good, Missy Audley . . . Missy Audley go go for market? . . . Walka good, walka good.'

'Is it the only market?' asked Peter, watching with fascination the streams of humanity they passed.

'Oh no. They have daily markets in the villages and a small daily market in Dzamandzar,' Audrey said, 'but this is the really important monthly one where you can buy anything from a cow to a peanut or a brass bed or a love potion.'

'They all look so clean and neat and well fed and prosperous; glossy, like horse chestnuts,' said Peter.

Audrey laughed, tooting her horn at a confusion of cattle and goats.

'Basically they are prosperous,' she said. 'Nearly everyone has a little farm or a business of some kind. They're not rich, of course, but they are certainly not poor, judged by other islands like this. And it's really all due to the Amela tree keeping the economy on an even keel. Without it, I dread to think what would happen. We're too far away from the world for the world to take any interest in us. That's fine when you're self-supporting. But if you suddenly want a handout the world doesn't want to know.'

There was a sudden rift in the brown tide of goats and cows and Audrey expertly nudged the nose of the vehicle into the gap and they were soon through, their lungs full of pink dust, their nostrils full of the pungent smell of goat and the sweet smell of cattle. Audrey took a narrow turning off the main road and the market crowd thinned to a trickle and they could increase speed. The girl drove fast, but well, her elegant hands resting negligently on the wheel. She was wearing a blue checked shirt, jeans and sandals and her hair hung free. Peter looked at her bewitching profile and wondered about her.

'At nineteen, I got me a degree in the Arts at Dublin University,' said Audrey, smiling mockingly, her words cutting uncannily across his thoughts. 'I thought I was a cross between Leonardo da Vinci and Picasso. I was pretty good, but to be only pretty good in such a crowded profession is not really good enough. Anyway, from the tender age of twenty until last year I spent a grandmother's inheritance, tiny but sufficient, and hitchhiked all across Europe, then Africa and through quite a bit of Asia. It was wonderful. But the more I saw, the more I realised I would never be Picasso, and so I learnt to be content with what talent I had.'

'Why did you come back here?' asked Peter.

'It's my home. But the real reason is that my mother died and I came back to make sure that Daddy didn't either drink himself into the grave or starve himself there by paying too much attention to the damn paper and not enough to his stomach.'

'Are you sorry?'

'Good Lord, no. I love Zenkali. Before, when I was a child, I loved it but accepted it all as quite normal. It was only coming back to it that I realised how eccentric and free it all was. Now I think you'd have to use dynamite to get me out of here.'

'Do you help your father with the paper?' he asked.

'A bit,' she said, 'but apart from that I give art lessons at the local school, I collect local music and give guitar and piano lessons and, with the aid of Hannibal, I've worked up a tiny but quite lucrative business translating obscure scientific papers. I speak six languages fluently, so that helps.'

'Good heavens, you do believe in using your talents,' said Peter, appreciatively.

'My father is a fanatic about that. He says it's your duty to explore all your talents. There are so many untalented people in the world that if you have any aptitude you should use it, otherwise it's criminal, you know, like being in a country of the blind and not using your eyes. I am going to take you to meet a lady who not only uses all her talents but invents new ones at every available opportunity.'

'Who's that?'

'The Reverend Judith Longnecker of the Church of the Second Coming. Headquarters: Ploughkeepsie, Virginia. Naturally she is known to the godless Hannibal as old Longknickers, Dangle-bloomers and similar irreverent sobriquets, which she loves. The rest of us just call her the Rev.'

They had turned off the road into a neat compound in which stood a small bungalow and next to it a tiny church, which was only half walled so that the congregation, when

73

seated, could see the view. The compound stood on the edge of an escarpment and looked down over a great sweep of green farmland and Amela plantations to where the sea, enamel smooth, lapped the land. Far out lay the great, white, crumpled, restless ribbon of reef foam and beyond that the deep sea, so dark a blue it was almost black. The compound in which the bungalow and the church stood was spotless. It was filled with flower beds and brilliant creepers had been encouraged in their exuberant climb over both house and church. By one of the flower beds drooped a tall, crane-like figure in a shapeless purple satin dress, concluding a lobotomy on a flowering shrub.

'Good morning, Rev,' called Audrey, as they stopped. The tall, angular figure turned. It was wearing a gigantic straw hat, held in place by a length of chiffon and a number of old-fashioned hatpins which looked as if they had been plunged into the Reverend Longnecker's skull to keep the hat in position. In the band of the hat were stuck innumerable bits of folded paper fastened in place with pins. Under this extraordinary headgear the Reverend's face, long, earnest and wistful as a giraffe, was burnt to a fine biscuit-brown and the skin had wrinkled so delicately and in such profusion that it looked as though she had walked into an intricate spider's web that had settled upon her face. Embedded in this lacework were two large, intelligent and sparkling dark eyes, a strong beaky nose and a wide, mobile mouth.

'Well, hi there!' cried the Rev. 'Godammit, I was just thinking of you and here you are. And who's your beau? Come on, tell the Rev. You know I can't stand secrets – can't keep them. It's really one of the reasons I couldn't be a Catholic, you know. No, not for Judith. I'd be out of that little ol' confessional and spreading it around the island before the poor person got home. Not, of course, that I've got anything against the Catholics, poor dears. No, no, they've got a grand design – just lacking in a few component parts. But I think it's wrong to burden a priest with so many of other people's secrets – I mean going around a community knowing all the dirt and not being able to tell it – for land sakes, it's not human – it leads directly to religious dyspepsia, I reckon.'

As she talked, she had rushed forward, embraced Audrey, wrung Peter's hand in her own brown calloused ones, and was propelling them towards the bungalow without making any attempt to let them speak. Peter wondered dazedly what her sermons were like.

'Leonardo da Vinci,' she shouted to a Zenkali gardener who was mowing the lawn, 'come here and finish pruning this bush, there's a good boy.' She stamped up the verandah, throwing out her limbs at wild angles.

'Come in, come in,' she said, 'come in and sit awhile. I'll get some drinks. Beethoven, *Beethoven*, which side you dere? *Beethoven*.'

She rushed off into the kitchen quarters and returned triumphantly a few minutes later followed by a diminutive and very fat Zenkali, almost invisible behind an enormous tray of drinks.

'Rum punch, that's the stuff,' said the Rev, busying herself with the tray. 'Nothing like rum punch.'

She poured out the drinks and then sat down, leaning forward eagerly.

'Now,' she said, 'tell me . . . you must be the new boy.'

'Peter Foxglove,' said Audrey. 'I'm just showing him the island and this is our first port of call.'

'You mean you brought him here before the Church of England and the Catholics can corrupt him?' asked the Rev. 'I think that's real neighbourly of you, Audrey, yes siree. It's not often in my line of business that you get a potential convert delivered on the hoof as it were before mid-morning drinks.'

Peter chuckled. 'I'm sure you could convert me to anything,' he said.

'We can try, we can try,' said the Rev, gulping at her drink.

'Tell me, d'you like Zenkali? You're just in time to see the last of it.'

'The last of it?' said Peter. 'What d'you mean?'

The Rev raised a long, bony forefinger.

'The island is doomed,' she said sepulchrally. 'Doomed and damned and there seems no way of averting it.'

'You mean the airfield?' asked Peter, who was now getting used to the idea that there seemed to be only one topic of conversation in Zenkali.

'I mean the airfield,' said the Rev, nodding portentously. 'If that goes through we are doomed.'

'Come now, Rev. You're worse than Hannibal,' said Audrey.

'This is one of the few things Hannibal and I see eye to eye on. As the whole disastrous thing is really a *fait accompli*, I have been thinking of last ditch stands,' said the Rev. 'And I tell you, Audrey, I am convinced that the good Lord must be against it, too, for He's been filling my head with the darnedest ideas. As you know, I've only got a small, but a very devoted congregation. Now I've been thinking that I could perhaps form them into a small guerrilla band and we could sabotage work on the airfield and the dam. With that end in view I sent away for a few books to get some ideas, and they sent me some splendid stuff.'

The Rev got up and darted to a corner of the room like a great disjointed dragonfly and came back with her arms full of books. 'Lookee here, there's some splendid information in these. *Secret Agent in Hitler's Germany* has some useful stuff on blowing up bridges. Here's another – *Rossignol of the French Resistance*. Did you know that a teaspoonful of sugar in a petrol tank could have a more detrimental effect on a vehicle than a woman driver? Here's another – *Fifty Years of Spying and Sabotage* by Count Marvrofalcon. There's a lot of stuff on invisible writing which won't help us, but he's got a first class recipe for Molotov cocktails, and a splendid drawing of a limpet mine. Captain Pappas has promised to get me all the necessary ingredients for a really good gunpowder and I think, with the aid of the Lord, we could give them a good run for their money.'

Peter stared at her. She appeared to be serious.

'Er, have you discussed this with Hannibal?' he asked.

'No, no, not yet. But I've got a note on the subject for him,' said the Rev excitedly, gazing round wildly. 'Now, where did I put my filing cabinet – where in Heaven's name have I put my filing cabinet?'

'Over there, on the chair,' said Audrey, who was taking the whole thing remarkably calmly, Peter thought.

'Ah, yes,' said the Rev retrieving her huge hat and twirling it round on her hand like a carousel. 'Let's see, let's see . . . ah, there's that jam recipe Lady Emerald wanted . . . shopping lists . . . what's this? Ah, yes, my sermon for tomorrow . . . here we are, "A brief plan for Insurrection in Zenkali".' She produced a slip of paper from her hatband and handed it to Peter.

'Give that to Hannibal,' she said, 'and tell him I could have my guerrilla force marshalled in a month. And if he knows of a source of good cheap hand-grenades he's to let me know.'

'I'll certainly do that,' said Peter, very seriously, and put the missive carefully in his pocket.

When they were eventually back in the car and had driven away, the Rev waving after them, Peter turned to Audrey, who was laughing immoderately.

'Now, look here, Miss Damien,' he began severely.

'I'm sorry,' she said, 'but you looked so startled. I wish you could have seen the expression on your face.'

'Well, what do you expect?' asked Peter aggrievedly. 'I'm not used to ministers of the Gospel suggesting guerrilla warfare as a means of settling problems. She can't be serious, surely?'

'Oh, yes, the Rev's always serious about everything. It doesn't mean to say she'll do it, but she'll plan it and put all the knowledge she gains to good use. If they ever have a demolition problem in Zenkali, the Rev will be in the forefront giving advice and she'll know exactly how much dynamite it would take to blow up Government House, or whatever. Rev never wastes anything. You know, when she goes on leave every two years she doesn't go home like the other missionaries do. She goes somewhere and learns something and then comes back and teaches the Zenkalis.'

'What kind of things?' asked Peter.

'Anything she thinks will be of use. She found that the sand here could make a rather nice greenish glass, so she went and learnt how to make glass and blow it, and now some of her converts run a tiny glass factory. She wasn't happy with the rather haphazard way they were building their houses so she went to Scandinavia and learnt the most up-to-date way of using wood and prefabricating things. Now her people have the best homes and furniture in Zenkali. She taught herself the most extraordinary things – she can take a car or lorry to bits and put it back together again; she spent one year learning new methods of agriculture. She went and learnt basket and cane chair-making and started another cottage industry with it. Her parishioners all adore her, and what I can't understand is why she has so few of them compared to the other religious groups. The Catholics have the most, then the Anglicans and poor old Rev makes do with the dregs.'

'What are the others like?'

'Awful. The Catholics are represented by Father O'Mally, who preaches fire and brimstone and eternal damnation by an all-loving God if you don't obey the rules of the Church. The Church of England is represented by Mr. and Mrs. Bradstitch. He is a pompous snob and pontificates. He doesn't really like the Zenkalis, smells of aniseed and beats his wife. She knits incessantly and is greatly given to doing incomprehensible good works, like teaching her Sunday School class to knit antimacassars. Now let's stop talking about missionaries and you admire the view. We're now three thousand feet up Matakama and I'm going to take you to picnic in the valley that all the hoo-ha is about. I should think it's your last chance of seeing it before they flood it.'

Since they had left the Rev's house, the road had meandered through Amela plantations and scattered farmland. Now it had started to climb in a series of loops and the higher they got, the wilder the forest became, thick and tangled with here and there a small clapboard homestead standing in a tiny garden of fruit and vegetables. Eventually, even these homesteads dwindled away, and they drove through thick forest.

'None of this is original forest, I gather from my guide book,' said Peter.

'No, there's nothing left of the original forest except a few species of shrub and the Amela tree. All this stuff is introduced: banyan, mango, traveller's palms and that damned Chinese guava, which grows everywhere and strangles everything. The fruit's lovely but the bush is a menace.'

The road swung round a corner and ahead lay a wide bridge. Audrey stopped the car in the middle. On the left towered a red and gold rock face some two or three hundred feet high and from its summit a thick jet of white water fell halfway down the cliff face in a shining plait to where it hit a projection of the cliff and burst into a rose of foam, rainbow garlanded, and it then continued its fall in two shining tangles of water. It hit the base of the cliff in a great tumble of rocks, each shiny with water, each green-wigged with lush vegetation. The water roared and foamed between the rocks and the air was full of fine mist and dozens of small but perfect rainbows. Then the waters rumbled beneath the bridge and fell down a further high cliff face in one great leap of water that crashed into the valley below.

'This is the Matakama river,' said Audrey, raising her voice above the roar of the waters. 'It's at the head of the top fall that they plan to dam it.'

They drove on and soon the road straightened out and ran alongside the river down the valley. Presently Audrey took the vehicle off the road and parked it under the trees on the river bank. They unloaded the food and drink and sat down at the water's edge. Here the river was wide and deep, running through rocks smooth like gravestones, each decorated with moss and yellow wild begonias. Brilliant kingfishers flickered like blue and scarlet flames in the gloom of the branches that overhung the banks, and the air was full of birdsong and the whirr and zither of insects and the plaintive peep and trill of frogs. The grass on which they sat was starred with small magenta flowers shaped like four-leaf clovers.

'What a gorgeous spot,' said Peter, brushing a green dragonfly off his sandwich. 'It's incredible that anyone should want to destroy it.'

'Progress,' said Audrey shortly, dissecting a small chicken. 'It's important to destroy this so we can have more electricity so that we can then have colour television to show us what the world is really like.'

'I still haven't quite got the geography right,' said Peter. 'How does this valley run?'

Audrey picked up a handful of earth and poured it out into a cone.

'That's Matakama,' she said. She took a stick and drew a curving line round one side. 'That's the valley we're in. Now, if you look at it as a sort of backbone you get a mass of smaller valleys running off it like ribs,' she said, and drew a series of lines curving off the main line on either side. The whole thing looked rather like a fish skeleton, slightly curved. 'When they flood this,' she said, pointing to the backbone, 'they also flood all these ribs. So, in fact, an enormous area of lovely mountain country will disappear.'

'What's in all these side valleys?' asked Peter.

'Nothing – I mean there's no habitation. A lot of them are inaccessible except by helicopter, I should imagine, and most of them are a terrible sweat to climb into, coupled with the fact that the soil is not good and so, from the point of view of agriculture, once you fell this forest the topsoil vanishes. This, of course, gives the pro-dam people a perfect argument – they're only flooding "useless" land – that's to say, land that's useless for farming. Wildlife and aesthetics have not even been considered.'

Their meal finished, they lay back and stared up at the blue sky through the shimmering tracery of leaves. Occasional gusts of warm wind stirred the trees, making petals from fragile unseen flowers high above in the canopy drift to the ground.

Half an hour later, they parked the car on the outskirts of Dzamandzar and took a Kingy Cart through the thickly-populated streets to a small building near the main square. On it was affixed an impressive notice which read *The Zenkali Voice – the only Honest Newspaper in the Island*. It was an odd claim to make, Peter thought, since it was the *only* paper on the island. Inside a tiny cluttered office they found Simon Damien. He was a tall burly man with his daughter's extraordinary eyes and a tangled mop of hair as red as a winter fox. It was apparent that he had drunk long and lovingly, but not wisely.

'I am more than delighted to meet you,' he said, in his broad brogue, wringing Peter's hand. 'Any man who can take that devil's spawn of mine off me hands for a whole day and give me the Peace of Paradise, free from nagging criticism, is a man in whose debt I stand.'

'I am more than willing to render you this service at any time,' said Peter.

Damien grinned at him. He had a pug nose like a bulldog's which wrinkled when he smiled.

'Have a drink,' he said, running his fingers through his hair and making it more wildly tangled than before. 'Have you ever tried an Appendectomy? Three parts Zenkali Nectar, one part Curaçao, one part white rum, one part vodka and a dash of soda to give it body. Sit you down – it'll take me but the twinkling of a fairy's eye to construct one for you.'

'No,' said Audrey, firmly, 'we can't stay, Father, we've got lots to do yet. We only popped in to say hello.'

'Are you sure?' said her father, disappointment in his face. 'Are you sure you can't, just for a wee glass, the size of half a wren's egg, now, are you sure?'

'Sure,' said Audrey, firmly. 'I know your wee glasses.'

'Audrey, me own daughter, talking to me like that,' he said, wounded. He turned to Peter. 'May God forgive me for saying it, but it's a hard and harsh world when a daughter denies her own father a wee drink when he stands here with his blackened tongue protruding from between cracked lips. It's a hard, harsh world, so it is.'

'And don't try your blarney with me,' said Audrey. 'You've had more than a wren's egg already.'

'I shware to you,' said Mr. Damien with a certain difficulty, 'by the holy big toe of the Apostle St. Paul, that the drinks that have passed my lips would scarcely have wet a leprechaun's toothbrush.'

'Liar,' said Audrey, grinning.

'Liar . . . *Liar?*' said Damien, as if doubting his ears. He turned to Peter. 'This must be painful for you to witness. Holy Mary, Mother of God, a daughter calling her own father a liar, and he must be the most honest and upright of Irishmen ever to have left the Emerald Isle as an emissary bringing truth and culture to the world.'

'Have you put the paper to bed?' enquired Audrey.

'Don't ask silly questions. Of course I have,' said Damien, abandoning his role as a misunderstood father.

'Well, I suggest you trot home and put yourself to bed, too,' said Audrey, practically.

'Sure and the girl had wondrous fine ideas,' said Damien, grinning. 'That's just what I was going to do when you stopped by.'

The girl went to him, kissed him and patted his cheek. 'Go home, you old reprobate,' she said. 'I'm just taking Peter to meet Carmen and then to see the Ombu – I'll be home about eight, I expect. And *don't* have more than a wren's egg or I'll murder you with my own hands, so I will.'

'Promises, promises,' said Damien, and then frowned. 'Oh, yes, I know. I had that little chap Droom in here looking for you.'

'What did he want?'

'I don't really know – you know how he drones on. Says

he's made an important discovery and must see Hannibal or Kingy.'

'They run a mile from him, poor thing. They say he's so boring.'

'Well, he wants you to use your influence to get Hannibal to see him; says it's very important, and for Hannibal's or Kingy's ears only. Said I'd tell you.'

'Okay. I'll see what I can do,' said Audrey. 'Goodbye, respected parent.'

'May the beard of the good King Wenceslas go with you, my daughter,' said Damien slowly, 'and all who sail with you.'

As they got into the Kingy Cart, Audrey sighed and then laughed.

'Poor Father,' she said, 'he's hit the bottle intermittently ever since Mother died. I do try and control him, but he's hopeless.'

'But drunk he's utterly charming,' said Peter.

'That's the trouble,' said Audrey, ruefully, 'he's so damned charming he gets his own way. Oh, well, now I'll inflict Carmen on you and then we can go and pat the Ombu. You're not bored, are you?'

'How could any man be bored in your company?' asked Peter. 'But to have your company and, as a bonus, to be introduced to such a dazzling array of eccentrics – it would take a very dull man to be bored.'

'Well, if you do get bored, you have only to say,' said Audrey and added, 'and then, out of spite, I'd take you to the English Club.'

The Kingy Cart raced through the narrow streets, filled with parrot-bright crowds, filled with the million scents that make up a conglomeration of human beings, filled with special scents of market day, the crisp scent of newly-laundered 'Sunday best' clothes, the smell of honey and herbs from a thousand glistening, sticky sweetmeats; the animals' smells, the avid, pugnacious smell of goat, the sweet smell of cattle, the rich filibustering aroma of pig, the dry, fusty smell of chicken feathers, the squat, damp smell of ducks. Then the vegetables and fruit, playing on your senses like an orchestra – the fine violin of lychees, the 'cello of mangoes, the piano of grapes, the massive organ music of a pineapple, and the throbbing drum of thatch-headed coconuts. Peter thought that there could be no experience more rewarding than being pulled through the streets in this ridiculous conveyance (which people gave instant passage to, as in other places they gave way to an ambulance) with a beautiful girl by your side and the whole of Zenkali, as it were, laid in layers within your nostrils.

Eventually they reached the waterfront and approached a building at the end of the harbour that hung over the water. It was a squat, two-tiered house built mainly of the indestructible Amela beams. But while the beams were indestructible, the other fabric wasn't, and so the building crouched, like a fragile old woman in corsets too large for her. On completion, round about 1800, someone, it appeared, had given the whole edifice a playful push, so that now, permanently caught off-balance, it leant out over the clear, seaweed-bright, fish-freckled waters. It had, attached to it, like a curious sort of parasite, a sign in coloured lights that stated *'Mother Carey's Chickens – Est. 1925'*. Peter and Audrey approached the large, black, misshapen door that looked as though it might be the entrance to some ancient castle's grimmest dungeon. On it was tacked a small sign in red which said, 'Welcome to a Home from Home – Gents on the left, Ladies on the right. No Spitting.'

'I wonder if Carmen is here,' said Audrey, as they pushed open the door. Inside there was a large room furnished as a bar, and looking – with its curious decor of mirrors, vases full of coloured ostrich feathers, fairy lights and slightly blurred and fly-spotted pictures of coy ladies in crinolines – rather like a raffish, nineteen-twenties night club that had gone to seed. Ten cats of assorted colours drifted, smoke-like, around the tables; five white rabbits with pink eyes, and several long-haired guinea pigs ambled to and fro; four patchwork dogs lolled about on the floor, panting gently. On half a dozen perches, parrots, cockatoos and a vivid royal blue macaw with yellow-rimmed eyes squawked and mumbled. In one corner stood a large cage in which a pair of greenish-grey vervet monkeys bickered.

At one of the plastic-topped tables that dotted the room was a curious tableau. On one side sat Captain Pappas, immobile, scowling blackly, a massive glass of beer in front of him. Opposite sat Carmen Carey. She was short and immensely fat, with glossy black curly hair, protuberant blue eyes and a mouth so perfectly shaped as a cupid's bow that it looked as though it had been painted on to her face. A pair of *pince-nez* grasped the end of her nose and were attached to her massive bosom by a chain. Round her neck was a string of pearls so big that no oyster known to man could have produced them without doing itself an injury, and her fat little hands had half a dozen rings embedded in the fingers. She was squeezed into a shell-pink silk dress with flying buttresses of lace. Her skin was smooth and unblemished and, before she had been overtaken by the avalanche of fat, she must have been a very pretty woman. As it was, she exuded an air of delicacy and good humour that made her attractive and feminine. At this moment, Captain Pappas was glowering at her darkly and she, her blue eyes clouded with anger, was pouting at him. In front of her stood a small glass of *crème de menthe*. Her flamingo-pink fingernails tapped out a rapid, irritated tattoo and then came to rest. She and Captain Pappas regarded each other like two chess players fossilised over an insoluble move. She took a long shuddering breath and began to speak.

'What Hi say, Captain Pappas,' she said, mellifluously and aristocratically, 'what Hi say his, you're nothing but a bloody Greek.'

Captain Pappas screwed up his little black-currant eyes.

'Greeks I am,' he conceded, 'bloody is a matter of opinion.'

''Ow hanyone who wasn't a Greek would dare to hask

me such a price for transporting my young ladies, Hi will never know,' said Carmen. 'Hit's 'ighway robbery.'

'You want I should bring you a lot of tarts,' Captain Pappas started aggrievedly, 'you have to pay . . .'

Carmen bristled and bright round spots of colour appeared in her cheeks.

'*Do* you mind, Captain Pappas,' she said with such aristocratic frigidity that even the Captain looked fairly contrite, 'my young ladies har *not* tarts, hif you please.'

'Well,' said the Captain, equably, 'if they're not tarts, what are they, eh?'

'They are gentlemen's companions,' said Carmen.

'To me, a tart is a tart,' said the Captain, shrugging, obviously not wanting to get bogged down in semantics. 'And I charges the same.'

'Hi 'ave no wish to be hoffensive, Captain,' she said, 'but Hi think you are nothing short of a crook. Heven a Greek must realise that dishonesty his not halways the best policy. 'Ave you never 'eard of the word "discount"?'

'Sure,' said the Captain, 'but not for the transportation of tarts.'

Silence fell again, and they eyed each other like two wrestlers, waiting for the moment when a quick turn of the wrist will lay one's adversary on the canvas. Out of the corner of her eye, Carmen suddenly caught sight of Peter and Audrey, and uttered a shrill squeak of delight.

'Miss Haudrey!' she exclaimed. 'Miss Haudrey, 'ow very nice. Now this his a treat.'

She got to her feet and came forward, bowing and cooing like a pigeon, her face wreathed in smiles.

'Hit his nice of you to come 'ere,' she said. 'Hi 'aven't seen you in hay hage.'

'I hope we're not interrupting, Carmen,' said Audrey. 'I just wanted you to meet Peter Foxglove.'

'Charmed, Hi ham sure,' said Carmen, extending her tiny fat hand, little finger raised. 'Hi do assure you, you his in no way hinterrupting. Hi was merely 'aving hay haltercation with the Captain 'ere. 'E his trying to charge me han hexcessive price for transporting some of my girls from Djakarta.'

'New girls?' asked Audrey. 'What about your old girls?'

'Ho, they're still with me, but I must 'ave some new ones, dear, now they're going to build the airfield. Ho, yes, all those new sailors hand hairmen, hand harmy, Hi've no doubt. My present girls 'ave got their 'ands full already, hif you know what Hi mean, with their regular gentlemen. We shall need some 'elp, that's for sure. Hi never want hit said that Mother Carey's Chickens didn't give full satisfaction. Hafter hall, Hi 'ave my reputation to consider.' She moved round behind the bar, her little feet moving so rapidly beneath her long dress that she appeared to glide rather than walk. 'Let me procure you some refreshment, dear,' she said, 'a *crème de menthe* hand something more substantial for the gentleman?'

'Two beers, Carmen,' said Audrey. 'We really can't stop. I only popped in because I'm showing Peter the Island and I felt he had to visit the M.C.C.'

'But of course, dear,' said Carmen, blushing and bridling. 'No cultural tour hof the hisland would be complete withhout a visit 'ere. Hand Hi 'opes, Mr. Foxglove, that hif hat hany time you're feeling hout of sorts or down in the dumps, you will look upon this as your 'ome from 'ome, where you may shed your cares, amid convivial companions.'

'Thank you,' said Peter, 'I certainly will.'

Carmen poured out the drinks.

'Well,' said Captain Pappas, 'I must goes.' He drained his glass and wiped the foam from his lips. Carmen watched him calculatingly.

' 'Ave another before you go,' she suggested. 'Hafter hall, we 'aven't reached hany agreement yet.'

'Thirty pounds a head,' said the Captain, slapping the table with his hand.

'Ten, not a penny more,' snapped Carmen.

'Twenty-eight, if you guarantees ten,' said Pappas.

They might, Peter reflected, have been discussing slaves.

'Hi will guarantee ten, but honly hat twelve pounds each,' said Carmen. 'You don't 'ave to feed 'em. They'll bring their own grub.'

'I can't do it under twenty-five a head,' said Pappas.

'Why don't you use Zenkali girls?' asked Audrey.

'My dear, they are charming,' said Carmen, 'nubile and all that, but when hit comes to personal hygiene, well, Hi meantersay, hit's not what you or Hi his used to, nor what my gentlemen expect. Pongy armpits and such is very offputting to the sort of clientele what Hi 'ave got. Mind, Hi'm not saying anything against them; they are pretty and they work 'ard, but clean they are not, God bless 'em. Hand when you 'ave an establishment such as this you soon realise that cleanliness his next to godliness, as they say. Only the hother day Hi 'ad to get rid of one – nice little thing, she was, big eyes and ever so eager to please. But the first gentleman said to me, "Carmen," 'e said, "I think she's a real little beaut, but she will keep blowing 'er nose hon the pillowcase." Put 'im off, you see, 'im being of a sensitive nature. Yes. You 'ave to take all that into consideration hin this line of work.'

Captain Pappas drained his beer with a flourish. 'Twenty pounds a head,' he said, 'not a penny less.'

'Done,' snapped Carmen. She filled a tiny copper shot measure with rum and poured it into the Captain's empty beer glass.

'That's a bargain, dearie,' she said.

'Bargain,' said Captain Pappas, and belched the small, soft, self-satisfied belch of a Greek who feels he has won.

'Well,' said Audrey, finishing her beer, 'now we know that the armed services have been taken care of, we must be off.'

'Must you really, dear? Oh, well, hif you must, you must. Look, can you and your nice gentleman come to dinner next Friday? Hit's me birthday and Hi am 'aving a small soirée. Nothing special – just an 'andful of guests, a few drinks and a singsong. The Captain 'ere his going to bring 'is bazouki, are you not, Captain?'

'You needs Greek music for a good party,' mumbled Pappas.

'We'd love to come,' said Audrey.

They picked their way out through the motley assemblage of cats, dogs, guinea pigs and rabbits, the parrots screeching a cacophonous goodbye, and re-entered their Kingy Cart.

'Now I am in a quandary,' said Peter. 'I thought I had lost my heart to the Rev, and now you confuse me by introducing me to Carmen, the girl of my dreams.'

'Carmen's special,' agreed Audrey. 'She is also one of the kindest people I know. If help is needed, she and her girls are in the forefront. Even when we had a ghastly smallpox epidemic some years ago she and her girls worked day and night, nursing the sick, without any thought for themselves.'

'Yes, I should think she's tough, but in the nicest way,' said Peter. 'Where are we off to now?'

'The Ombu,' said Audrey, 'and then I'll take you back home.'

'I would like to go up and explore those valleys before they go,' said Peter. 'Have they ever been explored properly?'

'I shouldn't think so,' said Audrey. 'The only person who ever comes up into them is Droom.'

'Who's he?' asked Peter.

'Professor sent out to do a complete study of Zenkali biology by the Min. of Ag. in England. He was the one who discovered the importance of the Amela Moth. He's now trying to find out where the damn thing breeds, so he trots about all over the island. He's a weird cove, but brilliant.'

'If I got my camping gear together and fixed up things, would you like to come up here for a weekend's exploring?' asked Peter.

There was a pause.

'Yes,' she said slowly. 'I would like that.'

'I'll organise it and let you know,' he said. He lay back and felt suddenly very contented.

Half an hour later, they drove down the road from Matakama and soon reached the outskirts of Dzamandzar where the Botanical Gardens lay. Laid down by the Dutch, they were not very extensive, but neatly kept and containing a wealth of plants and trees from Asia and Africa. The trees and shrubs were planted in neat rows or groups surrounded by pools full of multicoloured water lilies and papyrus. In the middle of this exotic vegetation was a low, rambling building which had a notice outside proclaiming it to be the administrative headquarters of the gardens. Audrey knocked on a door and a high-pitched voice cried out for them to enter. Inside the room – seated behind a desk almost obliterated by piles of dried plants, seeds and tottering mounds of scientific papers – was a very small, very fat man with a bare, shiny head. He was wearing the largest pair of spectacles Peter had ever seen with lenses so thick that they argued an eye condition only just this side of blindness.

'Audrey! Audrey! How nice of you to come,' squeaked the little man, rolling out from behind his desk and seizing her hands. 'How nice to see you. What may I do for you?' He stood on tiptoe, his fat body quivering, his absurd spectacles flashing.

'Peter, Dr. Mali Fellugona . . . this is Peter Foxglove, and I've brought him to see the Ombu tree, if we may,' said Audrey.

'So pleased to meet you,' said Fellugona, clasping Peter's hand, 'so very honoured, so very, very delighted. Of course you must see the Ombu. Poor, dear thing, it's all alone in the world now, you know, and it does so love visitors.'

Peter warmed to the little man. Fellugona armed himself with a giant key and they left the building and walked down a broad path lined with Royal Palms.

'Yes, you have no idea how this tree appreciates any little thing you do for it,' Fellugona went on, 'all trees do, of course, but especially this one. It simply loves music, for example, and luckily I play the flute. So every morning my first job, my first task – my first duty you might say – is to play a tune or two to the Ombu, poor thing. It seems to prefer Mozart and Vivaldi mostly. Bach, I think, it finds too complicated.'

He led them to an area of the garden where had been erected what looked like a giant aviary constructed of steel scaffolding on which was stretched fine mosquito wire. Fellugona opened a door in the side and they stepped in.

'Here it is, Mr. Foxglove,' said Fellugona, with something like a sob in his voice, 'the loneliest tree in the world.'

The Ombu tree was certainly strange. It stood on a squat trunk some ten feet high and about eight feet in circumference; a trunk that spread its massive curling roots out to embrace the ground like the talons of some strange mythological beast. The bark was streaked grey and silver and was pitted with holes and rents like magnified pumice stone. Small, glossy, green leaves like jade arrowheads hung from fat, twisted little branches that were all of such even length that it looked as if the Ombu had been polled at some time. The overall effect, Peter decided, was that of a fuzzy, green, oversized beach umbrella balanced on an outsized handle.

'Isn't it beautiful?' queried Fellugona, in a reverent whisper.

'Yes,' said Peter, although beautiful was not the word that sprang to mind. It was not beautiful, but it exuded personality almost as if it were a living mammal or bird. He stepped forward and ran his hands over the scarred and pitted bark, warm and rough like an elephant's hide.

'Oh, it loves to be scratched, to be massaged, to be rubbed,' said Fellugona. 'I'm afraid I haven't the time to give it the attention it deserves. What with one thing and another I can only get out to see it three or four times a day and it does miss the intellectual stimulus of frequent visits and exchange of ideas.'

'Do you keep it in this cage for any special reason?' asked Peter.

'Insect pests,' said Fellugona, his spectacles flashing as he expectorated the phrase as if it were a curse.

'Insect pests, dear Mr. Foxglove.' He glanced around nervously and held up a fat forefinger.

'They are all around us, poised ready to strike. Yield but one inch, open this door but one chink, vestige or, one might say, fissure, and they would stream in, ruthless and ravaging, worse than the hordes of Ghengis Khan, more savage than the armies of Attila, one might say more ruthless than the Roman legions. Ever since we discovered the economic importance of the Amela moth and were forced to give up insecticides our hands have been tied. We are at the mercy of every insect that crawls or flies.'

He paused, took off his spectacles and polished them feverishly. His eyes, deprived of their magnification, suddenly shrank to the size of a mole's but regained their size when he replaced the glasses.

'That is why, Mr. Foxglove, we keep Stella in this,' he said, waving his fat hand. 'We try not to call it a cage, which has all the unfortunate associations with captivity, bondage, one might say, durance vile. No, Stella prefers that we call it her boudoir.'

'I see,' said Peter, gravely. He tried not to catch Audrey's eye.

'The last of her kind,' said Fellugona, 'the last of her kind . . . when she goes, departs – one might say, passes on – the world will have suffered a botanical loss of incalculable magnitude.'

'Yes,' said Peter, 'I feel very privileged, Dr. Fellugona, that I have been allowed to meet Stella, very privileged indeed.'

'How kind, how kind,' said Fellugona, beaming. 'I'm sure it was delightful for Stella to meet you. New faces, you know, Mr. Foxglove. She gets very bored with the same old visitors, I'm afraid. You must come again, yes, yes indeed you must.'

Still expounding on the therapeutic value of visitors for Stella's health and well-being, Dr. Fellugona escorted them to the car and, standing on tiptoe, his spectacles flashing in the sun, he waved to them as they drove off. Peter leaned back in his seat and closed his eyes.

'I give up,' he said. 'Nothing will ever surprise me again after Stella's boudoir.'

Audrey chuckled.

'I thought you would enjoy that,' she said. 'Apart from the interest of Stella, Fellugona is one of my favourite characters here.'

'How you manage to gather such a collection of amiable nuts defeats me,' he said.

'It's Zenkali. I think they just wander round the world being square pegs in round holes, and when they finally end up here they find it's the perfect setting for them. Look at the Governor, poor old thing. For years they pushed him round the world from one blunder to another until someone had the brilliant idea of sending him here.'

'Zenkali got the Governor of its dreams.'

'Yes, they simply love him, and he potters about like a demented moth, opening vegetable shows and patting babies on the head and they all think he's great. They listen to his speeches with reverence.'

'Good God, he doesn't make speeches, does he?' asked Peter.

'Of course he does – dozens of them a year – they encourage him to. Hannibal calls them verbal icebergs because only one tenth are audible. But the Zenkalis think the Gov. is the greatest thing since Shakespeare.'

They drove back to Peter's house along the coast road. The sky was striped in green and scarlet and apricot by the dying sun, and the air felt cool after the heat of the day. Lines of women were coming back from the streams with baskets of washing on their heads, or returning from the fields with hoes tucked under their arms and baskets of fruit or vegetables on their heads.

'Coming in for a quick drink?' asked Peter, as they drew up outside his bungalow.

'A very quick one,' she said, 'I've simply got to get back and make sure Daddy has a decent meal.'

They went into the brightly lit living-room and Amos, brilliant in white and with a broad smile, came forward bearing a cleft stick with a message.

'Good evening, sah, good evening, Missy Audley,' he said. 'Masa get book from Masa Hannibal, sah.'

'Right, thank you,' said Peter, taking the missive. 'Pass drinks, will you please, Amos.'

'Yes, sah,' said Amos and disappeared.

Peter unfolded the note:

'Peter –

Bad news, I regret to say. They've passed the airfield idea, idiots that they are. However, one's not to reason why and so forth. Please be at my place for a council of war at eight tomorrow. Lots to do.

H.'

Peter read it out to Audrey.

'Damn them,' she said and her eyes filled with tears, 'Damn them, damn them, damn them to hell.'

'Maybe it won't be as bad as Hannibal and you all think,' said Peter awkwardly, not knowing how to be of comfort. Audrey gulped her drink down and put the glass on the table.

'It'll be worse than we think,' she said. 'I must go. Goodbye.' She walked quickly out of the house and before Peter could follow her, had climbed into the car and driven away.

Chapter Four

―◄ ❈ ►―

ZENKALI ASTOUNDED

The next day and for the fortnight that followed Peter worked exceptionally hard. He was constantly running between the Palace, Hannibal's house and Government House, making all the arrangements necessary for the signing ceremony, between the Government of Zenkali and the British Government. This agreement would, in effect, turn the island into an important military installation. The whole thing was made more complicated by Kingy insisting on the maximum pomp and ceremony. As he pointed out, he got so little chance of wearing his beautifully-cut uniforms that he was not going to pass up this opportunity. The British Government was sending from Singapore a battalion of troops, a naval band and a trio of reasonably obscure military people to represent the three services, a Brigadier, an elderly Admiral and an almost senile Wing Commander. To Peter's astonishment, his uncle, Sir Osbert, had been chosen to represent the Queen, and he was to be accompanied by Lord Hammer of Hammersteins and Gallop, the world-wide construction firm, who – it seemed inevitable – would get the job of building the dam, the airfield and any naval installation needed. What was, on the surface, a fairly simple ceremony, had so much detail and protocol attached to it that the work involved was considerable. Peter's task was not made any easier by Diggory Finn, the Governor's A.D.C., a slender young man with pink-rimmed eyes, sandy hair, an appalling stammer, no memory and a tendency to go into a nervous decline at the first sign of any trouble.

So, for a fortnight, Peter laboured, and, at the end of that time, everything had been solved satisfactorily; bedrooms had been allotted, dinners and dances and march pasts arranged; the Governor had written and practised in front of a mirror the various speeches he would have to make; flags and bunting had been washed and refurbished, the Zenkali band had practised in the most excruciating manner and one of the King's Guard set off an official cannon by mistake and blew a large hole in the side of the Palace, to Kingy's extreme annoyance. The whole of Zenkali was bordering on hysteria. Meanwhile a suicidal cobra got into the main generator and fused every light in the island for twenty-four hours before they could find an electrician brave enough to extract the body. The result was that the ice cream melted and many other perishables meant for the state banquet disintegrated. As a result, Captain Pappas had to do an extra run to Djakarta for fresh supplies. Owing to the lack of lights, a herd of cows on its way to the market in Dzamandzar stampeded and rushed en masse into one of the official marquees, bringing the whole thing to the ground, dragging it along and – owing to the nervous disposition of the cattle – leaving it in such a state that it took twenty-five washermen five days to scrub it back into a hygienic condition. By the time all this was over, Peter felt in urgent need of some sort of a break and so he phoned up Audrey.

'D'you want to come camping and explore some valleys? I feel if I don't go up into the mountains and hide for a while, my sanity will be in grave danger.'

'Fine,' she said. 'When d'you want to go?'

'I'll pick you up tomorrow morning,' said Peter. 'I'll be along at about eight, okay? We can live on tinned stuff for twenty-four hours and take plenty of fruit with us.'

'I'll make a large pie and we can take that,' said Audrey. 'Although I say it myself, my pies are famous.'

He had just finished talking to Audrey and was about to get himself a soothing drink when Amos appeared.

'Please, sah,' he said, 'Masa Droom done come.'

Peter groaned. Finding that neither Kingy nor Hannibal would see him because they were too busy with the forthcoming celebrations, Droom had turned his attention to Peter and not a day had passed without a cleft-stick message pleading for an audience, or else a telephone call asking for the same thing.

'God damn it,' said Peter, 'oh, all right, I'll see him, I suppose. Show Mr. Droom in, Amos.'

As Droom sidled into the room Peter watched him curiously. Droom was tiny, like a deformed schoolboy. He had a pigeon chest and bony legs and a slight curvature of the spine that made his head hump forward like a vulture's. His hair was lank and greasy and full of dandruff. His eyes protruded and were a very pale, watery blue with a crust of sediment gathered at the corners and he sniffed at regular intervals. Bobbing and cringing, he moved across the room like a crab, baring yellow and decaying teeth between bloodless lips in a ghastly travesty of a smile. Overlong Bermuda shorts covered most of his unlovely legs, and he was wearing a grubby singlet and over it a grey tropical coat that had once been white, the pockets bulging like swallows' nests with a strange assortment of tins, boxes, magnifying glasses, a small net, and coils of string. Peter thought that he had never before seen so many unattractive component parts assembled in one human being. He had to steel himself to take the large, dirty-nailed and slightly moist hand that Droom held out to him.

'Mr. Foxglove, I am charmed,' he said. 'It is so very kind of you to see me.' He sniffed and wiped his nose with the back of his hand. His voice was shrill and nasal, and he enunciated with the pedantic condescension of the professional academic lecturer.

'Delighted to meet you, I'm sure,' said Peter, who was taken aback by this awful charm. Given Droom's appearance he had expected him to be irritable.

'Won't you sit down and have a drink?' he asked.

'You are so kind,' said Droom, cringing into a chair and twisting his legs around each other like ivy stems. 'I do not believe in alcoholic beverages. No. But don't let me stop you, Mr. Foxglove. No. I will have a fruit juice while you imbibe.'

Peter poured himself out an unseemly large whisky and soda and made a lime juice for his guest.

'I must apologise for the fact that we've all been so elusive,' said Peter, untruthfully, 'but we've really all been worked off our feet.'

'No need for apologies, Mr. Foxglove,' said Droom, holding up a long, admonishing, dirt-engrained finger, 'no need for apologies at all. No. I understand the cares of government lie heavily upon the shoulders of even the old and experienced. Yes.'

'Well, what is it you want to see me about?' asked Peter, more shortly than he intended, since he did not like the implication that he was young and inexperienced. Droom sucked up a mouthful of his drink and wiped his mouth with the back of his hand. He smiled his graveyard smile at Peter.

'My request, my dear Mr. Foxglove, is simplicity itself. Yes. All you have to do – and I know you're a young man of influence, one who has, as they say, the ear of the Government – all you have to do is to procure for me a short interview with either His Majesty or Oliphant. Yes. It is, as I have tried to intimate, of the greatest importance that they see me. Yes. In fact, Mr. Foxglove, I cannot too strongly underline and insist upon the gravity of that which I wish to communicate to them. No.'

'Well, as you know, they are very busy,' said Peter, patiently. 'Perhaps if you told me what your problem is, I could then have a word with one of them. I see them both every day.'

A strange, crafty look spread over the unattractive face of Professor Droom. He held up his dirty finger again.

'Mr. Foxglove, what I have to divulge is of such

magnitude, such importance, that I could not, indeed, my scientific training would not allow me to, vouchsafe it to an underling. No. It must be for the ears of the King or Oliphant alone. I cannot risk it – my scientific training would not allow me to risk – this information being in the hands of the untutored.'

Peter had had a long, hard day and, patient though he was by nature, Droom was getting under his skin. He could quite see why everyone disliked and avoided him.

'Well, Professor Droom,' he said, 'since apparently you consider me untrustworthy, I can only suggest that you write whatever it is and communicate directly with Kingy or Hannibal. And now, if you'll excuse me, I've had a long day and I'd like to have my supper and go to bed.'

He got to his feet determinedly, but Droom put down his drink and held out his hands.

'Mr. Foxglove, Mr. Foxglove,' he whined, 'please hear me out. I must have audience. I cannot commit myself on paper, my scientific training would not permit me to commit myself on paper – until my experiment is finished and my hypothesis is unshakeable.'

'Well, wait until your experiment is finished,' said Peter, shortly, 'then commit yourself to paper and give it to somebody who is not an underling.'

'I can see you have no scientific training,' said Droom.

'No, I merely had training in good manners,' said Peter. 'Goodnight, Professor.'

Droom unwound his hairy shanks, picked up several test tubes and boxes that had fallen from his pocket and got to his feet.

'You'll be sorry for this, Mr. Foxglove, very sorry,' he said.

'I cannot do anything but repeat: tell me your problem or write it down and I will see it's delivered to the appropriate authorities. I can do no more than that.'

'If something should transpire in the next day or so – if my experiment is terminated – may I come and see you again?' asked Droom, all cringing, gargoyle smile, hands clutching convulsively at his pockets.

'Of course,' said Peter, reluctantly.

'Then I hope we will be in time,' said Droom. He wiped his nose with the back of his hand and held it out for Peter to shake.

'I must thank you for your kindness and your time,' he said, and sidled furtively out of the room.

Peter went to wash his hands and then poured out another whisky, bigger than the first. He decided that he had better phone Hannibal about Droom. It was his first experience of the vagaries of the Zenkali telephone system from outside town. As he lifted the receiver, there was a report like a pistol shot, followed by a strange, buzzing, bubbling noise, like a hive of bees immersed in a tub of water. He dialled Hannibal's number and then a sepulchral voice said, 'Yes, sah, Mr. Foxglove, which side you want to talk?'

'Who's that?' asked Peter, mystified.

'Napoleon Waterloo, sah.'

'Is Mr. Hannibal there?' asked Peter.

There was a long pause and Peter could hear Napoleon Waterloo mumbling to somebody.

'Jesus say Mr. Hannibal 'e no dere for house, sah,' said Napoleon Waterloo unexpectedly.

'Jesus?' asked Peter, who had still not quite got used to the names Zenkalis were christened.

'Yes, sah. Jesus 'e say Mr. Hannibal done go for Government House, sah. You like I go give you Government House?' asked Napoleon Waterloo.

Peter suddenly realised that the dial on his phone was useless and had presumably been put there as an ornament.

'Yes,' he said resignedly, 'give me Government House.'

He was connected noisily but with the utmost rapidity and efficiency to the main police station in Dzamandzar, the fish market and finally, in triumph, to Government House, where Hannibal came to the phone. Peter told him about Droom.

'Oh, that appalling man,' said Hannibal, 'I wouldn't mind if he wasn't so repulsive, because he is very bright when you get him on his own subject. But he loves to create mysteries, you know. The last time he started this cloak and dagger stuff and worried the hell out of Kingy and me, it turned out that he only wanted to divulge the earth-shattering news that he had found a species of jellyfish new to science and wanted to call it after Kingy. I wouldn't worry about him overmuch. I'm sorry he was rude to you, though. Still, he's been rude to all of us at one time or another, so I don't see why you should get preferential treatment.'

'Well, I just thought I ought to report,' said Peter.

'Yes, fine. But I'm in the middle of a domestic crisis here, so I can't worry about Droom,' said Hannibal.

'Anything I can do?'

'No. Not really. Lady Emerald has just discovered that she hasn't enough sheets for the V.I.P.s. I can see us all sleeping in blankets and getting prickly heat,' said Hannibal, irritably. 'I do wish the bloody British Government wasn't so parsimonious in furnishing Government Houses.'

'Well, I shall be away for the next couple of days. I'm going exploring the valleys of Matakama with Audrey.'

'Good. Wish I was coming with you, although I have a strange, probably unfounded, suspicion that you'd rather be alone together.'

Peter chuckled.

'Don't get lost in the valleys – they really aren't adequately mapped, you know, and it would be hell's own job trying to find you.'

'No, I'll keep safe,' promised Peter.

The next morning, he and Audrey drove up into the mountains. The weather was so beautiful that they had no need of a tent, but only warm sleeping bags, as the nights were cool in comparison to the day temperatures. Audrey had decided that four small pies were easier to handle than one big one, and Peter's knapsack was full of various tinned foods, matches, tea and other accoutrements to make life for the next two days bearable. Peter had also brought slender nylon ropes and his camera. It was a sparkling blue Zenkali day; Audrey was looking particularly ravishing. As they drove up the red road that wound along the broad flank of Matakama, mongooses at the side of the road sat up, their sly little faces watching the car with interest, before they slithered off into the undergrowth. At one point a small herd of feral pigs crossed the road, small, rotund and black with pot bellies and flop ears. They squealed and grunted and jostled each other with fright as the car approached them.

Presently, they came to the wild country where the small tributary valleys led off the main Matakama Valley and its river. Here, having consulted the maps Peter had brought, they decided to cross the main valley and explore first its three small northern tributaries. They crossed the Matakama River by jumping from rock to rock. This was dangerous as the rocks were very slippery and covered with mats of vegetation which clung to the rock faces by fragile rootlets. Kingfishers trilled with alarm at this invasion of their territory and flashed to and fro in the gloom. Having reached the farther bank the going was easier, though here and there, where the Chinese guava stems grew thick and straight, like walking sticks in a Victorian hat stand, they had to cut their way through. Peter carefully marked the trail so they could find their way back again. In places the forest was sparser and the ground was studded with pale magenta flowers and wild raspberry cane grew in great clumps like gigantic unravelled baskets, studded with ruby-red fruit the size of damsons, full of juice but having little taste. Small, demure doves, grey with bronze patches on their wings, fed in companionable pairs among the leaves and were so tame that they continued feeding until Peter and Audrey were within a few feet of them. Here and there the traveller's tree palms reared up, virulent green, incongruous, like some half-opened ladies' fans stuck in the middle of the forest. Their long tattered leaves made smooth sun-drenched beds for the *Phelsuma* lizards, dragon-green with scarlet and blue spots on their sides, who lounged there, elegant and beautiful, carefully keeping watch on their surroundings with golden eyes in gently tilted heads. As they pushed their way through the thicker forest they walked through a shower of fruit husks dropped by little Emerald Parakeets who, wheezing and squeaking, to each other, fed among the higher branches.

By evening they had explored the first valley and were halfway to the second one. They chose a small rocky promontory on which to camp for the night. Here, in a small clearing embraced on three sides by flame-of-the-forest trees aglow with bloom, they had a perfect view over the forest top to the distant sea. They lit a fire and ate the food they had brought while the sun sank. The wide, dark, leathery wings of bats beat the sky, as they flocked to somewhere in the forest below them to feed shrilly and noisily on wild mangoes. Later, the moon rose, bronze fading to primrose yellow and finally floating up into the black velvet sky, white as ice.

At dawn the next morning they were rudely awakened by the raucous screams and quarrellings of a troupe of macaques, with sly eyes and pink backsides. Peter crawled out of his sleeping bag, yawning and stretching.

'Good morning,' said Audrey. 'Are you going to make some tea?'

'I am,' said Peter, crouching over the embers of the fire and coaxing it into life with a handful of twigs. 'Moreover, I intend to cook some sausages which, in my wisdom, I put in my pack.'

'What a brilliant man,' said Audrey, admiringly, 'and on top of all that, he doesn't snore.'

'I,' said Peter, wagging a tin opener at her, 'I am a paragon of virtue, did you but know it.'

'I may agree with you when I see how you cook a sausage,' she said, sliding out of her bag.

'I am famed from Istanbul to Bangkok, from Peru to

Katmandu for my impeccable sausage cookery,' he said, 'Criticise me at your peril.'

Reluctantly they left the clearing and moved onwards towards the second valley. At noon they were still searching for it and were beginning to wonder if it had been marked on the map by mistake or if they had somehow walked round it. But then, suddenly, they hacked their way through a thicket of guava and came to the edge of a fifty-foot cliff. It was almost sheer and stretched away on both sides as far as they could see.

'Good thing I brought the ropes,' said Peter. 'It'll be easy enough getting down this – there are plenty of footholds.'

'It's not getting down, it's getting out again,' said Audrey, doubtfully.

'No, that'll be easy, I promise,' said Peter with confidence. He attached one end of the rope to a sturdy sapling and let the other dangle over the cliff. It reached to within a few feet of the ground, disappearing into a thicket of bushes.

'I'll go down first,' he said, 'then you lower the pack down and follow. Take it easy and test your footholds carefully, okay?'

'Okay,' said Audrey, trying to sound confident. She was secretly rather pleased that Peter assumed she could do this without maidenly hysteria.

Peter swung himself over the edge and started to descend the cliff slowly. There were plenty of footholds but the rock face was crumbly and he had to use caution. He was within twenty feet or so of the ground when a large section of the cliff that he had just trusted his weight to gave way with a rumbling hiss. It was so unexpected that the jerk broke his hold on the rope. Audrey, watching, saw him crash and bounce down the cliff face and then dive head first into the bushes and disappear from sight.

'Peter,' she called, 'are you all right?' But there was no reply.

Fortunately, the thicket of guavas into which he had fallen cushioned his fall. The only injury he sustained was a cut on his forehead, a twisted ankle and bruised ribs. He lay in the bushes, winded, and from the top of the cliff he could hear Audrey calling his name but he was too breathless to reply. Presently, when he could breathe again, he sat up with a groan and was just about to shout to Audrey and tell her that he was all right when there was a rustle in the undergrowth near him and through the leaves appeared a large bird. Peter gazed at it incredulously, for it was the last thing in life that he had expected to see. It was undoubtedly a living, breathing Mockery Bird.

As he sat there, dumbfounded, the Mockery Bird regarded him with a roguish eye, head on one side, and took a few slow steps into the clearing. With its head on one side and one foot tentatively raised, it seemed like some sort of lanky, avian dancing master. It stepped forward among the guava stems with a mincing delicacy and then shuffled its wings like somebody shuffling a pack of cards. He noticed that it had very long eyelashes, which it raised and lowered over its large, gaily-sparkling eyes. It did not appear to be half as surprised to see Peter as Peter was to see it. There was another complicated rustle and flurry in the undergrowth and then, projected into the clearing by its own nervous eagerness, came a female Mockery Bird, making strange, peeting noises, which became a soothing babble when she caught sight of the male. She went up to her mate and briefly preened his throat feathers as an over-zealous wife will straighten the tie of her consort. Peter sat and watched them and his whole being was flooded with an extraordinary excitement. Here in front of him, cosseting each other, were two birds which were thought to be extinct.

The male Mockery Bird made a deep vibrating noise, like somebody in a cellar dropping potatoes into a 'cello. The female, rearranging her plumage as petulantly as an elderly lady who had been caught in the lift doors at Harrods, responded with a few vague purring peets. Both birds looked at each other benignly and, equally benignly, at Peter. Then they moved towards each other, crossed beaks delicately like swordsmen starting a duel and rattled them together suddenly, like the sound of someone running a stick along a fence. This done they both raised their beaks to the sky and, closing their eyes, let forth a melodious and mocking sound.

'Ha! ha! *ha!*' they cried, their throats throbbing. 'Ha! ha! *ha!*'

They paused for a brief moment looking at the ground, and then the female executed a small but complicated minuet which resulted in her almost falling on her beak. This ritual over, the birds stared at each other with apparent affection, clashed beaks briefly and then started to wander about the clearing, peeting at each other gently and stirring the leaves for insects.

Peter brushed soil and moss from himself. The birds regarded him roguishly and came forward. They stood a foot away and stared at him with great interest. Presently the male, with the air of a connoisseur testing a new dish, leant forward and tentatively pecked at Peter's trousers. Peter held out his hand and the birds gathered around him and took his fingers in their beaks and mumbled them gently. Then they looked at each other and commented 'Ha *ha* . . . ha *ha!*' softly and melodically. They examined and pecked at his trousers and shirt and gazed with great intensity into his face, blinking their long eyelashes over their dark eyes. Then, having proved him harmless and welcome to their world, they moved off through the undergrowth, keeping in touch with each other by a series of deep vibrating sounds.

He lay back, letting the whole incredible experience melt over him. He heard Audrey's voice from on top of the cliff calling him again but he remained lying there, staring at the sky. He was, he realised, like someone who, going down to their W. H. Smiths for a postcard, had suddenly found a Gutenberg Bible. He was like someone who had discovered a Stradivarius in a dustbin. But it was more than that. It was possible that in the course of human history, one could construct another such Bible, but the birds he had just seen were unique. Once they vanished nothing could bring them back.

'Peter, Peter . . . are you all right?' Audrey was starting to sound desperate. Peter sat up, his mind still in a whirl.

'Audrey . . . can you hear me?' he called.

'Yes . . . are you all right?'

'Yes, perfectly. Look, get the other rope and fix it properly to a tree and then come down yourself. I've found something incredible.'

'You sound very funny. Are you sure you're all right?'

'Yes, yes,' he said, impatiently. 'Come down here.'

A few minutes later, she swung out of the sky and landed on the ground beside him.

'You gave me a hell of a fright,' she complained. 'Why didn't you answer when I called? I thought you'd broken your neck.'

'I was busy talking to a couple of birds,' he said.

She stared at him.

'A couple of birds?' she asked.

'Yes. Mockery Birds.'

Her vivid blue eyes widened incredulously.

'Mockery Birds?' she repeated.

'Yes,' said Peter, 'genuine, live, fully feathered Mockery Birds. Pecking my trousers.'

The girl looked at him in concern.

'Are you sure you didn't bang your head?' she asked anxiously.

'Of course I didn't,' said Peter. 'Come on and I'll show you.'

He seized her hand and dragged her off through the undergrowth in the direction that the birds had disappeared. They found them some fifty feet away, circling round a small clearing, gleaning for insects, thrumming cosily at each other. Audrey gazed at them disbelievingly.

'Holy St. Peter and all the Apostles,' she said at last. 'You weren't dreaming.'

'A genuine pair of fully fledged Mockery Birds,' said Peter, proudly.

'Peter, it's unbelievable,' she said.

The Mockery Birds displayed particular interest in Audrey. They had already inspected Peter pretty thoroughly, but now Audrey had to be peered at with heads on one side, her jeans and her fingers had to be gently pecked to see if they were edible and, when they had finally satisfied themselves about her, they clattered their beaks together, gazed up at the sky and said 'Ha! *ha!* . . . ha! *ha!*' in chorus. Audrey crouched down and, by clicking her fingers got the birds to approach. They stood by her while she scratched their heads, their eyes half closed, making faint thrumming noises indicative of excessive pleasure.

'Aren't they enchanting,' she said, smiling up at Peter delightedly. 'They're so tame . . . like domestic chickens.'

'That's why they were shot to hell in the first place,' said Peter. 'I wonder how many of them there are?'

'It's only a small valley. I shouldn't think very many could live in it,' said Audrey. 'Maybe they are the only two that are left.'

'I hope not,' said Peter, gazing around.

'Let's explore and find out,' Audrey suggested.

'Good God, look,' said Peter suddenly and with such vehemence that he startled Audrey and the Mockery Birds.

'What's the matter?' asked Audrey, surprised.

'All these trees,' said Peter, excitedly, 'they're Ombu trees.'

'Good Lord, so they are,' said Audrey. 'It's fantastic, Peter. Look there . . . dozens of them. The valley must be full of them. Won't Fellugona be pleased?'

'To say nothing of Stella,' said Peter. 'This whole thing's going to create some excitement when we tell everyone.'

'I think we'd better tell Hannibal first,' said Audrey. 'Let's explore the valley and see if there are any more birds,' she suggested.

The valley was about a mile and a half long and about

half a mile in width. A stream meandered down its length and at one point widened out to form a small lake. The sand and mud that formed the shore of this was fretted with dozens of Mockery Bird footprints, but it was some time before they found any more birds. It took them a little over two and a half hours to quarter the valley thoroughly but at the end of that time they had counted four hundred Ombu trees and fifteen pairs of Mockery Birds. They also found another way into the valley. The valley itself was long and slender like a knife cut, both sides formed by vertical cliffs some fifty feet high. By following the stream, they came to a fissure in the cliff face through which the waters slid. They waded into the crevice and it grew narrower and narrower until it was only just wide enough to allow their passage. Then they saw light ahead and heard the sound of a waterfall. They pushed their way out through a mat of creepers and found the stream fell in a series of little waterfalls down into the main valley of the Matakama. It was obvious from where they stood that once the main valley was flooded the Mockery Bird valley would be inundated as well.

'What will happen now?' asked Audrey, as they made their way back into the valley and towards the cliff face which they had descended. 'I suppose they'll have to catch the birds and move them, won't they?'

'Possibly. I'm not sure where they'd move them to. But I suppose they'd be all right in any valley, really. They'll have to watch points, though, otherwise they'll have a great religious row on their hands.'

'Religious? Why religious?' asked Audrey.

'Well, after all, it's the lost God of the Fangouas,' said Peter, 'unless of course they are now so damned Christian and civilised they want to ignore it.'

'I have a feeling that this whole discovery is going to cause a bit of an uproar,' said Audrey, thoughtfully.

She was right, but even then neither of them could visualise the full extent of the uproar that the resurrection of the Mockery Bird was going to create.

They reached Hannibal's house at dusk, just as he was sitting down to a vast curry. As they hurried, dirty and dishevelled, into his dining-room, he laid down his spoon and fork and stared at them.

'I take it from your disgustingly unkempt condition that you have just returned from your virile Boy Scout activities,' he said. 'You look in need of a square meal. Fortunately, my cook always makes enough curry to feed not only me, but, I suspect, all of his eighty-four living relatives, so there is plenty for you. Tomba, lay two more places, please.'

'Hannibal, we've made the most important discovery,' said Peter.

'We've found a valley on Matakama . . .' began Audrey, excitedly.

'Full of Ombu trees and Mockery Birds . . .' said Peter.

'Full of them . . . they're simply wonderful,' said Audrey.

Hannibal stared at them.

'I can only conclude that you have, most unwisely, been partaking of Zenkali Nectar,' he said, 'you know what a surfeit of that devil juice does to you, don't you?'

'Hannibal, we're serious,' said Peter. 'It's true. We found about four hundred Ombu trees and fifteen pairs of Mockery Birds.'

Hannibal looked at their faces and saw that they were not pulling his leg.

'Jesu, joy of man's desiring,' he said. 'Tell me all.'

While the curry lay congealing, untouched, in front of them they told him their tale. When they had finished, Hannibal took them into the living-room and spread a large-scale map on the floor. Poring over it, the excited couple managed to locate the area they were now referring to as Mockery Bird Valley.

Hannibal surveyed the area through a huge magnifying glass.

'Trouble is, the island was last surveyed so long ago and probably rather inefficiently, anyway,' he said, 'and a group of drunken surveyors couldn't be expected to recognise a Mockery Bird or an Ombu. But if you're right about the location, it means that when the main Matakama Valley is flooded, this one will flood too. My, my, as the Reverend Dangledrawers would say, you've certainly opened up a can of worms. I think the first thing to do is to get on to Kingy and tell him.'

He strode to the telephone.

'Oh, God,' he said. 'Is that you, Napoleon Waterloo?'

'Yes, sah, Masa Hannibal,' said a hoarse and penetrating voice.

'You go get me Kingy House one time, you hear,' shouted Hannibal.

'Yes, sah,' said Napoleon Waterloo, doubtfully, sounding like a frog croaking in a well. He rapidly connected Hannibal to the Docks, Government House, the Fire Station and the Docks again.

'God!' said Hannibal. 'Do you wonder Kingy invented the cleft stick?'

At last, with an explosion that almost shattered the receiver, the Palace was reached and eventually Kingy came on the line.

'Sorry to worry you so late,' said Hannibal, 'but Foxglove and Audrey Damien have made an extraordinary discovery and I think you should be the first to know. Can we come and see you?'

'Of course,' said Kingy, 'if it's that important.'

'I think it may be dynamite in every conceivable direction,' said Hannibal seriously, 'but I'd rather not talk on the phone. We'll be right over.'

When they reached the Palace, it was ablaze with lights. They were herded down long marble corridors until finally, great double doors were flung open and they were ushered into a huge drawing-room full of overstuffed couches and strange awkwardly-shaped Victorian furniture. Lying on one of the couches, almost dwarfing it, lay Kingy with his son and heir, Prince Talibut, aged two, leaping up and down on his stomach, uttering wild shrieks of delight as his father tried to tickle him. On one of the other couches sat Kingy's wife, a tall, slender and very beautiful Zenkali, the Princess Matissa. She rose and made them welcome, saw they had drinks and then taking her over-excited son by the hand she gracefully took her leave.

'Well,' said Kingy, as she left, 'tell me your news. I do hope it's not another jellyfish you've discovered. I can't be named after more than one.'

'No, not a jellyfish,' said Hannibal, 'something a good deal more important. These two have been exploring the valleys on Matakama and they've found one which is full of Ombu trees and Mockery Birds.'

There was a long silence while Kingy stared at them, wide-eyed. 'You must be pulling my leg,' he said at length.

'No, it's true,' said Peter. 'I know it's incredible, but it's true.'

'Fifteen pairs,' said Audrey, 'and they're so tame. You'll love them, Kingy.'

'About four hundred Ombus,' said Peter.

Kingy and Hannibal exchanged long and meaningful looks.

'But don't you think it's a wonderful discovery?' asked Audrey in amazement.

Hannibal and Kingy rose simultaneously to their feet and started to pace up and down, passing and repassing each other like sentries. Though Hannibal was not a short man, he was dwarfed by Kingy's bulk. As they walked they talked to each other, each in turn appearing to play the part of devil's advocate.

'It'll be a grand thing to have your old god back again,' said Hannibal.

'It'll cause trouble with the missionaries,' said Kingy.

'On the other hand, it'll cause a problem about flooding the valley,' said Hannibal.

'You can't flood it. World opinion wouldn't let you do it even if you wanted to,' said Kingy.

'You could catch the birds up and put them elsewhere.'

'But there are the Ombu trees. You can't just dig them up and move them,' Kingy pointed out.

'If you don't flood the valley the whole scheme with the U.K. falls through.'

'Yes. And Looja catches a cold,' said Kingy, with satisfaction.

'On the other hand, the U.K. Government's not going to be pleased. They'll try and bring pressure to bear.'

They continued to pace in silence for a while.

'Of course,' said Kingy at last, 'there is a way round it.'

'What?' asked Hannibal.

'Well,' said Kingy blandly, 'just don't tell anyone and go ahead and flood the valley.'

'True,' said Hannibal.

Audrey and Peter looked at each other, speechless.

'On the other hand,' said Kingy judiciously, 'have we the right to deprive the world of part of its biological heritage, as well as the establishment of an old god?'

'Speaking for myself, I cannot see a shadow of an excuse for it,' said Hannibal.

Kingy sighed a deep, despairing sigh.

'It seems to me that we'll simply have to crush our finer feelings under foot and sacrifice Looja,' he said mournfully, and then turned his great grin of delight on them.

'So you're for it?' asked Hannibal.

'Of course I'm for it,' said Kingy indignantly.

'Good,' said Hannibal, with relief.

'But,' warned Kingy, wagging a huge, chocolate-coloured finger, 'there'll be a frightful row. Looja won't take this lying down, you know. We'll have to handle the whole thing with great care or I'll find I'm out-voted and then there'll be trouble.'

'Can't you just issue an edict?' asked Audrey. 'After all, you are the King.'

'Unfortunately, no,' said Kingy. 'I do my best to be a dictator, but just occasionally we have to show just a tiny flash of democracy.'

'Catch 'em off guard is my advice,' said Hannibal. 'After

all, the very last thing anyone will expect will be this. Release the story to local and world press first thing in the morning and I guarantee there will be such an uproar that no one will be able to advocate the continuation of the dam.'

'You don't know Looja,' said Kingy.

For an hour, while Kingy and Hannibal paced the floor, they discussed the strategy. Then, when they were all agreed on what was to be done they swept into action. Audrey was dispatched to get her father to stay up all night and bring out a special edition of the *Zenkali Voice*. Kingy's private secretary, Amos Gumbaloo, was told to defy the telephone system and call every member of the legislative council to a special meeting at noon on the following day. A Book Boy was dispatched to the local photographic shop in Dzamandzar to get all Peter's films developed, and he was accompanied by a Royal Guard to make sure he did the job properly. Meanwhile, Hannibal and Peter hammered out a press release which could be cabled to Reuter's Correspondent in Djakarta the following morning. Having done this, they went round to the offices of the *Zenkali Voice* to see if they could help. They found Damien and his staff, who were all Fangouas, in a state of great excitement. Damien and Audrey, covered in printer's ink, were working out the front page. Round about ten that night the presses rolled and soon they were gazing with pride at the first sticky black copy of the *Zenkali Voice* with its scarlet banner saying *Special Edition* and under it the headline that Damien, in a fit of wild Irish enthusiasm, had worked out and set up without consulting anyone. It was straightforward but confusing, and a bit mystical. Under a huge photo of the Mockery Bird it said:

GOD REDISCOVERED

THE BIRD HAS NOT FLOWN

It was the headline that was going to rivet world attention on Zenkali.

Of course, the rediscovery of the Ombu and the Mockery Bird were of sufficient biological importance in themselves to be newsworthy. But when you added to this the additional ingredients that they were rediscovered in a remote valley, and a valley, moreover, just about to be drowned in the construction of a dam, and that the bird was the lost god of the Fangouas, then you had a story that could only be outclassed in any newspaper-man's eyes by a really good world war. Add to all this that the *Empress of India* was due to arrive in two days' time, bringing troops, bands and the armed services' V.I.P.s, and the situation in Zenkali could only be described by an unprejudiced historian as one fraught with interest.

Early the next morning, Audrey and her father joined Hannibal and Peter and they made their way to the building in Dzamandzar that housed the parliament. It was a large and beautiful room with scarlet leather seats curved in two half moons. Where they joined was an immense wooden throne, on the canopy of which were carved the Dolphin and the Mockery Bird. Crimson carpets lay on the white marble floor and crimson curtains hung in thick folds at the huge windows that lit the chamber. The four of them took their seats on wooden benches in a small gallery, which hung like a large swallow's nest at one end of the chamber. This was for V.I.P.s and the Press.

Amos Gumbaloo, Kingy's secretary, had done his job well and the assembly was packed. On the left sat the Fangouas, on the right the Ginkas. Most of the chiefs wore traditional white or multicoloured robes with small heavily embroidered skull caps, but a few were in European dress. Conspicuous among these was Looja, clad in an exquisite midnight blue suit with a pale primrose-coloured shirt, a heavy blue silk tie and pale primrose-coloured spats.

At precisely midday the trumpeters outside the assembly building played a fanfare and Kingy's own Kingy

Cart – bigger than any other and very ornate – drew up at the steps and Kingy got out. He was dressed in a pale lavender robe and elegant black sandals with gold buckles. On his head was a small gold skull cap. On one hand he wore a ring with a square amethyst in it the size of a postage stamp. In his other hand he carried a scroll. His face was smooth and unruffled. His expression gave nothing away. Peter thought that he looked so relaxed and rested it was hard to believe that he and Hannibal had been up all night working on the statement Kingy was now to deliver. Tall and stately, he walked into the chamber and down the crimson carpet that led to the throne. Everyone rose, everyone bowed. Kingy inclined his head infinitesimally from left to right as he progressed. Every inch of his six foot four was majestic, and for all his bulk, he seemed to glide rather than walk. He mounted the steps to the throne, turned, inclined his head to the assembly and sat down. There was a rustle and creaking as everyone followed suit. Peter saw Looja, his reptile eyes expressionless, one slender finger gently tapping his knee. Peter wondered how he would take the news. Kingy, with slow deliberation, took out his spectacle case and placed his spectacles on his nose. Then, slowly, he unrolled the proclamation.

'He certainly knows how to ham it up, the old devil,' whispered Hannibal.

Kingy adjusted his spectacles carefully, gazed for a moment or two at what he was about to read. The silence was intense. Kingy cleared his throat and began:

'Friends,' he said, peering at the assembly over the tops of his spectacles. 'Friends, we are gathered here today, thus suddenly called together, so that I may give you some news of the utmost importance to Zenkali. The magnitude of what I am about to reveal to you can scarcely be exaggerated. What has happened is something of such importance that it is unequalled in Zenkali history. Indeed, it is possible that nothing quite like it has happened in the history of the world.'

Here Kingy coughed, took out his handkerchief and

polished his spectacles carefully. The silence was almost tangible. He put his spectacles on again and peered over the tops of them at the chamber.

'As everyone knows,' he said sonorously, 'during that unfortunate period of time when we were under French rule the Fangouas suffered a grievous loss, the loss of their ancient and most respected deity, Tiomala, who inhabited the island in the shape of the Mockery Bird. In spite of its importance to the Fangouas, the French on this occasion let their culinary enthusiasm override their *politesse*, and the Mockery Bird soon became a thing of the past.'

Kingy paused.

'Apparently,' he said.

He took out his handkerchief and polished his spectacles again.

'At the same time that the Mockery Bird vanished,' he went on, 'the Ombu tree, another species unique to Zenkali, was lost to us. So, during the French occupation Zenkalis lost two species of great biological importance. But – more important still – the Fangouas were deprived of their deity which led, I regret to say, to a considerable amount of animosity between Fangouas and Ginkas, since the Ginkas still possess their god.'

Here he paused and looked fixedly and rather ferociously at the Ginka side of the assembly, who swayed quietly.

'However,' said Kingy, holding up one enormous hand, palm out, as if giving a blessing, 'the news I have to give you is, to say the least, miraculous.' He turned on his huge, smile and dazzled the assembly with it.

'Both the Mockery Bird and the Ombu have not vanished. No. They are still with us,' he said.

Uproar immediately overtook the chamber. The Fangouas rose in a body, hysterically incredulous, excited and vociferous; the Ginkas hissed and huddled and gesticulated. Kingy allowed the cackling cacophony to continue for a minute or so, and then held up a huge hand. The chamber fell silent.

'Let me tell you how this remarkable discovery came about,' he said. 'You all of you know Peter Foxglove and Audrey Damien. While exploring valleys up on Matakama they came across one remote and secret one in which they found no less than fifteen pairs of Mockery Birds and four hundred Ombu trees.'

There was a hiss of indrawn breath from the Fangouas. Peter, watching Looja, saw his eyes narrow infinitesimally, saw the tapping forefinger come to rest.

'Now,' said Kingy, taking off his glasses and waving them, 'although this news is of the greatest importance both biologically and religiously, I cannot conceal from you the fact that it presents a problem. A grave problem.'

He paused. Looja edged forward imperceptibly on his seat.

'The problem is this. If we should go ahead with the dam that we are planning, we run into a great difficulty. That is, that in constructing the dam we have to flood the valley containing both the Mockery Bird, symbol of Tiomala, and the Ombu tree.'

Looja seemed to coil into himself and become as impassive as a cat who is addressed out of turn.

'On their way to join us and take part in the festivities that were to have taken place to celebrate the signing of our agreement with the United Kingdom Government are many dear friends of Zenkali. Yet the whole thing is fraught with difficulty. The whole problem will have to be carefully investigated before we can come to a final decision on the dam. But since all these people are arriving, since all the great festivities have been planned, we cannot cancel them. So, I suggest we use them as a means of celebrating the rediscovery of our god, Tiomala. After the celebration we will work out what is best to be done about the dam. But I must confess to you that I do not hold out great hopes for it.'

Kingy paused and smiled beatifically. Looja seemed to crouch slightly, like a small black snake about to strike.

'Now, at last, after three hundred years,' said Kingy,

rising massively to his feet, 'I can give you the old greeting, the old blessing.'

He paused and looked round the chamber.

'Tiomala be with you,' he thundered.

Then through the excited, bowing, chattering assembly, he sailed majestically out of the chamber.

Chapter Five

————◄ ❊ ►————

ZENKALI TURBULENT

Hard on the heels of Kingy's speech the special edition of the *Zenkali Voice* hit the streets and the whole population of the island received the extraordinary news. To say that it caused an uproar would be euphemistic; it had ramifications which even Hannibal had not foreseen.

The Ginkas, long secure and smug in the knowledge that they were the only ones with a true God, became loudly and belligerently hostile to the new discovery. As a minority group, the only way of proving their superiority to the Fangouas was the fact that they had a God and the Fangouas had not. They felt their rivals had no right to resurrect the Mockery Bird, when it had been extinct for so many years. The Ginkas' one source of satisfaction, this feeling of immense religious superiority, was undermined. So they treated the news with anger and did their best to discredit it, loudly and bitterly claiming that the whole thing was a hoax, that there was no Mockery Bird. They said the newspaper had been bribed. They said the announcement was a typical example of the high-handed way the Fangouas tried, by dishonest means, to trample over the wishes and finer feelings of a minority group. They said it was a subtle plot to try and gain more power for an already too powerful group.

The Fangouas, on the other hand, had always felt a twinge of inferiority at their lack of a God, and so they treated the news of the Mockery Bird's resurrection with immense joy and, it is to be feared, a certain amount of brash conceit. Naturally, therefore, they did not take too kindly to the Ginkas' attitude. In Dzamandzar itself and in all the outlying villages where, for centuries, the two tribes had been living together in comparative peace, feeling started to run high. At first it took the form of vulgar abuse, but soon the insults became so viciously personal that fights started to break out. They started comparatively innocuously; a fair amount of teeth were knocked out and a few noses broken but nothing more. However, when things started to assume more ugly proportions, the Zenkali Police Force suddenly found themselves with a serious role to play. After years of nothing more exhilarating to do than arrest the odd drunk or track down someone's stolen chicken, they were in the firing line. Ex-Chief Superintendent Angus MacTavish of the Glasgow Police, the leader of the Zenkali police force, was, at first, delighted that at last 'his boys' had something to get their teeth into. He felt he would now show the island what he had worked for years to achieve. The islanders would realise that all those interminable Burns' Nights he had organised with his boys giving exhibitions of gymnastics and unarmed combat were not just show. Those who had jeered at him for these displays would have to swallow their words. Unfortunately, as is always the case when you have two warring factions, the referee who tries to come between them immediately becomes the target of the bitterest animosity. The ferocity with which both Fangouas and Ginkas, their quarrel momentarily forgotten, turned upon the police was so great that the Hospital in Dzamandzar was soon full to overflowing with constables suffering from everything from broken legs to fractured skulls.

Thus it was, when the *Empress of India* arrived in port and the Brigade of Loamshire Light Infantry, the Naval band, and the Physical Instruction Team sent by the R.A.F. all trooped happily ashore in the most convivial of moods, they suddenly found themselves being turned into a peace-keeping force. Instead of being greeted with smiles and cheers from the Zenkali population, they were greeted by scowls, insults and numerous badly aimed rocks. The troops found it very disheartening, having looked forward to a sojourn in a lovely island with nothing more strenuous to do than play 'God Save the Queen', salute a bit and relax at Mother Carey's Chickens, to be suddenly handed a lot of hastily commandeered dustbin lids and have to chase a host of recalcitrant Ginkas and Fangouas through the exceedingly hot streets of Dzamandzar.

Sir Osbert and the military V.I.P.s found themselves hustled away to Government House and kept there, guarded by a group of the King's own bodyguard. The situation in Government House became somewhat tense. The cook, who was a Ginka, had his head laid open with a meat cleaver by the butler, who was a Fangoua. As a result, the cook-mate took over the culinary arts and, though he did his best, he produced meals that were gastronomically frightening by any Government House standards. Added to this was the fact that Lady Emerald, once they had got the news through to her, was convinced that the islanders would attack and eat her Guinea Fowl. This slight misunderstanding was due to the fact that she had grasped the information that some kind of bird was responsible for the uprising but was unsure of the species. Not wishing to take any chances, however, she decided to bring her forty-odd Guinea Fowl inside for safety and released them in the drawing-room. In these turbulent times it did help to alleviate some of Peter's irritation with the whole silly situation to be treated to the sight of his Uncle, the Air Marshal, cobweb frail and senile, the Brigadier who looked an unprepossessing pickled walnut, the Rear Admiral, strawberry of face with round blue seafarer's eyes of impressive vacuity, and Lord Hammer (aptly named) picking their way through a carpet of Guinea-Fowl droppings to take their after-dinner coffee.

The situation for everyone got steadily worse. Both the Catholic and Church of England missionaries suddenly found themselves deprived, in one fell swoop, of all their faithful adherents who had, for the most part, been

Fangouas. The only one who retained any of her converts was the Rev. So when Father O'Mally and the Reverend Bradstitch decided to go to the Palace to utter a protest they insisted that she accompany them, which she did with the utmost reluctance.

'It's disgusting . . . it's blasphemous . . . this worshipping a bird,' said Father O'Mally to Kingy, his brogue coming as thick as porridge as his indignation increased. 'You as Head of State should set an example by putting a stop to it, so you should.'

'Yes, indeed, yes indeed,' bleated Reverend Bradstitch, mopping the sweat from his tallow-coloured face, 'I cannot begin to tell you what an undermining effect it's having. Yesterday I preached to a congregation of four.'

'It's disgraceful, so it is,' said Father O'Mally.

Kingy lay back in his chair and stared at them blandly. Then he looked at the Rev who had not spoken.

'And what about you, Reverend Longnecker?' he enquired.

'Aw, shoot,' said the Rev, slightly embarrassed, 'it doesn't affect *me*. I just told my congregation they could do what they liked with the Mockery Bird, as long as they still belonged to my church. You see, the way I figger it is that God *created* the Mockery Bird in the first place, and it's His wish that we should have it back. If you want to worship the bird you're worshipping one of His creations, so it's kinda like worshipping Him it seems to me.'

'It's idolatry,' snapped Father O'Mally.

'A disgraceful attitude for a responsible Christian to take,' said the Reverend Bradstitch, 'I'm surprised at you, Reverend Longnecker.'

'It's a vicious undermining of the true faith,' snarled Father O'Mally, 'it's got to be stopped.'

Kingy, who had been lying back in a billow of white robes, sat up sharply at this.

'I do not presume to tell you what you should or should not worship,' Kingy said coldly, 'we of Zenkali would consider it presumptuous to do so. Would you care for it if

I issued an edict stating that henceforth every foreigner in the island was compelled to worship the Mockery Bird or else leave?'

Father O'Mally flinched as though the King had struck him.

'After all my work here, all the souls I've saved?' he said.

'It would be a . . . um . . . a . . . a terribly retrograde step,' gasped Bradstitch.

The Rev grinned ruefully at Kingy.

'The way I look at it is that it's your island,' she said, 'but I would be mighty sorry to have to leave.'

Kingy looked at them for a long moment, then he sighed.

'You may rest assured that I will issue no such edict,' he said, and the missionaries relaxed.

'However,' he went on, holding up a huge, pink palm, 'let me just say this so that you know where you stand. If you want my personal view I do not think it matters what you worship providing what you worship does no harm to others. I feel that, of the three of you, the Reverend Longnecker's attitude is the correct one. I have not the slightest intention of interfering with my people's religion to fit in with your rather quaint notions of deity. If any of my people wish to embrace your faith they are quite at liberty to do so. They are also at liberty to believe in anything else they like if it does no harm to Zenkali. You must remember always that one man's God may be another man's fairy tale, but both Gods and fairy tales have their place in the world.'

'Kingy, you're as sharp as a tack,' said the Rev with satisfaction.

'Thank you,' said Kingy majestically.

He rose from his chair to signify that the audience was at an end, and the dispirited representatives of the Catholic and Protestant faiths left, taking with them the ebullient Rev.

'Well, boys,' she said, when they were outside the Palace, being of a mind to rub a little salt into their wounds, 'I have to hurry back. All my converts are waiting for me

'. . . we've got a big choir practice today.'

In a complex situation like this, with everyone jockeying for position, most people confused and nearly everyone seeing the worst in their fellow men, people come to believe curious things which, in normal circumstances, they would have dismissed. So, when someone started the rumour that the entire population of Mockery Birds had been secretly captured and confined in – of all places – the English Club, no true Zenkali doubted this for a moment. So it was that an evilly disposed band of Ginkas (bent on destruction) and a group of stalwart Fangouas (bent on rescue) converged on the Club at that sacred hour of the day when all the English residents of Zenkali, some thirty-five souls in all, were sipping iced drinks, flirting ponderously with each other's wives, reading month-old copies of *Punch* and *The Illustrated London News*, playing billiards or croquet, or merely sitting and deploring the recent behaviour of the natives. In spite of the way the Zenkalis were behaving, however, there was not a single resident who did not feel secure behind the bastion of tall, immaculately clipped hibiscus hedge that surrounded the English Club. Whatever the Zenkalis did outside, Club members felt safe in their well-tended bit of Heaven. So it naturally came as a surprise to the assembled Club when the neat, tall, protective hedge was knocked flat by a human avalanche of Ginkas and Fangouas rolling through it, locked in combat.

Tubby Fortescue, an old Rugger Blue with enormous brawn and practically no frontal lobes, succeeded in fracturing several Ginka and Fangoua skulls with his croquet mallet. It took five stalwart Zenkalis of both tribes to subdue him and duck him unconscious in the lily pond that was one of the horticultural features of the Club.

Melanie Treet, a frail spinster, who painted blurred water colours of Zenkali life, was backed into a corner by a short-sighted, highly inebriated Fangoua and kissed; an experience which was forever after reflected in the increasingly phallic content of her paintings.

Sandy Shore, an Amela planter of substance and standing, had his glasses knocked off and trampled on, which reduced him to a state bordering on blindness. In consequence he attacked the Club Secretary, Bill Mellor, with a croquet mallet and knocked him unconscious under the mistaken impression that he was a Fangoua brave. Mrs. Mellor, normally a placid woman whose hobbies included crochet and jam-making, was so infuriated by this attack on her husband that she went to the unprecedented length of hitting Shore over the head with a bottle of *crème de menthe* which not only knocked him out but also caused a nasty scalp wound.

The confusion was total. The croquet lawn and the bowling green, for years so carefully rolled and cut and cosseted, were ploughed up by groups of Zenkalis and Club members rolling over them. Machetes, billiard cues, spears, bottles, wooden clubs and croquet mallets did irreparable damage to the pampered turf. It was at this point that the English Club, an attractive white clapboard building with wide verandahs, had a match applied to it by an enthusiastic and malicious Ginka. It went up in a grand conflagration, taking with it stuffed animal heads, ancient bound copies of *Punch*, yellowing group photographs of apparently senile former members and a filing cabinet of membership as intricate and complicated as the family tree of any minor European Royalty. By the time the police, a contingent of the Loamshires and the Fire Brigade had arrived to restore order, only the blackened and glowing shell remained, while the grounds looked as though a herd of water buffalo had been disporting themselves in the flower beds and across the lawns. It took the two Zenkali ambulances ten trips to remove all the combatants to the Hospital where things got so cramped that one of the marquees that had been erected for the festivities had to be commandeered, taken down and re-erected in the hospital gardens. The same state of congestion prevailed at the main prison, where the lesser offenders had to be sent home after the police had extracted a solemn promise from them that they would reappear in due course for punishment.

Both the Ginkas and the Fangouas claimed the attack to be a major victory as did the members of the Club, who felt that their rearguard action and subsequent vanquishing could be treated as a tactical victory equal, if not superior to, Dunkirk.

A new form of disgruntlement now emerged. The military contingents already on the island were reinforced by the arrival of H.M.S. *Conrad*, a frigate that had been doing a long spell of service at sea and whose crew, in consequence, were greatly looking forward to the delights of Mother Carey's Chickens. Their alarm and anger may be imagined when they learnt from the peace-keeping forces ashore that all the young ladies had been called out on strike by Carmen as a protest against drowning the Mockery Bird.

'Hi don't care what hanyone says, dears,' she confided to Peter and Audrey, 'Hi ham a hanimal lover and Hi will not tolerate cruelty, ho dear me no. When Hi think of all them poor little birds up there getting drowned hit makes my blood fairly boil, Hi can tell you. Hand hit makes my young ladies' blood boil likewise. So Hi says to them Hi says, "Girls, we will not service another gentleman until the matter his resolved hand hall them poor dumb creatures are saved."'

In consequence the rage and frustration of the military forces became so great that they would willingly have slaughtered the Mockery Birds if they had known where to find them.

Captain Pappas arrived back from Djakarta with the six reinforcements for Mother Carey's, who were immediately put into purdah by Carmen, and an assorted bunch of journalists and television people. They all looked somewhat jaded so it was obvious that the new recruits to Carmen's band of young ladies had not let the grass grow under their feet during the voyage. The arrival of the Press and Television in such quantity created a housing situation which Peter had to solve by commandeering a small hotel, The Rising Moon, run by Zenkali's only Chinese family. The proprietress of this hotel was called by the unlikely name of Pinponshe Chang. Peter was delighted by Audrey's explanation of her Christian name. Pinponshe's parents had been unable to read or write when they arrived from Hong Kong. In Zenkali they had thought it expedient to embrace the Protestant faith and, when their first daughter was born, they duly took her to be christened. They wished to call her Pleasant Spirit of the Chrysanthemum Flower and so they got one of their neighbours, a man of letters, to record the name on a slip of paper and this was then secured to the baby's shawl with a large safety-pin. It was unfortunate that the then Protestant Minister was newly arrived in the island and in consequence had not got to grips with pidgin English. He asked the proud parents what they proposed to call the child. 'It pin pon she,' said the father, meaning the name was pinned on the shawl. Before anyone could stop him or explain, the Minister had christened the child and from that day forward Pinponshe she remained. In due course she became very proud of her name, to such an extent that she had her son christened Albert Pinponhim Chang.

So Pinponshe and her son, Pinponhim, scrubbed and swept out their little hotel and coped with a motley collection of Press and T.V. personnel. Daniel Brewster was well known for his endless series of excessively boring television travelogues entitled 'Abroad with Brewster'. He arrived wearing heavy tweeds and a deer-stalker hat. He had a round, pasty face, pale eyes, a sycophant's oily smile and excessively large, damp red hands. The cameraman, Stephen Blore, was a paunchy man with puffy, disgruntled eyes and bad teeth which he had a habit of sucking loudly and vehemently when in thought. In spite of his repellent appearance he thought of himself as a ladies' man.

'You've got a lovely lot of tit, I'll say that for this dump,' remarked Blore to Peter as they drove towards the Rising Moon.

'Really?' said Peter, coldly.

'Yes, I'll say,' said Blore, rubbing his hands, 'lovely lot . . . look at that one there . . . cor! I bet she'd make you look up, eh? Well, my motto is that there's plenty of it about and it's a mug what pays for it.'

'Steve's a real card,' explained Daniel Brewster, giggling, 'keeps everyone in the B.B.C. in stitches, I can tell you. He's the life and soul of every party, but you've got to mind the girls, eh, Steve?'

'Yes, there's plenty of it about,' said Steve, as though discussing influenza.

'A real card,' repeated Brewster with pride.

'I think you'll be all right in this hotel,' said Peter, changing the subject, 'it's small but comfortable. It's run by Chinese.'

'I hope it's clean,' said Blore moodily, 'I know what these Chinks are like. And I don't want any of that muck they eat, either.'

'Chinese cuisine has been famous for centuries,' Peter pointed out.

'Not with me it hasn't mate,' said Blore, 'you can keep that muck. No, I've been around a bit and I know you can't beat decent English food, don't care what anyone says. Fish and chips . . . eggs and bacon . . . steaks . . . stuff like that. That's good enough for me. Good enough for anyone, I reckon. No, I don't go for this gourmand lark, myself. Can't stand mucky foreign food.'

'Steve's a real Englishman,' said Brewster admiringly.

'There's enough foreigners in the world to eat the muck, so why should we have to, that's what I say,' said Blore.

Peter wondered if all the pleasure he had got from re-discovering the Mockery Bird was going to be tainted by a never-ending influx of people like Blore.

'When we've settled in I'll interview you and this Damien girl,' said Brewster, as if conferring an honour, 'and then Steve and I will nip up into the valley and get the background stuff on the birds and the trees.'

Peter took a deep breath and tried to keep his temper.

'First of all, I'm not sure that Miss Damien wants to be interviewed,' he said, 'and secondly the position of the valley is being kept a close secret for the moment.'

'But not from me, surely?' asked Daniel Brewster in wounded astonishment. 'Why, one of my programmes on the box will put Zenkali right on the map.'

'Zenkali is already on the map without your help,' said Peter. 'Anyway, if you want to get into the valley you'll have to see Oliphant and the King.'

'I'm sure they won't refuse,' said Brewster, 'they *must* have seen my programmes.'

'I doubt it,' said Peter. 'We don't have television here.'

'You don't have a T.V. station?'

'No, it's one of the more civilised aspects of the island,' said Peter.

They drove the rest of the way to the hotel in a chilly silence. Peter then went back to the docks and ferried three reporters to the Rising Moon.

'What were you and Miss Damien doing up in the mountains together when you made the discovery?' asked Sibely of the *Daily Reflector*, with lascivious interest. 'Are you engaged or what?' He was a cadaverous man with very long greasy hair and bitten finger nails.

'Or what,' Peter replied shortly, deciding that he disliked Sibely as much as the T.V. boys. 'We were simply exploring the valleys before they were flooded.'

'You spent the night up there?' asked Sibely eagerly.

'Yes,' said Peter, and regretted it instantly. He regretted it more later, for his honesty resulted in the front-page story in the *Daily Reflector* having the headline, 'Mountain Lovers Get the Bird', which, as Hannibal observed, could be interpreted in several different ways.

The other two reporters, Highbury and Coons, were from *The Times* and Reuter's respectively. They seemed inoffensive enough and genuinely concerned and interested by the rediscovery of the Mockery Bird and Ombu, and displayed no interest in Peter's sex life, which was a relief. No sooner had Peter bedded down the Press than he had to turn his mind to a series of fresh problems.

When the *Empress of India* had reached Djakarta after depositing the military, her owners told her to about-face immediately and head back for Zenkali, for she now had an unprecedentedly full complement of passengers.

The first to lead this new deputation ashore was Sir Lancelot Haverly-Egger, Chairman of the World Organisation for the Protection of Endangered Species, known to its friends as WOPES. Sir Lancelot was a repentant big-game hunter, an all-round naturalist and a diplomat of the smoother variety. He was a short, stocky, bald-headed man, with pale green eyes, a heavy ginger moustache and an aura of self-importance. He was accompanied by the Secretary for the World Naturalists Trust, the Honourable Alfred Clatter, who resembled an inebriated praying mantis in a frayed straw hat, clutching a pile of bird books under one arm and a huge brass telescope under the other. Then there was Hiram F. Harp, in a scarlet coat with white flannels, President of the American League of Ornithology, a man whose brown face and white teeth appeared to be twice life-size and who carried slung around his bull neck enough camera equipment to make even a Japanese tourist envious. Following him, in an ill-fitting and somewhat crumpled white duck suit and looking slightly out of place among the titled gentry and the rich Americans, was Cedric Jugg, owner of one of Britain's biggest Safari Parks, Jugg's Jungle. Following him on to the dockside came another dozen or so assorted humans, all of whom were associated with one or other of these various organisations. They had been described in the telegram warning Zenkali of their arrival as 'secretaries' or 'assistants'.

Peter had purloined Diggory from Government House and pressed him into service, and he now scuttled round the docks like a red-headed, stammering sheep dog, herding everyone together and forming them into a semi-circle round Peter so that he could address them. 'Ladies and gentlemen,' Peter said, raising his voice slightly to quell the chattering. 'Ladies and gentlemen, my name is Peter Foxglove and I am the assistant to Her Majesty's Government's Political Advisor, Mr. Hannibal Oliphant. I am here to greet you on behalf of His Majesty King Tamalawala the Third.'

There was a buzz of excited chatter, instantly stilled as Peter continued.

'The King would like me to say that he welcomes you most warmly and hopes you will all enjoy your stay here in Zenkali. However,' Peter went on, 'owing to the rather troubled situation that has arisen in Zenkali recently, His Majesty wishes to make it clear that, although we will do everything in our power to make your stay comfortable and to ensure your protection, you do stay here at your own risk.'

The word 'risk' ran like a snake's hiss through the group. The Honourable Alfred Clatter, his eyes large and horrified behind his immense horn-rimmed spectacles, turned sharply to the man on his right to discuss this unnerving announcement, and thus hit Cedric Jugg a severe blow on the elbow with his telescope.

'See here, young fella,' said Hiram F. Harp in trenchant tones, alarm showing plainly on his massive brown face, 'what's all this about risk . . . what situation has arisen . . . why weren't we told . . . what I want to know . . .'

'Mr. Harp, just a moment please,' said Peter, holding up his hand, 'you see, since the Mockery Bird was re-discovered, various religious difficulties have emerged that have caused a certain amount of friction between the two tribes that live in Zenkali.'

'Religion, religion?' said Harp, bemused. 'What's religion got to do with ornithology, for crying out loud?'

'It would take too long to explain now,' said Peter, 'but you will all get a detailed handout when you are settled which will give you full details of the complex situation.'

'But what's all this about risk?' asked Harp. 'You said risk. Do you mean danger, young fella? I demand an answer. What's going on here, eh? After all, don't forget, we have ladies in the party.'

'I assure you that everything has been taken into consideration,' said Peter, soothingly. 'Most of you will be in a large house on the outskirts of Dzamandzar, a house that will be well protected by a detachment of the King's own bodyguard and a detachment of the Loamshires. Everything will be done to ensure that at no time will you be in any danger.'

'I don't like it, I don't like it one bit,' trumpeted Hiram F. Harp, 'we men, of course, can look after ourselves, but if anything were to happen to any of these little gals here . . . well!'

He blew out his cheeks and rolled his huge eyes expressively, while the gathering of 'little gals' gazed at him admiringly.

'Believe me,' said Peter earnestly, hoping he was speaking the truth, 'things are already settling down and within a few days we are confident that we will have the situation back to normal.'

'Has there been any bloodshed?' demanded Harp. 'Tell me that, young fella. Has there or has there not been any bloodshed?'

Peter smiled his most charming and calming smile.

'Let us say a few heads have been broken,' he said deprecatingly, 'but there has been no loss of life.'

'A few *heads* broken?' said Harp, aghast. 'A few *heads* broken . . . well, for God's sake . . . er . . . excuse me, little ladies . . . well for Land's Sakes, what does that mean . . . a few heads broken . . . a fractured skull can last a lifetime, I'll have you know young man.'

'I think Mr. Foxglove was merely using that as a figure of speech,' said Sir Lancelot, speaking for the first time in a soft purr like a cat musing over a mouse. 'I am sure we all must know that His Majesty King Tamalawala is doing his very best to welcome us and also to point out that in such troubled times it behoves us all to move with caution and not to rock the boat, as the saying goes. I am quite sure that His Majesty would not allow us ashore if he thought we were in any very grave danger.'

Peter had a momentary mental picture of Kingy that morning saying in exasperation, 'We could do without that crowd of animal lovers at this juncture, but we can't stop them. With a bit of luck someone will stick a spear into one of them.' This memory, however, he did not communicate to the group.

'I think,' continued Sir Lancelot, having neatly commandeered the situation, 'we should all do exactly what Mr. Foxglove tells us to do, as I am sure he has the situation well in hand.'

'Thank you, sir,' said Peter.

'Yes, I suggest that you all go to this house that Mr. Foxglove has so kindly arranged for us,' Sir Lancelot continued and he turned to Peter, smiling blandly. 'I will be staying at Government House?'

It was more of a statement than a question. Peter swallowed and took a deep breath. He had been warned that Sir Lancelot took his position in life very seriously indeed.

'I'm afraid not, Sir Lancelot,' he said, mollifyingly, 'you see, owing to the present unusual situation, Government House is full. Sir Adrian and Lady Emerald asked me to convey their apologies to you and to explain that their limited accommodation is already occupied by the people sent out by the British Government to deal with this airfield affair.'

'Oh!' said Sir Lancelot, compressing into that one monosyllable a degree of disgust, disappointment, disbelief, chagrin and long-suffering that was a masterpiece of expression. 'Oh, well, in such times as these we all have to learn to take the rough with the smooth.'

'Yes, sir,' said Peter, smiling. 'You and the Honourable Alfred Clatter are to be my guests. I will do my best to make you comfortable. Now,' he added briskly, 'if you will all kindly follow me, I have a fleet of Kingy Carts waiting.'

Eventually Peter managed to get the party safely billeted and Sir Lancelot and the Honourable Alfred installed on his verandah with a large drink apiece. He then excused himself, telling them that he had to attend a special meeting at the Palace.

'The Palace?' asked Sir Lancelot, not troubling to disguise his surprise, his eyes gleaming. 'Ah, yes. Just so. So you go to the Palace, do you?'

'When I'm asked, sir, yes,' said Peter with a perfectly straight face.

'Just so. I should very much like to meet King Tamalawala,' said Sir Lancelot, 'I am great friends with the Duke of Penzance who went to school with him I believe.'

'Yes, yes, and I know Lord Grottingly who also went to school with him, I believe,' said the Honourable Alfred, not to be outdone.

'And I am also on very good terms with Prince Umberto Cellini whom I believe the King knows,' Sir Lancelot went on, neatly checkmating the Honourable Alfred, 'I am sure the King would like news of his friends.'

'Well, I'll certainly mention it, sir,' said Peter, 'and now if you'll excuse me I must rush.'

Because of the trying times, Kingy had temporarily lifted the ban on motor vehicles in the centre of the city, to be used by Government officials only. Peter had borrowed a Land Rover from the police. He soon found, however, that the population of Dzamandzar were so used to the harmless Kingy Carts that they could not get used to the idea of a lethal vehicle in their midst. They drifted about the streets in their normal languid fashion, stopping in little groups to argue or throw dice in the road. This, to Peter's irritation, meant that his pace had to be slowed down to that of a Kingy Cart if he did not want to kill half the inhabitants of Dzamandzar. He arrived at the Palace half an hour late and in a great state of nerves.

He was ushered into the State dining-room which Kingy sometimes used as a conference room. It was a lovely room in cream and green, with a bronze carpet and an ornate stucco ceiling. At one end of the huge dining-table, the company had assembled. Kingy, in pale yellow robes, sat at the head of the table, looking, as always, massively self-assured. On his right slouched Hannibal, smoking a cigar, his eyes half closed. On his left Sir Osbert sat stiffly, his monocle screwed into his eye so firmly that it seemed to be an integral part of his anatomy. Next to him sat Lord Hammer, a large, fleshy man with soot black hair and a round pink baby face, whose innocence was only belied by large, violet eyes as sharp as a fox's. His big, pudgy hands were forever building and rebuilding a variety of structures with his note pad, his gold pencil, an ashtray, his spectacle case and his cigar case. They all looked up as Peter hurriedly entered the room.

'Ah, Peter,' said Kingy, beaming, 'good morning. You got here at last . . . good, now we can begin.'

'Good morning, Kingy,' said Peter, taking a seat next to Hannibal, 'I'm sorry I'm late but it took some time to sort the new batch out.'

'Ah yes,' said Kingy, gloomily, 'the redoubtable Sir Lancelot. I have no doubt we shall be hearing from him in due course.'

At the mention of this name, Lord Hammer's hands became still and Sir Osbert started.

'Sir Lancelot?' he asked sharply, screwing his monocle more firmly into his eye and surveying Kingy as if he were a slovenly private on the parade ground. 'You don't mean Sir Lancelot Haverly-Egger, do you? That damned chap's not here is he?'

'Do you know Sir Lancelot?' Kingy enquired.

'Know him? Of course I know him,' said Sir Osbert with feeling, 'the chap's a bloody menace. One of these damned fluffy-minded animal lovers, always interfering and causing trouble. You can't set a spade in the ground anywhere but up he pops with all his namby-pamby henchmen to tell you you can't build here because of a stoat or weasel or some such damned animal and you can't drain that swamp because of some awful creepy-crawly thing that's got to be saved. I tell you, that man is against progress: he's a menace.'

'I fear that he is in Zenkali for these very reasons,' said Kingy. 'It is too much to hope that he will look with favour on this airfield scheme, now that we have rediscovered the Mockery Bird.'

'The whole situation is perfectly ridiculous,' said Sir Osbert angrily, 'and now we have that fool Haverly-Egger interfering.'

Lord Hammer heaved a great sigh.

'Shall we discuss the airfield now, Your Majesty?' he asked in a curious soft, plaintive, piping voice like a child's.

'By all means,' said Kingy benignly, 'but, if you will excuse my saying so, Lord Hammer, I find your presence in Zenkali puzzling. Firstly, we do not know if the work is going ahead and, secondly, it has not as yet gone out to tender.'

There was a moment's silence. Sir Osbert shifted uncomfortably in his chair. Lord Hammer rearranged the items in front of him carefully with fat hands.

'On big and complicated jobs like this – though I trust my men, you understand – I always like to see the job for myself before we tender,' he said at last, and smiled beguilingly as a baby with fox's eyes.

'I see,' said Kingy.

'Most commendable,' snapped Hannibal.

'Well,' said Sir Osbert, 'I do think it's about time to get down to brass tacks about this whole thing. You really can't keep Her Majesty's Government hanging about like this over such a vital issue. If you take my advice you will flood the valleys. The sooner this is done the sooner everyone will forget about this damned bird.'

Kingy looked at him coldly.

'By "damned bird" I suppose you mean the ancestral God of the Fangouas?' he enquired.

Sir Osbert reddened.

'I only meant . . .' he began.

'Tell me, Sir Osbert,' interrupted Kingy, 'what would your reaction be if I suggested bulldozing St. Paul's or Westminster Abbey to make way for an airstrip?'

'Not quite the same thing . . .' began Sir Osbert.

'Of course, of course,' said Kingy, 'one is the God of a lot of black heathens and the others are sacred edifices of the civilised white man. How could they resemble each other?'

There was a short and pregnant silence.

'I must inform you, Sir Osbert, and you too, Lord Hammer, that before this matter can be resolved it must go to Select Council for a decision,' said Kingy. 'I can do nothing until they reach a conclusion.'

'I thought the King had absolute power?' said Sir Osbert, the faintest ripple of a sneer in his voice.

'Oh, no,' said Kingy smiling, 'we do try and be democratic. Surely you have not forgotten how long your country spent trying to inculcate the principles of democracy into Zenkali, Sir Osbert? Surely you would not have us discard them because you find them inconvenient?'

'When can you give us a decision?' asked Sir Osbert, his eyes glittering angrily.

'The day after tomorrow,' said Kingy, 'you have my word.'

After Sir Osbert and Lord Hammer had left, Kingy poured out drinks and they all sat in silence for a moment.

'What d'you think the Select Council will advise?' asked Hannibal at last, lighting a cigar.

Kingy spread his huge brown hands as if doing a conjuring trick.

'My dear Hannibal, I have not the least idea,' he shrugged.

'Is Looja on it?' asked Peter.

'Our Constitution states that in the rare event of a Select Council being set up to consider an important affair that affects the safety and future of the island, then it must consist of an equal number of Ginkas and Fangouas,' said

Kingy, 'so Looja and his henchmen make up half the committee.'

'Can you override them?' asked Hannibal.

'I can guide but not override, I'm afraid,' said Kingy, 'no, I'm afraid we cannot speculate at the moment. We must wait and see and play it off the cuff when the time comes.'

Peter drove home in a very depressed frame of mind. When he got to his house he was pleased to find Audrey waiting for him. She came up to him, kissed him quickly and then looked into his face.

'God, you look tired,' she said, 'shall I get you a drink?'

'Please,' he said, flopping into a chair, 'a large one. Where are Sir Lancelot and the Hon. Alf?'

'They're in the bathroom making themselves beautiful. They're very thrilled because they've been invited to Gov. House for dinner, so that will keep them out of our hair for this evening. I thought we could have a couple more drinks, a quiet swim and then dinner and early bed for you.'

'Wonderful,' said Peter, sipping his drink.

He was telling her about the day's events when Sir Lancelot and the Honourable Alfred appeared, resplendent in dinner jackets.

'Ah, Foxglove,' said Sir Lancelot jovially, 'back from the Palace? And what did His Majesty have to say?'

'Oh . . . er . . . he sent his salutations to you, sir, and said that, as soon as things calmed down a bit, he would have the pleasure of seeing you.'

'Excellent, excellent,' said Sir Lancelot in his purring voice.

'Splendid,' said the Honourable Alf.

'Well, we must be off,' said Sir Lancelot, beaming, 'we're having dinner at Government House.'

'Oh, good, I do hope you enjoy it, sir,' said Peter.

When they had left, Audrey poured herself out a drink and sat down beside Peter.

'What d'you think's going to happen?' she asked. 'Or don't you feel like talking about it?'

'God knows,' said Peter gloomily, 'I don't think anyone knows. The whole situation is so damn complex.'

'But surely they won't flood the valleys?'

'They're stupid enough for anything,' said Peter, 'but no, I don't think they'll do that. It's a question of finding a compromise, that's the difficulty. I've been racking my brains but I can't think of one.'

'Another drink and then some food, that's what you need,' said Audrey, getting to her feet. At that moment Amos appeared.

'Please, sah, Mr. Looja 'e done come,' said Amos with distaste.

'Looja?' asked Peter in amazement. 'Are you sure?'

'Yes, sah, for true, sah,' said Amos stoically.

Peter looked at Audrey.

'Now what?' he asked softly.

'I don't know,' she answered, 'but beware.'

'Show Mr. Looja in, Amos,' said Peter.

Looja, wearing elegant white ducks and his Rugby tie, walked briskly into the room, smiling a bland smile, his eyes expressionless. He checked slightly in his stride when he saw Audrey, but continued across the room, his hand held out.

'My dear Foxglove, Miss Damien,' he said, bowing slightly, 'forgive this intrusion.'

'Not at all. Please sit down and have a drink,' said Peter.

'Thank you. That is kind. I'll have a snifter of the old B. & S. if I may,' said Looja.

'Amos, a brandy and soda for Mr. Looja, please,' Peter said.

When the drink was served Looja cosseted it in his tiny hands. He carefully crossed his legs with anxious concern for the razor crease in his trousers, and fixed his tar-black eyes on Peter.

'I will confess, Foxglove – with no disrespect to Miss

Damien – that I had hoped to find you alone, for the matter I wish to discuss with you is . . . well, shall we say delicate and private?'

'I'll go if you like, Mr. Looja,' said Audrey, sweetly.

'I think that anything Mr. Looja wants to say to me can quite safely be said in front of you,' said Peter firmly.

'Quite so, quite so, my own thoughts exactly,' said Looja, 'for I realise now, of course, finding you both here, that the matter I wish to discuss concerns you both. So I would be grateful if you would stay, Miss Damien, as I should value your opinion as well as Foxglove's in this matter.'

He sipped his drink and slid a silk handkerchief from his sleeve and dabbed his mouth fastidiously.

'The matter I wish to discuss concerns – as you no doubt will have guessed – this remarkable discovery that you and Miss Damien made,' he went on.

'Well?' said Peter bluntly. 'What about it?'

'A truly remarkable biological discovery,' Looja went on, 'and one that does you both great credit. But nevertheless, one is forced to admit, it is a two-edged sword.'

'How so?' asked Peter.

'Well, between ourselves, Foxglove – you're a man of the world and Miss Damien here is a highly intelligent young lady – between ourselves we know that, however important, biologically speaking, this discovery is, it cannot benefit the island as the airfield would. Therefore, it is ridiculous to suppose that we should let it stand in the way of the development of the island which, after all, means so much to the people of Zenkali.'

'Financially, you mean?' asked Peter.

'But of course,' said Looja, his dark eyes gleaming, 'it will make the island rich.'

'And will make you rich at the same time,' said Peter.

Looja sat back in his chair, nursing his glass.

'I would not dream of trying to deceive you, Foxglove, old man. I do stand to gain a bit financially from this project,' said Looja gravely. 'Then, so do hundreds of other Zenkalis. Even the most unlikely people, such as yourself, might benefit ultimately.'

Looja watched Peter over the rim of his glass. Before Peter could comment, he went on. 'As you know, we have the Special Council. I tell you frankly, old man, I don't know how things will go. Everyone has got over-sensitive and hysterical over this whole business, and it is more than likely, in this tense climate, that even the Special Council might make a mistake and cancel the airfield project. That of course would be a disaster for the island, a complete disaster. No one is thinking very clearly at this juncture, and it is more than likely that, quite by mistake, the wrong solution to the problem may be arrived at. So, what is to be done?'

This was obviously a rhetorical question, for Looja hurried on before Peter could offer any suggestion.

'Now it seems to me,' said Looja, trying to look benign, 'it seems to me, old man, that the simplest thing to do would be to remove the obstacle, as it were. With that removed the airfield can go ahead as planned.'

There was a short silence.

'I see,' said Peter, 'and how would you propose to go about that?'

'That's just the point,' said Looja, smiling, showing his tiny white puppy teeth, 'I cannot, of course, achieve success without the full co-operation of Miss Damien and yourself, since I do not know the whereabouts of the valley in question. But the matter need not involve either of you at all. If I simply had this information I would take care of the rest of the procedure myself.'

'Let me get this clear,' said Peter, 'you want me and Miss Damien to tell you the whereabouts of Mockery Bird Valley and then you will proceed to – how did you put it – remove the obstacle?'

'Perfectly correct,' said Looja.

'How?' said Peter.

Looja shrugged delicately and brushed an invisible speck of dust from his knee.

'There are ways,' he said.

'What ways?' Peter persisted.

'Fire and shotguns can be very persuasive,' said Looja, 'and sufficient evidence can be planted to make it look as though a raiding party of Ginkas stumbled on the valley and . . . er . . . eliminated the obstacle.'

'And what would be in it for me?' asked Peter.

Looja's eyes gleamed like a fisherman who feels, trembling through the rod and line, the first fragile nibblings of the fish.

'I know what your job pays, of course,' said Looja silkily, 'and so I can sympathise with your desire to – shall we say? – cash in on your discovery. I assure you you would not find me ungenerous, Foxglove.'

'Yes, but it would still be nice to know what your generosity would consist of,' said Peter gently.

'Shall we say . . . five thousand pounds?' suggested Looja.

Peter looked at him and laughed.

'What, with all you're going to make out of the airfield?' he asked scornfully. 'That's chickenfeed. And what does Miss Damien get out of it?'

'Shall we say six thousand then, six thousand apiece?' said Looja, his eyes glittering.

'Listen, Looja, you're going to make several hundred thousand pounds out of that airstrip, aren't you?' asked Peter.

Looja shrugged.

'Let us say that I shall be well satisfied if the deal goes through,' he said, 'but come now, Foxglove, the offer I am making is not ungenerous, considering that I am taking all the risks.'

Peter just sat and looked at him. Looja now had the air of a man in a poker game who knows that his hand bristles with aces. He drained his drink and placed the empty glass carefully on the table at his elbow. Then he leant forward, ingratiatingly.

'Well, well, Foxglove old fellow,' he said, 'I am not a

man to quibble when I want something badly enough. No one could ever call me stingy. How would it be if I paid you – and Miss Damien, of course – twenty-five thousand pounds for this little secret, eh? Now you can't say that's not a fair price, eh? And, who knows, if the whole thing works out as we plan there might be other little remunerations in the future, eh? What d'you say, old man?'

He leant forward eagerly, his silver hair shining, his black eyes gleaming, his forefinger tapping his knee, supremely confident of Peter's reply.

Peter drained his glass and stood up.

'The trouble with you, Looja,' he said kindly, 'is that you're an overdressed little blackamoor with a cash register for a mind. You work on the stupid principle that every man has his price. Well, let me tell you, *old boy*, that I wouldn't tell you the whereabouts of Mockery Bird Valley for twenty-five million, let alone twenty-five thousand.'

Looja had shrunk back in his chair, his face a sort of livid yellow, his eyes blazing.

'Furthermore, I must confess that I dislike you more than I can say,' said Peter, getting into his stride. 'I really do not know what poor Zenkali has done to deserve such an undersized, malignant little runt like you who, by rights, should have been quietly strangled at birth, but I do assure you that I will do everything in my power to make sure this airfield does not go through. It will give me great pleasure to upset your nasty little apple cart. Now please leave. Miss Damien and I are particular about the company we keep and we have already had a surfeit of yours.'

Looja got to his feet and walked to the door, where he turned. His face still had the curious livid sheen, but his eyes no longer blazed. They were dark and expressionless.

'You will regret your attitude, Foxglove, you will regret your insults. No one speaks to me like that. And, remember this, I let no one stand in my way, no one. Particularly someone as paltry as you.'

He went out, slamming the door behind him. Peter sank back into his chair.

'Well,' said Audrey, 'you certainly know how to win friends and influence people.'

'Yes. I got the distinct impression that friend Looja didn't care for me overmuch,' said Peter grinning.

'Seriously, though, he makes a bad enemy,' said Audrey, 'what do you think he will do?'

'Unless he knows where the valley is he can't do anything,' said Peter.

In this he was greatly mistaken.

Chapter Six

ZENKALI VOCIFEROUS

The next day Peter came out to breakfast to find both Sir Lancelot and the Hon. Alf installed on the verandah demolishing bacon and eggs and a huge bowl of fruit. After Peter had taken a seat, Sir Lancelot launched forth.

'The whole situation is fascinating, fascinating, you know, Foxglove,' he said, waving an eggy knife at Peter, 'so many factors involved.'

'Yes, sir,' said Peter. He did not feel like starting the day discussing the situation in Zenkali, but he could not very well say so.

'Extraordinary, quite extraordinary,' said the Hon. Alf, struggling with a mango the size of a small melon. 'I was saying to Sir Lancelot that something very similar occurred when I was staying with the Maharajah of Kumquat. In that instance it was sacred monkeys that threw a wrench in the works – one might almost say a monkey wrench in the works, eh, what? Ha! Ha!'

'Quite,' said Sir Lancelot, having considered whether to laugh or not and having decided against it. 'As I was saying to my friend Arthur Mendal – the Home Secretary, you know – well, he came down for the weekend not long ago with the Marquis of Orkney and Lord Bellroyal, and I was saying to them that when politics and religion get mixed up with conservation, then you have a very delicate situation indeed.'

'I said a very similar thing to the Maharajah of Kumquat,' said the Hon. Alf, but you could tell that his heart was not in it.

'The Special Council meets today, doesn't it?' asked Sir Lancelot.

'Yes, at eleven-thirty,' Peter replied.

'Do they hold it in the Parliament Building?'

'No, they hold it in the Palace.'

'I see. By lunchtime we may hope to be told the results of their deliberations?' asked Sir Lancelot.

'I would imagine so, yes,' Peter replied, 'but it's hard to say as the situation is so complex. It may take longer.'

'Quite, quite,' said Sir Lancelot, 'best not to rush into such an important decision – best to hasten slowly, as they say.'

'Exactly,' said the Hon. Alf, delighted with this homily, 'well said, indeed.'

'Well, if you'll excuse me, I must be going. I've got to make sure all your people are all right and then get along to the Palace for the meeting,' Peter said.

'Oh, you're going to the meeting are you?' said Sir Lancelot with ill-concealed surprise.

'The King specially asked that I and Hannibal Oliphant should be present as observers. Normally the meeting of a Special Council is *in camera*.'

'Most interesting,' mused Sir Lancelot, 'I shall look forward, therefore, to hearing your first-hand account.'

As Peter walked across the verandah and then down through the gardens he heard the Hon. Alf say: 'This reminds me very much of the situation in Rio Muni, when I remember saying to the Duke of Pelligroza . . .'

Leaving them to their game of *Debrett* or *Almanac de Gotha*, Peter drove rapidly down to his office and from there, later in the morning he made his way down to the old Dutch planter's house he had commandeered to make sure that the rest of his flock were in good fettle.

When he arrived he was somewhat surprised to find Captain Pappas seated on the broad, cool verandah, imbibing large glasses of Zenkali Nectar with Cedric Jugg. They were apparently halfway through a bottle and the spirit had already taken its toll.

''allo, 'allo, 'allo,' cried Jugg, ''ere's Foxglove, very blighter we wanted to see. Talk of the Devil and in you walks, eh? Har, Har!'

His fat, grey face was speckled with tiny beads of sweat, and his sparse, lank hair was dishevelled. He climbed unsteadily to his feet, waddled across the verandah and took Peter's arm in an affectionate grip. At the table Captain Pappas sat immobile, his little dark eyes unwavering.

'Come 'an 'ave a drink and let me 'splain you what I've been workin' out,' said Jugg, smiling widely, his eyes slightly unfocused, 'come an' 'ave a drink . . . Zenkali Nectar . . . wunnerful stuff . . . great stuff . . . puts hairs on your chest . . . puts hair all over you.'

It suddenly occurred to Peter to wonder why Jugg was in Zenkali at all. The poor man was obviously completely out of place with the rest of the group. Wanting to learn more he allowed himself to be dragged across to the table and pressed into a chair.

'What'll you 'ave?' asked Jugg, seating himself and gazing at Peter with great earnestness. 'What'll you 'ave? Anythink you want . . . I'm buying . . . anythink you want . . . brandy, rum, gin . . . you jus' name it . . . I'm buying.'

'It's too early for me, thanks,' said Peter, 'I'll just have a coffee, if I may.'

With great precision and in a loud voice to ensure that he was understood, Jugg relayed this request to the Zenkali steward. Then, this linguistic triumph over, he sat back in his chair and beamed at Peter, mopping his face with a scarlet handkerchief.

'Funny thing you should come along jus' as I was talking about you to the Captain 'ere. You know the Captain, don't you? Good ole pal of mine.'

'Yes, I know the Captain well,' said Peter, smiling at him. Captain Pappas acknowledged this with the merest flicker of agate eyes.

'Now, I was telling the Captain 'ere as 'ow I could 'elp

you out of the 'ole you've got yourselves into, see? I got wot you might call the key to the 'ole bleedin' problem,' continued Jugg, unsteadily pouring himself out another Zenkali Nectar.

'Really?' asked Peter, fascinated. He glanced at Captain Pappas who did not appear to be even breathing and whose eyes were expressionless and unwinking.

'Yes,' said Jugg expansively. 'I 'ave the key. I don' know what you know about me, Mr. Foxglove, but I'm Jugg of Jugg's Jungle, d'you see. Finest Safari Park in the world, though I says it meself as shouldn't.'

'Yes I knew you were the owner of Jugg's Jungle . . .' Peter began.

'Owner *and* creator,' said Jugg solemnly, 'don' forget that.'

'Of course,' said Peter, 'but I don't quite see how it helps us?'

'Solves your bleedin' problem, don't it?' said Jugg smugly.

'I'm not quite sure I follow you,' said Peter, puzzled.

'Look 'ere,' said Jugg, leaning forward and waving his glass under Peter's nose, 'you've got a problem, ain't you? Can't flood them bleedin' valleys because of them bleedin' birds, eh? S'right, ain't it? An' if you don' flood the bleedin' valleys you don' get no airfield. You get my meaning? What the French calls a cul-de-sac. And I got the key to it. You get my meanin'?'

Peter nodded.

'Now, this is where I come in . . . an' you, too,' said Jugg. He glanced about and lowered his voice. 'Now, what I'm going to tell you is in strictest confidence, eh? Strictest confidence. 'Cos we don' want any of them bleedin' conser . . . conser . . . conser . . . any of that crowd gettin' in on the act, eh? So, be like dad, keep mum, eh? Har! Har!'

He took a large draught of Zenkali Nectar to fortify himself.

'Now,' he said, wiping his mouth with the back of his

hand, ''splain to you what I 'ave in mind. If you gets rid of them birds you can 'ave the airfield, right?'

'Well, more or less I suppose,' said Peter, cautiously.

'Right,' said Jugg, stifling a belch, 'well, I'm the man what'll get rid of them for you, see? Not only get *rid* of 'em but put a nice profit into the pocket of that Cannibal King of yours.'

He leant back, winked at Peter slowly and nodded his head portentously. He took another gulp of Nectar.

'Yes, got it all worked out,' he said, 'want you to go an' tell this black boy of yours not to worry any more. Jugg will take care of it, tell 'im. Jugg will fix it. All I've got to 'ave is 'is permission and I'll whip up into that valley and catch all them bleedin' birds up and before you can say Bingo they'll be in Jugg's Jungle. Yes, five 'undred apiece I'm offerin' and a generous price it is too, you'll 'ave to admit. Considering the mess wot you're in, your King chap ought by rights to be payin' me to take 'em. Yes, by rights 'e ought to be beggin' me to 'ave 'em. Still, that's not the way Jugg's does business. Oh, no. Fair's fair. An' I won't deny for a minute that them birds will make a nice bit of publicity and a nice bit of profit for me. Yes, I've got the advert worked out now: EVEN THE EXTINCT COME TO LIFE IN JUGG'S JUNGLE. 'Ow d'you like that then? That'll grab 'em. We'll get thousands through the gate, thousands.'

'But you know nothing about them,' Peter protested, 'you don't even know what they eat.'

'Wot they eat? . . . well . . . they're birds, ain't they? . . . they eat things like other birds, I 'spect,' said Jugg, waving a vague hand, dismissing this quibble, 'like an ostrich, I shouldn't wonder.'

'But what if they eat something . . . something special . . . that you can't get in England?' asked Peter.

'Learn 'em to eat something you *can* get,' said Jugg, 'jus' school 'em, see? They'll eat if they're 'ungry enough, mark my words.'

'And what about the climate?' asked Peter. 'It's very hot here, remember. Supposing they can't stand the cold?'

'Well, now,' said Jugg, and his bleared eyes grew pensive, '"ow many did you say there were?'

'We counted fifteeen pairs,' said Peter, 'there may be more.'

'Thirty birds, eh? Well, that's a goodish number. Supposin' you lose 'alf gettin' 'em to England. Well, that would still leave you fifteen. An' supposing they was to last a fortnight. That would mean . . .' Jugg closed his eyes, screwed up his face and did some mental arithmetic, 'Yes, well . . . I reckon if they lasted a fortnight – and, blimey, I would 'ope they'd last a bit longer – with the right sort of publicity I reckon we could clear fifty thousand profit, easy. Maybe more.'

Peter felt slightly sick.

'And if all the Mockery Birds died?' he asked.

'Well, we got along without 'em before you found 'em, didn't we?' said Jugg. 'No doubt we could get along without 'em again. But it would be damn bad luck if they all died, damn bad luck. But there's no doubt about it, the animal game's chancy. The profit is good but there's no denying it's chancy.'

'In what way?' asked Peter, feeling he should hear everything.

'Well, I'll give you a for instance,' said Jugg. 'Last winter we imported a batch of leopards, see? Ten of 'em. Cost me a packet. Got 'em all safely to the Jungle and then wot d'you think happens? Damn fool in charge – 'e'd only been with us a short time of course – well, 'e shuts 'em out in the paddock all night. The 'ole lot dead in the snow in the morning. You wouldn't credit it, would you? But the 'ole bleedin' lot died. No, I tell a lie. Two of 'em were still alive, but they died that same day. You wouldn't credit 'ow difficult they are, leopards.'

'What happened to the man?' asked Peter incredulously. 'Did you sack him?'

'Sack 'im?' said Jugg, looking at Peter pityingly. 'Lord love you, it would be more than my life's worth to sack 'im. 'Ave the Union down on me like a ton of bricks if I did. No, it was just a little mistake, could 'ave 'appened to anyone, and in this life wot I say is one 'as to learn by one's mistakes. No, young Bert's shaping up very well now, considering. But, like wot I was telling you, these damn animals are real chancy.'

'So I can see,' said Peter dryly, 'but at least they don't have Unions.'

Jugg laughed so heartily at this that it brought the tears to his eyes.

'Unions? Animals 'aving Unions. Oh, dearie me, that is a good one and no mistake. We would all be in a pretty pickle, wouldn't we, eh?' he said, wiping his eyes with his scarlet handkerchief. 'Anyway, like I was saying, I'll take these birds off of your 'ands and the Captain 'ere is going to give me a good price for runnin' 'em to Djakarta. Now, what I want you to do is to put my proposition to your King chappie. Tell 'im five 'undred on the nose for every bird I get – 'e gets the money and I 'ave all the problems, savvy? An' you can tell 'im that if I get 'em all back an' make the profit I think I will I'll send him a bonus . . . you know, a bag of coloured beads or somethink.'

Jugg lay back in his chair and laughed uproariously.

'Yes,' said Peter, standing up, 'well, I'll convey your proposition to His Majesty, I'm sure he'll be most interested. And now I must go and see the other members of your party. Thanks for the coffee.'

'Nice to 'ave 'ad a chinwag with you,' said Jugg earnestly, holding out his hand, 'nice to talk to a fellow 'oo knows wot's wot.'

As Peter went in search of the rest of the group he reflected that it was a waste of time him getting annoyed with Jugg. The main thing was that under no circumstances would Jugg be allowed to pull off his coup and spirit the Mockery Birds off to the horrors of Jugg's Jungle.

He found the rest of the party sunbathing in the garden behind the house.

'And what I say is,' Harp was saying decisively as Peter approached the group, 'we must take a very firm line with

His Majesty, yes sir, very firm indeed. We must let him see that the conservation movement will not be trifled with, no sir . . .'

He broke off as he caught sight of Peter and, beaming his innocent, large-toothed smile, he hastened forward, hand outstretched. 'Well, Mr. Foxglove, sir, how nice to see you,' he said, engulfing Peter's hand in both of his.

'Don't let me interrupt,' said Peter.

'Interrupt? No, no, not at all . . . just yacking a bit with the boys and girls,' said Harp, 'come and have a drink. What can we do for you?'

'Well, it's more what I can do for you,' said Peter. 'I've come to see if you're happy and comfortable and if there is anything you want that I can organise for you.'

'Well, now, that's mighty nice of you,' said Harp. 'We don't want to plague you, you know. We realise you're a very, very busy man, yes sir, very busy.'

'Not at all,' said Peter, smiling, 'it's part of my job.'

'Well, we hesitate to worry you,' said Harp again, pulling from the pocket of his shorts a formidable-looking list, 'but it so happens that I did run around the boys and girls this morning to make sure everything was okay and we've come up with a short list of a few suggestions. Just suggestions, you understand. We'd be glad of your views.'

For the next hour Peter tried to cope with the few suggestions.

There was Miss Alison Grubworthy's complaint about the cockroaches, ticks, wasps, moths and geckos which were inhabiting her room. There was Adolf Zwigbuerrer's comprehensive criticism of everything on the grounds that it was never done like that in Sweden. There was Senorita Maria-Rosa Lopez's desire for a new lock on her door to allay her suspicion that the Zenkali majordomo of the establishment possessed a duplicate key for the present lock and was making preparations to enter her room one night and rape her. As Senorita Lopez was a seventy-year-old hunchback, wrinkled as tripe, Peter felt this fear was scarcely justified. However, he endeavoured to satisfy all their whims and fancies, from Harp's desire for more ice and a more strenuous washing of the salads, to the desire of Herr Rudi Meinstoller to know a place in Dzamandzar where he could get his watch repaired. This dour representative of the World Organisation for Nature Preservation seemed to think it would be detrimental to Switzerland to have a Swiss going about with a defective timepiece.

By the time Peter arrived at Hannibal's house he had a raging headache and an even more raging thirst. He found Hannibal sitting in his giant rocking chair in the long, bright living-room cooled by whirling fans. Surrounded by his retinue of dogs, Hannibal had a table in front of him piled high with files and a further scattering of them lay on the floor. He was writing assiduously, his glasses perched on the end of his nose. He looked up as Peter came in and pointed to the table of drinks without speaking and then returned to his writing. Peter poured himself a drink and took a chair near Hannibal. He sat, sipping his drink, until Hannibal had finished writing, read his composition through, taken off his glasses and raised his drink.

'Your health,' said Hannibal.

'Cheers,' said Peter.

They drank in companionable silence for a moment.

'Well,' said Hannibal at last, 'what news?'

Peter took a long pull at his drink and then told Hannibal about Jugg's proposition. Hannibal roared with laughter, rocking backwards and forwards in his great chair.

'The tyke!' he exclaimed joyfully. 'The appalling, cheeky little tyke. Cannibal King indeed . . . by Jove, Kingy'll love that.'

'You're not going to tell him, are you?' asked Peter, alarmed.

'Of course, why not?' said Hannibal. 'The poor old boy's not had a good laugh for days . . . he'll adore it.'

Peter refilled their glasses and sat down again.

'But that's just a lot of idiocy, like that American Harp

and his damned ice and that servile Swiss and his watch,' he said.

'Do you realise that by belittling an American's ice and a Swiss's watch you are cutting deep at the cultural roots of those two great countries?' enquired Hannibal solemnly.

'Well, anyway,' said Peter, grinning, 'let me tell you about that nasty little creep Looja. That's much more important.'

'Looja?' said Hannibal. 'And what has he been up to now?'

Peter told him about Looja's visit and the outcome. Hannibal whistled.

'He must be feeling nervous to try and bribe you,' he said. 'It's such a silly thing to try and do. I wonder if a certain pressure is being brought to bear.'

'Pressure from whom?' asked Peter.

'Your uncle for one,' said Hannibal. 'I never have liked that Siamese-twin act between Sir Osbert and Hammer, and as soon as I found out that Looja knew your uncle I smelt a rodent of considerable proportions.'

'You mean my uncle stands to gain by the airfield? That he's getting a rake-off?' asked Peter incredulously.

'Stranger things have happened,' said Hannibal. 'Of course, we've got no evidence . . . nothing that would stand up in a court of law.'

'Could we get evidence, d'you think?' asked Peter excitedly. 'If what you think is right it would put paid to the whole airfield idea, surely?'

'I'm not so sure of that, though it would give us a breathing space,' said Hannibal, 'but I don't see us getting any evidence unless that unpleasant trio walks in here and hands us a full, signed confession. Anyway, there's nothing we can do for the moment, so let's cut along to the Special Council and see what they have to say.'

The Special Council consisted of all the minor and major chiefs of both the Ginkas and the Fangouas, twenty of each, with Kingy being allowed the casting vote. They sat, in their brightly coloured robes, tightly packed round the long polished table. Kingy looked magnificent in a robe of royal purple with gold embroidery at the neck and cuffs. The only jarring note was Looja in an immaculate lounge suit, wearing his Rugby tie. When Hannibal and Peter had taken their seats, Kingy started.

'I think, at the outset,' he said, speaking with his rich rolling voice that lent itself well to rhetoric, 'this Special Council must realise one thing. That is that there is no possibility of depriving the Fangouas of their newly rediscovered God, any more than there would be a possibility of depriving the Ginkas of their Fish God. The problem that faces us is that both the Mockery Bird and the Ombu tree will perish if we go forward with our plans to flood the valleys, and yet we have already agreed in Parliament that the airfield should go forward. So what we have to decide today is how the airfield can be created without detriment to the religious susceptibilities of the Fangouas. To start with, I shall go round the table in turn and ask you to state your individual views. Then we might have a general discussion.'

Slowly Kingy worked his way round the table, getting the ideas of each individual. Some were succinct and to the point, but most were rambling and vague, using the opportunity more to revel in the sound of their own voices than to offer any concrete solution. Hannibal kept uttering tiny grunts of impatience and at one point passed a scribbled note to Peter which said: 'They are all going round in circles . . . told Kingy they would. But I've given Kingy some delaying ammunition which may work. Remind me I want to see that creep Droom.'

Finally, two hours later, after endless discussion and acrimony, with people leaping to their feet, banging on the table and trying to shout each other down in the most democratic fashion, Kingy held up his hand for silence.

'All of you have been heard and all of you have made suggestions that have been recorded,' he said, and he beamed round the table in a fatherly way, 'and I would like to thank you all for taking this matter so seriously and for making such sensible and intelligent suggestions.'

He paused, put his spectacles on and glanced at a piece of paper in his hand. Then he took his glasses off and looked at the Special Council benignly.

'However, intelligent and helpful though your suggestions were, they none of them really solved our problem. Therefore, if you will allow me, I would like to put up a suggestion of my own which I think may serve the case.'

The Special Council sat and watched Kingy, hypnotised by his giant personality. Only Looja, Peter noticed, watched the King with slightly narrowed eyes, one fragile forefinger tapping the polished table top.

'Now,' Kingy continued, 'our problem is to save both the bird and the tree. How should we best go about it? The thing that obviously springs to mind is that if you don't want them where they are you must move them. In the case of the bird a full biological investigation of its needs would have to be made so that a suitable area for the translocation could be chosen. In the case of the tree it is slightly more difficult and very much more expensive. In America, as you know, they have perfected methods of moving fully grown trees and so I suggest we investigate the possibilities of moving the Ombu trees and planting them in the same area to which we will remove the Mockery Bird.'

A murmur of excited speculation ran through the two groups. Only Looja remained silent, a faint sneer on his face. During the general discussion, he had offered no suggestion, merely saying with a shrug that he would go along with a majority decision.

'I realise, of course, that this programme will be slow and costly, but I do believe that it is the only course we can adopt. I am sure that financial help will be forthcoming from many quarters to help us in this important rescue operation.' Kingy went on, 'I would therefore propose that we institute a Fund to be called the Mockery Bird Fund and that I get Professor Droom to start immediately on investigating the basic biology of the Mockery Bird and the logistics of moving the Ombu tree. I presume you would all be in favour of this method of circumventing our problems?'

So captivated were the Council by Kingy's novel approach, there was a stunned silence for a moment, and then they held up their hands and chanted yes to a man. They looked at each other, wreathed in smiles, nodding their heads and laughing as if the whole problem had now been solved.

'Good,' said Kingy, 'then we will not disband this Council, but we will have another meeting in, say, two months' time when I am sure Professor Droom will have some news for us.'

He rose and led Hannibal and Peter into his own apartments, while the chattering, excited Council broke up. In Kingy's private study a large Thermos of 'Lèse-Majesté' awaited and in silence Kingy poured out the drinks and in silence they toasted one another.

'Well,' said Kingy, having drunk the first gulp of well-laced coconut milk. 'Thank God for your brainwave, Hannibal. It seems to have worked.'

'Let us not rate it too high,' said Hannibal. 'It's given us a much-wanted breathing space, that's all. The bill for transplanting a forest of Ombu trees will be astronomical, and it's quite possible that those birds will pine and die for some reason if they're removed from the valley. I foresee difficulties with the whole thing, probably insurmountable. But it's given us a few weeks to try and think of an alternative – that's something, I suppose.'

'Droom will be delighted he's coming into his own,' said Peter.

'Yes,' said Hannibal, 'as soon as you've finished that drink I'd like you to zoom off, find Droom, and bring him to my house.'

'Right,' said Peter, draining his drink and getting up. 'I'll go right now. If he's there I'll get him to your place in about half an hour. Okay?'

'Fine,' said Hannibal. 'Just give me time for another of Kingy's lethal drinks.'

When Peter reached the small house on the outskirts of Dzamandzar in which Droom had lodgings, he was greeted by Droom's landlady, an elderly and very fat Zenkali lady, who informed him that Droom had gone off the previous day with his collecting bag and a supply of food and had not yet returned.

'You savvy which side 'e go go?' asked Peter.

'No, sah, I no savvy which side 'e go go,' said the lady, twirling her toes in the dust. 'For true, sah, Masa Dloom never tell me which side 'e go go.'

'You say 'e done take chop with him?'

'Yes, sah, he take plenty chop. I done cook um, sah.'

''E done take enough chop for maybe two-three days?' asked Peter.

'No, sah,' said the lady firmly. 'His chop no go pass two days, for true, sah.'

There was only one thing for it and that was to leave a message, Peter thought.

'You go take me to Masa Droom's room, Mammy,' he said. 'I go write a book for Masa Droom and when 'e go come from bush, you go give 'um, you hear.'

'I hear, sah,' said the landlady, and led him into Droom's rooms.

Unlike Droom's personal appearance the rooms were, to Peter's astonishment, immaculate. There were shelves of reference books, ranks of thick files all carefully labelled, rows and rows of jars and gauze cages in which various insects sat imprisoned, and a table with a great, gleaming microscope and microphotographic equipment on it, all meticulously arranged. On the desk Peter found a jotting pad and on it he wrote a short note to Droom, asking him to come to Hannibal's house without delay. This he gave to the landlady, who tucked it for safety between her massive bosoms and promised him she would deliver it faithfully when Droom returned.

When Peter got to Hannibal's he found to his astonishment that he was holding a press conference. Seated out on the broad verandah in a circle of chairs sat the representatives of the Press and Television, all clutching large drinks and listening to Hannibal avidly.

'And so I tell you gentlemen that the rediscovery of the Mockery Bird and the Ombu tree constitutes one of the major biological discoveries of this century – perhaps of any century. You do not, after all, discover a god every day of the week.'

'Why were there these disturbances?' asked Highbury of *The Times*, whose face was flushed purple with a combination of heat and Hannibal's hospitality.

'Historically speaking . . .' Hannibal began, and then he caught sight of Peter. 'Ah, Peter, get yourself a drink and join us. I'm just trying to inject a little truth and culture into the Press and T.V. boys – an uphill struggle, I might say, but no matter. Just another burden we Empire-builders have to shoulder. What was I saying – ah, yes, disturbances – well, historically speaking, almost every new discovery, every new departure in thought, even, has created a disturbance. You remember, I've no doubt, how they behaved in the North of England when the Spinning Jenny was introduced.'

Those members of the Press who knew their history looked confused. Hannibal carried around a jug containing a potent-looking liquid and refilled their glasses.

'But the disturbances here?' began Coons of Reuter's.

'A mere schoolboy romp,' said Hannibal, airily.

'But . . . but . . . they burned down the English Club,' exclaimed Sibely of the *Reflector*, as though discussing the fate of the great library in Alexandria.

'It was long overdue for demolition,' said Hannibal blandly. 'They, in fact, did the English community a favour by ridding them of that insanitary old club-house. Now, with the insurance money, they'll be able to build a nice new one, all chromium plate and glass, more in keeping with the image of Great Britain.'

'You say it was just a schoolboy romp,' said Highbury,

'but the hospital is full to overflowing with the wounded.'

'My dear fellow, you have, with the unerring accuracy of an experienced reporter, put your finger right on the very crux of the whole thing. Wounded, you said. Precisely. Where else in the world would you have a romp like that and only have a few wounded at the end of it? Not a single death. Why, I've seen rugger matches that ended up with more casualties than that.'

'I still say there were a hell of a lot of wounded for what you describe as a romp,' said Highbury truculently.

'My dear chap, be reasonable,' said Hannibal, smiling warmly and reasonably at Highbury. 'After all, as the Spanish say, you can't have a romp without breaking heads.'

Highbury chuckled and raised his glass.

'Is it true that one of the English ladies was raped by one of the niggers?' asked Sibely, hopefully, licking his lips.

'A Zenkali would be a happier way of describing the person,' said Hannibal. 'No, I assure you that the affair did not get beyond fisticuffs aided and abetted by a few spears and a croquet mallet or two. People were too busy fighting to give much thought to sex.'

'What was the King's reaction to this?' asked Coons.

'He was most upset,' said Hannibal. 'He has worked for years to bring the Ginkas, Fangouas and foreign residents closer together, and so naturally he was dismayed at this stupid and quite unnecessary outbreak of violence.'

'Is it true that you have the King in the palm of your hand?' asked Sibely.

'The King is six foot four and weighs eighteen stone,' said Hannibal. 'I would have to have a pretty large hand to fit him into the palm of it.'

They all laughed. The atmosphere, from being that of a rather uncomfortable press conference had turned into a cocktail party with Hannibal acting as a warm, humorous and attentive host.

'And what has the Special Council decided?' asked Coons.

'Well,' said Hannibal, lighting up a cigar, 'I think they've come up with a most brilliant solution to the problem.'

Hannibal outlined the plan the Special Council had agreed to, stressing at all times that the idea came from Kingy aided by the members of the Council, and hinting in the most delicate way that if Great Britain was so anxious to have this airfield then she must be prepared to pay at least a goodly proportion of the costs involved in translocating the Mockery Birds and the Ombu trees.

'I don't think anything quite like it will have been attempted before. At least I know of no other instance to compare with it,' said Hannibal. 'We will, in effect, be moving both the Mockery Birds and their habitat.'

'What wonderful television it will make,' cried Brewster ecstatically.

'Yes, I expect T.V. throughout the world would be interested,' said Hannibal. 'I've no doubt we can negotiate.'

'But . . . but . . . you must let me . . . I mean, the B.B.C. have it,' said Brewster in horror. 'You couldn't let anyone else have it. I mean to say, when all is said and done, you are a colony.'

'Within a few weeks we will officially have self-government,' Hannibal pointed out, 'but even so I'm sure your offer will be viewed most sympathetically.'

At last the Press, slurring its words, but effusively grateful, made its departure.

'Phew!' said Hannibal, seating himself in his rocking chair. 'Give me a drink, dear boy. I need one. I found all those blighters clamouring on my doorstep when I got back, so I had to say something. God knows, they make a bad enough job of it when they're quoting you verbatim, so one wants to avoid letting 'em use what they believe to be their imagination.'

'I'm delighted,' said Peter. 'It's saved me a job. But I still ought to get out an official statement, oughtn't I, for the Press and the *Zenkali Voice* and Sir Lancelot?'

'Yes, do that,' said Hannibal, drinking deeply. 'What news of Droom?'

'Off in the forest somewhere. I left a message for him to come here.'

'Good. You had any lunch?'

'No,' said Peter, suddenly realising he was very hungry.

'Well, cut along home and have some. Work on the Press release. Oh, and tell Sir Lancelot and the Hon. Alf that I'll be glad for them to come to dinner tonight. You and Audrey, too, of course.'

'Thanks,' said Peter, 'I'll tell them. They'll be delighted. I think they're feeling a bit neglected.'

As Peter drove back to his house he reflected that he had not seen Audrey for twenty-four hours, since the epic meeting with Looja. He found suddenly that he missed her presence and took a firm grip on himself. Audrey was a charming girl and a delightful companion, but nothing more serious, he assured himself. He intended to remain a bachelor. Not for him the supposed joys of marriage with a nagging wife, in a cloud forest of damp nappies. Not the effort of trying to make ends meet on his pay while his wife went out and got them into debt by buying chinchilla coats. (He was not quite sure why his wife would go out and buy a chinchilla coat, but in some way it seemed to him to be the worst marital sin next to infidelity.) But still, he thought, he did miss Audrey. She was such fun to be with. He decided that he would call her as soon as he got in.

He found, to his relief, that Sir Lancelot and the Hon. Alf were snorkelling on the reef. He could concentrate on his belated lunch and the Press release. He was just about to telephone Audrey when his guests appeared, dripping, from the sea. He told them of Hannibal's invitation and they were delighted.

'So at last we'll get to meet the power behind the throne,' said Sir Lancelot with satisfaction.

'I think he would prefer it if you didn't call him that,' said Peter. 'Obviously he makes suggestions, but it's up to the King to accept or reject them.'

'Quite, quite, I understand,' said Sir Lancelot. 'Tell me, what news from the Special Council? Did they reach a decision?'

'Yes,' said Peter, 'a sort of stop-gap decision.'

He went on to explain what had happened. Sir Lancelot frowned and pursed his lips.

'I'm not at all sure that W.O.P.E.S. could go along with that idea,' he said, gravely.

'No, indeed not,' said the Hon. Alf, rolling his eyes behind his spectacles, 'neither would my organisation.'

'Why is that, sir?' asked Peter, stifling a sigh of exasperation.

'Well, our job in W.O.P.E.S. is to make sure not only that animal species are preserved, but that their habitat is preserved, too,' explained Sir Lancelot. 'This idea of the Special Council of transplanting all the Ombu trees and relocating the Mockery Bird goes against all our principles. We believe that animals should be preserved *in situ*, as it were. No, speaking as chairman, I think I can safely say that W.O.P.E.S. would not countenance this scheme at all. Something else will have to be thought of.'

'And that, of course, goes for W.N.T. as well,' said the Hon. Alf determinedly.

'Well, I'm afraid you'll have to talk to the King about it,' said Peter, 'it's his idea. But really it's just to give him and Hannibal a breathing space so they can think up something better, though what, God only knows.'

'You mean that they really have no intention of undertaking this wild scheme?' asked Sir Lancelot.

'I suppose they would have to, if there was no alternative,' said Peter, 'but the expense would be enormous.'

'I think I shall have to speak quite frankly and seriously to the King about this,' said Sir Lancelot, pursing his lips and looking grave. 'This idea of playing fast and loose with Nature – well, it's reprehensible.'

'Indeed, indeed,' bleated the Hon. Alf. 'You can't play fast and loose with Mother Nature.'

'Well, I should discuss it with Hannibal this evening,' said Peter, 'and now I must go and phone Miss Damien.'

With a pleasant feeling of anticipation, Peter, through the good offices of Napoleon Waterloo, was connected to the local pawn shop, Government House, the fish market and finally, triumphantly with a sizzling noise like three very large gangsters being electrocuted simultaneously, to the offices of the *Zenkali Voice*.

'Hello, Simon?' said Peter. 'Peter Foxglove here. Could I speak to Audrey?'

'Oh, hello Peter,' said Damien. 'What d'you mean, you want to speak to Audrey? Isn't she with you?'

'With me?' said Peter blankly. 'No, what gave you that idea?'

'Well, I knew she was coming over to see you last night and when she didn't come back I naturally assumed she spent the night at your place.'

Peter went cold.

'Let's get this straight,' he said. 'You haven't seen Audrey since she came over here last night?'

'That's right,' said Damien, 'I haven't seen hair nor hide of her. If she's not with you I don't know where the devil she could be.'

'I think I do,' said Peter grimly.

'You sound awfully queer,' said Damien in alarm. 'D'you think something happened to her?'

'No, don't get excited,' said Peter soothingly. 'Just let me phone round a bit – I'll come back to you with whatever I discover.'

'All right,' said Damien reluctantly, 'but if you find the witch's orphan will you tell her she'll be getting the rough edge of my tongue?'

An hour later, aided, abetted and frustrated by Napoleon Waterloo, Peter had phoned up Government House, the Botanical Gardens, Mother Carey's Chickens and various people in the English community that she might have gone to visit. The only person he could not get through to was the Rev. Her phone remained stubbornly silent. Eventually, exceedingly worried, Peter phoned Hannibal and explained the situation.

'What d'you think happened?' asked Hannibal.

'I don't know,' said Peter worriedly, 'but I don't like it. She may be with the Rev, but I'm not sure. If she's not there, I can only think of one thing – Looja.'

Hannibal whistled and was silent for a moment.

'I can't conceive of him being so stupid,' he said at last. 'I mean, dammit, he couldn't be such an imbecile. This is not Chicago, for heaven's sake.'

'But he must have been pretty desperate to try and bribe me,' said Peter, 'and he was in a very ugly mood when he left.'

'Look,' said Hannibal, 'don't do anything precipitous. Let me scout around and then I'll come over and we'll hold a council of war. In the meantime see if you can get hold of the Rev.'

'Okay,' said Peter, 'but if this is Looja's doing, I warn you, Hannibal, I'm going to break his neck.'

'I'll help you,' said Hannibal.

Peter tried the Rev's number again, but the phone rang and rang and there was no answer. Irritably he slammed the phone down and paced up and down the room. Then he went and poured himself a drink. His mind was in a turmoil. He could not bring himself to believe that, however unpleasant and desperate he was, Looja would be silly enough to do anything to harm Audrey. But where was she? Had she gone swimming and met a shark? Had she crashed on one of the remote mountain roads and was bleeding to death in the wreckage of her car? Peter broke out in a cold sweat at the thought, and poured himself another drink. Suddenly he heard a car draw up with screeching brakes and then there was a trampling of footsteps in the hall, a cacophony of voices and the door burst open and in loped the Rev, red-faced and excited, her hat over one eye. She was followed, to Peter's astonishment, by Captain Pappas and Leonardo da Vinci Brown.

'Ha!' said the Rev, without preamble, pointing a long

finger at him. 'I can see from your face you've just discovered she's missing, eh?'

'Yes,' said Peter. 'Where is she, Rev, d'you know?'

The Rev squatted down in a chair, took off her hat and fanned herself.

'Looja's got her,' she said simply.

Chapter Seven

ZENKALI APPALLED

Outside it was growing dark; the crickets chimed, tinkled and squeaked, and the geckos called 'tock-tock' in tiny voices. The air was warm and redolent with flower scent and sunshine, and in the gloom of the bushes the fireflies gleamed like floating opals. But all this was lost on Peter.

'What d'you mean?' he asked at last, 'Looja's got her?'

'Just what I say,' said the Rev, staring at him owlishly. 'Looja got her – kidnapped her last night on her way home.'

'Where is she?' demanded Peter, starting to his feet. 'Is she at Looja's house? I'll strangle that nasty little illegitimate –'

'Now, now, now,' said the Rev, soothingly, 'don't go spitting chips like that. She's not at Looja's house and neither is Looja, so you can calm down and stop looking so darn malevolent and give me a drink.'

'I'm sorry,' said Peter, pouring out drinks for them all, annoyed to see his hands were shaking, 'but please tell me, where the hell is she and how d'you know all this?'

'To begin with,' said the Rev, taking a deep pull at her drink, 'she's safe, so you can stop worrying. Now, how I come to know all this is because of Leonardo da Vinci Brown here.'

'But I thought he was your gardener . . .' began Peter.

'He is, he is,' said the Rev, 'but he's also one of my better spies.'

'Spies?' said Peter, bewilderéd.

'Yes,' said the Rev, 'I felt I ought to keep a finger on the pulse of this airfield thing, so I appointed several of my more intelligent parishioners as spies to find out what was going on. Well, from Leonardo here I learnt that your Uncle and Lord Hammer had been having secret meetings with Looja. He heard Sir Osbert and Hammer tell Looja that something must be done about the valley immediately or their bargain was off. Sir Osbert said to Looja, "I don't care how you do it but clear those damned trees and ridiculous birds out of that valley, and do it quickly." This panicked Looja, so he came to see you and tried to bribe you, didn't he?'

'How the hell did you know that?' asked Peter, astonished.

'Tulip, your small boy, is also one of my informants,' said the Rev, with a gleam of satisfaction in her eye.

'Good God, you're worse than the Communists,' said Peter.

'Much, much worse,' said the Rev, with pride. 'I believe in the old Biblical phrase about fighting fire with fire and an eye for an eye, and all that really rich stuff. Christians, in my view, have become much too sloppy. Anyway, I decided that Leonardo here ought to get closer to Looja and so he managed to join Looja's little band of roughnecks, who have been the ring-leaders in the unrest and who were really responsible for the fire at the English Club. Anyway, Leonardo joined them and it was just as well he did, because the first job he and the others had to do was to snatch Audrey. They got her on her way back from you, last evening. Apparently Looja's band wasn't very happy about the whole thing because they all know Audrey and like her, but Looja has such a stranglehold on them they had to obey. They took her up into the forest to one of those small huts the deer hunters use. Then Looja came to talk to her. But, before that, Leonardo had managed to attract Audrey's attention and conveyed to her by signs that he was going to let me know.'

'Well, thank God for Leonardo,' said Peter, fervently, 'now, can he lead us there?'

'Yes, he'll lead us there,' said the Rev. 'Captain Pappas and I will come, too, in case you need help.'

Captain Pappas cleared his throat.

'I would like to help, Mr. Foxtrot, sir,' he said. 'Miss Audrey is a fine girl, a fine lady and that black bastard Looja has gone too far. I want to help you fix the bastard good, eh?'

'Thanks,' said Peter, with relish, 'when I get my hands on him I'll use him as shark bait.'

'No, I think he'd serve us better alive,' said a voice.

They all looked round and there, in the doorway, stood Hannibal.

'Hannibal!' cried Peter. 'You're just in time – do you know what that swine Looja has . . .'

'Yes,' said Hannibal, taking off his giant sola topi and sitting down, 'you were all so vociferous and so loud that I could hear everything standing in the hall. It's a good job I wasn't Looja.'

'We were just going to go up and rescue Audrey,' said Peter, 'will you come?'

'Certainly,' said Hannibal, 'but not now.'

'What d'you mean, not now?'

'What I say,' said Hannibal. 'At this hour, seven o'clock, every good Zenkali is crouching over his cooking pot and he will not have finished before eight-thirty, when he will promptly fall asleep. It's one of those curious eating habits the Zenkalis inherited from the French. If you go up to the deer hunter's hut now, you will find them all awake and on the *qui vive*. So it would be better to leave it until about one o'clock.'

'That's all very well,' said Peter, 'but what if Looja tries to make Audrey tell him about the valley and we're all here twiddling our thumbs?'

'You mean torture?' asked Hannibal. 'No way. None of Looja's band would stand for it. Aren't I right, Leonardo?'

'Yes, sah, Mr. Hannibal. Looja tell um all they no go hurt Miss Audrey at all or 'e go humbug 'em too much,' said Leonardo earnestly.

'Well,' said Peter, reluctantly, for he knew how the waiting would play on his nerves, 'I suppose you're right.'

'Now,' said Hannibal, 'I'm going to take your two guests off your hands, because I don't suppose you want to come to dinner and I'm sure you don't want them hanging about, eh? So I'll be here to pick you up at midnight. How long does it take to get to this hut, Leonardo?'

'Is no far, sah,' said Leonardo, 'is close to Missy Rev's place, sah.'

'Pick me up at my house,' said the Rev, 'it's about half an hour from there.'

Hannibal looked at Peter.

'How long would it take you to get into Mockery Bird Valley?' he asked.

'How long? Well, it depends which way you go. If you go via the cliffs, as we did, it takes you about half a day. But the way to get in there is through the cleft under the waterfall. Then the whole thing would take about an hour from the road. Why?'

'I just wondered. Have you ever asked the way of an Irishman?' he asked.

'No,' said Peter, mystified.

'It's an education, I do assure you,' said Hannibal, but he would say no more. He left, taking Sir Lancelot and the Hon. Alf with him. The Rev followed with Leonardo and Pappas.

On the stroke of midnight, Hannibal reappeared with his two guests, both flushed of face, with a tendency to stagger. Having sent them to bed, Peter and Hannibal set off for the Rev's house. The night was cool and redolent of a thousand scents, and above, a canary-coloured moon flooded the forest with brilliant light. Occasionally their headlights would pick out the diamond sparkle of mongoose eyes, quickly quenched as the animals dived for the under-growth, and the darker patches of forest were decorated with pulsating myriads of fireflies.

'How did you get on with His Nibs and the Hon. Alf?' asked Peter, curiously.

Hannibal chuckled.

'Not bad,' he said, 'at least they're genuine in their desire to do good, so I suppose one has to overlook their more objectionable foibles. Still, during the course of dinner I managed to beat Sir Lancelot's score of V.I.P.s by three minor royalty, eight Dukes, fourteen Sirs and several Prime Ministers. He was so impressed, he asked me to call him Lance.'

Peter laughed.

'It seems a harmless eccentricity,' he said, 'anyway, I'd rather have it than the smug self-satisfaction of Daniel Brewster.'

'Amen to that,' said Hannibal, with feeling, 'by the by, did you bring a gun?'

'No, I didn't,' said Peter, ruefully.

'Well, it's probably just as well,' said Hannibal. 'I brought my little Smith and Wesson. It makes a nice loud bang, but it's difficult to hit anything with it. Still, they won't know that.'

Presently, they reached the Rev's house. The Rev and Pappas and Damien were all clad in khaki bush jackets and trousers. The Rev was also wearing an outsize black cowboy hat, and slung over her shoulder was a leather bandolier of cartridges. She had a powerful-looking shotgun under her arm and a very large and intimidating bowie knife on one hip.

'Good, good, we're all ready now,' she exclaimed. 'Simon, will you pour us all out a drink? While you're doing that, I'll just go and get the bombs.'

'Bombs?' said Hannibal. 'Steady on, Rev, this is not a full-scale war we're trying to instigate.'

'Hannibal, there are times when, for an intelligent man, you display gross stupidity,' said the Rev, severely. 'I don't mean killing bombs, for crying out loud, I mean smoke bombs. I found a book called *A Hundred Japes and Jokes and Jollities for Young Folk* and there was a recipe for smoke bombs in it. I got Cap. Pappas to get me the ingredients in Djakarta and put 'em in some long test-tubes I had.'

'Pappas, you should know better than to encourage her,' said Hannibal with some asperity.

'Sure, and she's the most bloodthirsty and belligerent Christian I've ever come into contact with,' said Damien, pouring out liberal tots of brandy, 'I swear to you if she was an Irish Catholic, she would have beaten the British Government to its knees by now and got Northern Ireland back for us.'

The Rev, delving into a cupboard, had produced four opaque glass globes which she stuffed into her pockets.

'Now,' she said, knocking her drink back in one gulp, 'are we all set? Fine, let's be off and bring that poor child back here so she can have a bath and a decent meal.'

They drove some two miles down the road and then, under Leonardo's instructions, parked under a giant banyan tree at the edge of the forest. Lighting their torches and with Leonardo taking the lead, they set off along a narrow, winding path that zig-zagged through the trees and the straight stalks of the guava bushes. They had not gone far when Pappas stopped and, with a machete he was carrying, lopped down four saplings, cut them into convenient six-foot lengths and handed one each to Damien, Hannibal and Peter.

'Good for fight with,' he explained. 'You hit man on the legs, he no run away. You hit him on the head, he no run away also.'

'Well, where's mine?' asked the Rev, indignantly.

Reluctantly, Pappas cut her a staff, and she whistled it around her head with great enthusiasm, almost decapitating Peter in the process. They moved on, and after walking for three-quarters of an hour, Leonardo halted and crouched down on the path.

'We very close now, sah,' he whispered and turned, directing his torch downwards so it cast a puddle of light on the path. He rapidly drew a map in the dust of the path with a twig.

'Dis na house, sah,' he said, 'on side of river. House 'e got two rooms. For dis room they get Missy Audley, in dis room they get four men for guard Missy Audley.'

'Are there any other guards?' asked Hannibal.

'Yes, sah,' said Leonardo, 'they get two guards, sah. One 'e stay for *here* and dey get another one *here*.'

'All right,' said Hannibal, 'Simon and I will go and tackle this one, while Peter and Pappas fix the other. We'll rendezvous outside the hut.'

'Okay,' said Peter, and he and Pappas moved off through the undergrowth.

'What about me? What do *I* do?' asked the Rev indignantly.

'Come with me,' said Hannibal, 'and try not to blow my head off with that gun.'

Peter and Pappas followed Leonardo through the trees. They were forced to move slowly for they could not use their torches, and the risk of snapping dry twigs and giving the alarm was considerable. Presently, Peter could make out a dim glow ahead of them that flickered and pulsed between the tree trunks. It puzzled him at first until he realised it was the light of a small fire which pin-pointed the guard's position perfectly. Leonardo stopped and whispered in Peter's ear.

'De guard 'e sit for dat small small fire, sah,' he said, 'you like I go beat him?'

'No,' Peter breathed, 'he's my bird, I think.'

Taking a firmer grip on his quarterstaff, he edged forward, his eyes constantly searching the shadows that flickered and moved in the light of the flames from the fire. Slowly he inched forward. Then, suddenly, what he had taken to be a tree stump stood up and revealed itself to be a very large Zenkali, wrapped in a blanket, carrying a huge spear. Fortunately, his back was to Peter and as he stretched and yawned, preparatory to turning round, Peter realised he would have to act fast. He took three quick steps forward, his staff whistled through the air and, just as his victim was turning to ascertain the source of this strange sound, the thick staff caught him across the back of the head. The huge Zenkali gave a surprised grunt, dropped his spear and his blanket, pitched forward on to his face, and lay still. Peter felt the tingle of the blow run through his arms.

'Good, Mr. Foxtrot, you hit the bastard good,' whispered Pappas hoarsely, 'with luck you kill him.'

'God!' exclaimed Peter in alarm. 'I hope not.'

Agitatedly he went down on his knees and placed his hand on the broad chest of his fallen adversary. To his relief, the man was still breathing and his heart was still pounding under his massive rib cage. It seemed as though he would be unconscious for a long time, but Peter was taking no chances. He quickly cut the man's blanket into strips and bound his hands behind him and then lashed his feet securely to a sapling. In the forest to their left they heard a cry, cut off by a crack like a breaking branch. Obviously Hannibal had dealt equally effectively with the other guard. Now all that remained were the five men in the shack.

Peter passed by the little fire and not far beyond, the forest ended and he came to a clearing through which twinkled and whispered a tiny river. On the far bank of the river was the deer hunter's hut. It was quite large and as Peter edged his way cautiously round it, he saw that it had two doorways and two heavily shuttered windows. One of the doors was held shut by a massive bar across it and this, he thought, must be where Audrey was a prisoner, for the other door was merely shut and not barred. Over on the other side of the clearing, he saw Hannibal, Simon and the curious figure of the Rev appear, and so he stepped out into the moonlight and waved. Hannibal waved back and they hurried across the clearing to join Peter and Pappas.

'Everything under control?' whispered Hannibal. 'Did you get your man?'

'Yes. He's all tied up in the trees there.'

'Good. Mine turned round just as I was creeping up on

him and he tried to loose a yell but I got him in time. Did you hear him?'

'Only faintly,' Peter said. 'What's the plan of campaign now?'

'Well, the hut's obviously got two separate rooms and so I think this is where the Rev's bombs come in handy. If we can open that door and lob them in, the surprise element will make them play right into our hands,' said Hannibal.

'You can only use my bombs if I can throw them,' said the Rev.

'All right, all right, you bloodthirsty harridan,' said Hannibal. 'Now, Simon, if you open the door the Rev can chuck her bombs in. Then, slam the door shut and put that beam across it. After they've been incarcerated for five minutes they should be in no fighting condition. Then we'll let 'em out and bop 'em.'

'I haven't had so much fun since I took up all-in-wrestling and judo,' the Rev confided in Peter.

They moved across the clearing until they reached the hut and then Damien took his place by the door, his hand on the latch.

'Are you ready, Rev?' he whispered.

The Rev had removed the bombs from her pocket and held them in her large hands.

'Yes, sirree, right and ready,' she nodded. Damien pulled up the latch and flung the door wide. As soon as it was open, the Rev lobbed her four bombs into the dark interior. There was the crack and splintering of glass, and a wild yell of fright from inside the room, and then Damien slammed the door shut and the next moment the solid beam had locked it in place. From inside the hut rose a cacophony of muffled cries, coughs, and the steady beating of desperate hands on the door.

As soon as the bombs had been thrown, Peter made his way swiftly to the door leading into the second room, and lifted out the bar that held it closed. He threw open the door and there stood Audrey, laughing and unharmed. He took her in his arms and kissed her.

'Have you been kidnapped enough?' he enquired at length. 'I mean I don't want to drag you home against your will or anything.'

'My hero,' said Audrey, and started to laugh at the sight of her rescuers.

'It's an ungrateful devil's brat she's always been,' said Damien, kissing his daughter, 'here we risk life and limb to rescue you and all you do is laugh.'

'But you all look so funny,' Audrey protested, 'and what have you done to my poor kidnappers?'

'Gassed 'em,' said the Rev with relish.

'*Gassed* them?'

'The Rev invented some bombs,' said Peter, 'and so we lobbed them in there. That's what all the noise is about.'

'And now, be Jesus, we're going to let them out and bop them on the turnip,' said Damien, rubbing his hands.

'But you can't do that,' said Audrey, indignantly.

'Why ever not?' asked Peter.

'They've been perfectly sweet to me, the poor things,' said Audrey, angrily, 'and I'm not having them bopped anywhere,' Audrey repeated. 'And if you've gassed them all, Rev, I shall never forgive you. You must let them out at once.'

'As a rescue this seems to be as much of a fiasco as anything else that has been happening round here lately,' said Hannibal.

'But you didn't have to hurt them,' said Audrey, 'all you had to do was to come here and they would have handed me over.'

'Handed you over?' asked Hannibal, incredulous.

'Yes, of course.'

'But why?' asked Hannibal.

'Because they knew you were coming,' said Audrey, impatiently; 'Hannibal, you are dense sometimes.'

'But who told them? How did they know?'

'Because I told them.'

'*You* told them? Good God,' said Hannibal, 'I give up. D'you mean to say we've been carrying on all over the forest like a cross between a Commando raid and a badly organised Boy Scouts' outing, and they knew we were coming all the time?'

'Of course,' said Audrey, 'they didn't want to do it, they were forced to by that unspeakable little runt, Looja. Now hurry and let them out before you kill them.'

As Peter opened the door, the four frightened Zenkalis reeled out, groaning, gasping, coughing in great paroxysms, with tears streaming down their faces and fell on all fours on the ground, spitting and vomiting. The clouds of white, suffocating vapour that poured out of the hut had a nauseating smell of rotting eggs and elderly blocked drains.

'What the hell did you put in it, Rev?' asked Hannibal.

'Well, the first batch I made seemed to lack something,' the Rev confessed, 'so I added the recipe for stink bombs as well, to give it flavour.'

'I don't believe you're a Reverend at all,' said Hannibal, 'you're more like a witch from Salem.'

'I think it works pretty darn well when you consider they're the first bombs I've ever made,' she said, a trifle aggrievedly.

Meantime, Peter and Audrey had been giving first aid to the unfortunate kidnappers. With the help of water from the stream and a hip flask of brandy, reluctantly contributed by Damien, they were soon more or less their old selves, though they still tended to breathe rather stertorously and cough a lot. The two guards, when Peter went to look for them, had recovered considerably and, although they were muzzy with egg-sized contusions on the backs of their heads, they seemed none the worse.

'Now,' said Hannibal, 'if you are satisfied that none of the opposition are going to die, perhaps you could tell me what this is all about?'

'Yes, but let's get back to the Rev's first,' said Audrey, 'we haven't much time and we must phone the Palace.'

When they got back to the Mission, Audrey told her tale over a fortifying drink.

'I was a fool,' she admitted wryly. 'I was driving home when I found a large tree across the road and a few Zenkalis standing about aimlessly with machetes as if trying to clear it. I was about to wait patiently for this to happen, when Garutara – you know, Looja's first cousin who always says he hates Looja – drove up on the other side of the tree, and got out and there was a lot of shouting. Then Garutara climbed over the tree and came to my car and said they had sent for a saw, and clearing the tree would take several hours so he was returning to town, could he give me a lift.'

'And so you accepted the lift?' said Hannibal.

'Yes, and before I knew where I was, we had turned off into the forest. Well, there was no point in resisting and, anyway, I felt that if I went with them, I might learn something useful.'

Peter sighed and raised his eyes to heaven.

'Well,' Audrey continued, 'when we got to the hut there was Looja, looking very like Gunga Din in his bush jacket and Tyrolean hat. He was very polite but oily and menacing. As soon as I stopped being sarcastic, he smiled and then cut the ground from under my feet by expounding his plans.'

She paused to drink.

'If I did not tell him where the valley was, he said the airfield, dam and all would not go through and he would stand to lose a lot of money. He said he was not a vindictive man but if this happened, he would see that, over the years, harm would come to all those I loved and respected. He said he would not threaten me directly as he knew I would not respond to that. But he felt that the slow torture of never knowing when harm would come to my friends might help to sway me.'

'Evil little swine,' said Hannibal.

Peter said nothing – he was watching Audrey's face

which was now beginning to show something of what she had been through.

She gave him a crooked smile.

'I tried to bluff him,' she shrugged, 'it was useless. I said that even if I told him where the valley was and he destroyed it, this wouldn't do him any good because all Zenkali would be up in arms against him. He gave one of those awful little laughs of his and said he didn't give a damn for Zenkali. Once the valley was destroyed, he would have done what he'd been asked to do and he would go to Djakarta where his money would be awaiting him.'

'I hadn't thought of that,' said Hannibal. 'So that was why he was so desperate.'

'Yes,' said Audrey, 'desperate but confident.'

'So what did you do?' asked the Rev.

'I told him where the valley was,' said Audrey.

There was a moment's silence.

'You did *what*?' demanded Peter.

'May God forgive you, my own daughter,' bellowed Damien.

'Audrey, my dear, how could you?' squealed the Rev.

Only Hannibal remained unmoved, a gleam in his eye.

'I have a feeling that Audrey did the simplest and most intelligent thing,' he said. 'Come on, you Irish Machiavelli, now, out with it.'

'Oh, I told him where to go, all right,' she said, grinning, 'with a few tiny misdirections to help matters. But I told him the long way round and I specified how dangerous it was and how difficult to negotiate. He was satisfied with this and I heard him telling Garutara that he would get into the valley with thirty men just after dawn. I had told him it only takes six or seven hours. As I knew from Leonardo you all would rescue me, I felt that gave us a breathing space.'

'Brilliant,' said Hannibal, 'hoist him on his own petard.'

'Sure and it takes an Irish girl to outwit a thieving wog

any day, so it does,' said Damien with pride, slapping the Rev on the back in his enthusiasm.

'What's your plan?' asked Peter.

'Kingy,' she said, 'can tell his Guard to go through the waterfall entrance. We can be waiting below the cliff long before Looja's men get there. Then when they climb down, we . . .'

'Bop them on the onion,' squawked the Rev, delighted with the idea.

Hannibal grinned and rose to his feet. 'I'm going to call the Palace.'

'And I'm going to make some more bombs,' said the Rev with relish, as Hannibal left the room.

'Oh, no, Rev. You can't throw bombs about in the valley,' exclaimed Audrey, 'you might disturb the birds.'

The Rev's face fell.

'Do you think you ought to come, Rev?' asked Peter, 'after all, there may be quite a fracas and we don't want a Reverend rolling about in the valley in a vulgar brawl. It would be bad publicity for the Church.'

'Rubbish,' said the Rev, 'I've been in this thing from the start and I intend to see it through. Anyhow, I reckon the Church needs a little bit of militant publicity.'

Hannibal came back.

'Sorry it took so long,' he apologised, 'but Napoleon Waterloo and Jesus are not at their best this late at night.'

'What did Kingy say?' asked Audrey.

'He'll have his full Guard waiting at the crossroads to Mockery Bird Valley in the hour. He's delighted that this is the downfall of Looja and asked me to convey his apologies to you that any Zenkali should have behaved in this way to you, and to congratulate you on your achievement.'

'Well, it's nice of Kingy but it's not an achievement yet,' said Audrey.

'It will be,' said Peter.

'Certainly,' agreed Hannibal, 'and now, Rev, coffee please, gallons of hot coffee and we must be off.'

They rendezvoused with the King's Guard at a point in

the road some quarter of a mile from the waterfall that concealed the entrance to the valley. The King's personal guard was an elite body of men, picked for their enormous and intimidating size, and trained and led by one Captain 'Crackling' Summerville, late of the Brigade of Guards. He was a clipped and efficient officer and had his little force under perfect control.

He came up to Hannibal and saluted, while his men stood at attention in the background.

'I've briefed the men, sir,' said Crackling, 'there's to be no bloodshed unless necessary, and the valley is to be saved at all costs.'

'Quite right,' said Hannibal, 'and disturbed as little as possible.'

'Quite so,' said Crackling, 'I've stressed that. By the way, sir, are the . . . er . . . ladies coming too? There may be some rough stuff, you know. Not the place for females, sir, really. Men's work and all that.'

'It is obvious that you don't know these ladies,' said Hannibal with amusement, 'Miss Damien here is responsible for discovering this whole plot, and the Rev Longnecker has a way with bombs that makes her the perfect Christian guerrilla.'

'Well, if you say so, sir,' said Crackling, still doubtful and thinking that Hannibal was being facetious, 'but I hope they'll keep in the rear, out of the line of fire.'

'I will be personally responsible,' said Hannibal.

They made their way to the waterfall with the utmost caution, Peter leading, Crackling and his men following, and the rest of the party bringing up the rear. It was unlikely that Looja's force, who should be some miles away in the forest, could see or hear them but they did not want to take any risks. On reaching the waterfall and the narrow cleft that led to the valley, Crackling posted six men on guard. Then the King's Guard and their strangely assorted companions scrambled into the cleft and made their way, splashing and stumbling, into Mockery Bird Valley. As they entered the valley, dawn was just breaking. In the pale, pearly half-light, the Ombu trees stood with veils of mist entangled in their branches and, as the light grew stronger and turned from pearl to pale primrose, they could hear the Mockery Birds on all sides of them, calling 'Ha *ha,* Ha *ha,*' in gentle derisiveness.

Finally they reached the cliff down which Audrey and Peter had first descended into the valley. It was here that Looja's men would descend for they would be following Peter's trail and Audrey's instructions.

Crackling deployed his forces with care and the rest of them took up a position where they could see the outcome of the action without getting into the line of fire. The morning air was cool and Audrey shivered, partly with cold and partly with anticipation, and a strange fear that Looja, by some clairvoyance, would realise she had tricked him, and not appear. The last skeins of mist, like drifts of swans-down, were drawn up into the sky and this was now a rich and lovely blue.

'They should be here soon,' whispered Peter, looking at his watch, 'my only worry is that friend Looja won't come down with them – I don't want him to get away.'

Captain Pappas, sitting there like a great, scowling bear, shifted his bulk and glanced at Peter with something like a glitter of satisfaction in his black eyes.

'Don't worry yourself, Mr. Foxtrot,' he said in a rumbling whisper, 'even if he gets away from here, he can't get off Zenkali.'

'Why not?' asked Peter.

'Because he paid me five hundred pounds for me to take him to Djakarta,' said Captain Pappas simply, 'and I won't take him now, after what he did to Miss Audrey.'

'You mean you would have let him destroy this valley if he hadn't kidnapped Audrey, and then helped him to get away?' asked Peter, incredulously.

The Captain's eyes gleamed.

'No. He was stupid enough to pay me in advance. He's no businessman. No Greek would have done that. It is a disgust. So I would have informed Mr. Hannibal here of what Looja was going to do. Then they would catch him, the valley she would be okay,' he shrugged.

'And the five hundred?' asked Hannibal.

Pappas looked at him and scowled.

'You think I go give five hundred to a crook?' he asked, indignantly, 'that is not the way we Greeks do business.'

Before they could further investigate this curious business ethic, Crackling appeared suddenly in their midst.

'No more talking, please, sir,' he said to Hannibal, 'one of my men I posted up a tree has just signalled us they have arrived.'

Peter looked at Audrey. They both felt triumphant that Looja had walked into the trap she had set for him. The Rev rubbed her hands together slowly, and even the usually imperturbable Hannibal looked tense. Only Captain Pappas remained impassive, looking like a man who is trying to decide the best way of spending five hundred pounds.

On the cliff top they heard the arrival of Looja's men who, obviously thinking they were quite alone, talked, sang little snatches of song and laughed amongst themselves. When they reached the top of the cliff, there was a lot of noisy altercation about how the ropes should be fixed and who should carry what down the cliff face. They could hear Looja's voice issuing instructions and snapping out reprimands. Obviously, his contingent were much more happy-go-lucky and undisciplined than the King's Guard who crouched, immobile, in the bushes at the foot of the cliff. The first three ropes came snaking down the cliffs, and the excitement among the watchers was intense. Gradually Looja's cohorts swarmed down the ropes carrying machetes, cans of petrol and a selection of firearms ranging from repeating shotguns to ancient Arab muzzle-loaders, which would probably have been as dangerous to their owners as to any Mockery Bird. Forty men descended and stood in a chattering group, awaiting their leader and further instructions. To Peter's surprise, when Looja swung down the rope to join his men, he displayed surprising agility and litheness for such a dandified little man. As he landed, he wiped his hands fastidiously on a white silk handkerchief, readjusted the set of his Tyrolean hat and turned to address his men. In that moment, a solid, menacing half-moon of the King's Guard, rifles held casually, rose from the bushes and stood there, silent and implacable, pinning Looja and his men against the cliff.

Looja, for a moment, looked stunned. He looked from side to side and his pink tongue flicked across his lips. Crackling stepped forward.

'Throw down your arms in the name of the King,' he said, his voice throbbing with the pride of a job well done, 'you're under arrest.'

After a moment's stunned silence all of Looja's men threw down their guns, machetes and canisters of petrol and fled back to the ropes, fighting and kicking and pushing in an effort to climb up to the top of the cliff and escape.

'Guard forward, arrest those men,' shouted Crackling, his voice shrill with excitement. The King's Guard lumbered forward, a great avalanche of khaki-clad black flesh, and in a moment all was turmoil at the base of the cliffs. As their adversaries had dropped their weapons, the Guard did likewise and drew their short but powerful truncheons instead against the squealing and running men.

Looja stood, dapper, tiny and deadly, in the midst of the fracas. At first, Peter thought that Looja was so stunned by the sudden turn of events and the undermining of all his plans that he was going to concede defeat and give up with as much grace as possible. He was mistaken. Looja waited until it appeared that every Guardsman had his hands full trying to subdue and manacle a hysterical and recalcitrant member of his band, and then he seized his chance. Because he had remained motionless, the Guard had assumed, like Peter, that this was a tacit act of surrender and so had ignored him to concentrate on the rest who were obviously trying to escape. Looja's active and cunning mind had anticipated this. Suddenly, he crouched and ran with astonishing speed through the Ombu trees It was unfortunate for him that he was still unaware of the presence of Hannibal and his party, who had remained concealed in the bushes. The moment he started to move, Peter leapt to his feet and ran to intercept him. Looja's course took him, zig-zagging through the trees and bushes, parallel to where Hannibal and the Rev were positioned. Peter was having a hard time in shortening the distance between himself and his quarry, who proved to be unexpectedly fleet of foot. Hannibal decided to lessen the odds a trifle, though he felt that, by rights, Looja was Peter's prey. As Looja passed, therefore, Hannibal raised the useful fighting quarterstaff that Pappas had cut when they rescued Audrey, and, aiming carefully, he threw it like a spear with all the force of his powerful arm. The staff flew through the air and struck Looja just between the shoulder blades with a thwack that they could all hear, knocking him flat and driving the air out of his lungs in a great retching gasp.

'Bravo, excellent shot,' applauded the Rev, hopping up and down with delight.

Looja rolled on the ground, his face grey, his breath coming in strangled gasps. He was as much shocked by the sudden massive blow on his back as he was by the sight of Peter, dishevelled and panting, running up to him, followed by Audrey and the rest of the party.

'Foxglove!' he croaked, his eyes malevolent.

'Yes, my precious,' said Peter, unpleasantly, leaning over and picking up Looja by the front of his bush jacket, 'and I think I owe you something, you little monster.'

Peter, with care and precision, hit Looja on the point of the jaw and sent him reeling and stumbling backwards to end in a sitting position, blood trickling down his face, his eyes blazing. The jarring of the blow sent a pleasant tingling along Peter's arm. He had packed all the worries and frustrations of the past weeks into that uppercut and felt it could be described as a beauty.

'That was for me,' said Peter, approaching Looja again,

seizing him by his lapels and picking him up like a toy, 'and now one for Miss Damien, I think.'

He drew back his fist to hit the little man again, but quickly as a snake striking, Looja drew a thin-bladed knife from his sleeve and stabbed Peter in the chest. It was the small silver flask that he had borrowed from Damien that saved Peter. He had slipped it into the breast pocket of his bush jacket and now, owing to the angle from which Looja was striking, the blade snicked through the cloth, ricocheted off the silver and slid up to slash Peter's jawbone from chin to ear. Surprised, Peter let go of the little man and, looking down, saw the blood running in torrents down his jacket front. He looked up stupidly just as Looja, his little white teeth showing in a bloodstained snarl, leapt at him again, the knife held low for the stomach. Peter was just trying to gather his wits for a defence, when a large brown hand, covered with a thick black pelt of hair, materialised and enveloped Looja's hand like a vice. Looja screamed in pain. Simultaneously another hand came down on the back of Looja's neck in a vicious karate chop. Looja dropped instantly and lay like a discarded doll.

'Huh!' said the disgusted voice of Captain Pappas, to whom the massive hands belonged, 'the bastard didn't even know how to use a knife properly.'

'Peter, are you all right?' asked Audrey, running up. Peter turned to her a face masked in semi-congealed blood, from which rivulets still flowed. The cut, from his chin to his ear, was like a sabre slash and had bared his cheek to the bone.

'Knife,' said Peter succinctly, trying to grin, 'looks worse than it is.'

'If it was worse than it looks you'd be dead, you idiot,' said Audrey, and burst into tears. 'Why the hell did you have to tackle him?'

'Because he was half my size,' said Peter, facetiously.

'Come here and let me clean up that cut,' said Audrey.

'No, no,' said the Rev panting up to where they stood,

'let me. It's got to be done carefully if you don't want him scarred for life.'

She cleaned up the blood from around the wound with a small first-aid kit she was carrying, and then put two tiny strips of plaster across to keep the gaping wound more or less closed.

'Now, my dear,' she said to Audrey, 'you're to get him down to hospital as quickly as possible. Doctor Mafoozi is a real humdinger with a needle – yes, sir – real humdinger. He's not much of a doctor, of course, but put a needle in his hand and – well – he'll have your boy looking like a Bayeux tapestry in five seconds and twice as beautiful. Now, take your father with you in case Peter faints and be off with you.'

'Faint?' said Peter, indignantly, 'I'm not going to faint. I'm just waiting for that little bastard to come round and then . . .'

'You'll do no such thing,' said Audrey, firmly. 'The Rev's right.'

'Leave Looja to us,' said Hannibal, 'I fancy a charge of attempted murder will settle his hash as well as everything else.'

'Amen,' said the Rev.

As she said it, all around them, the Mockery Birds started calling, 'Ha *ha* . . . ha *ha* . . . ha *ha* . . .' in the undergrowth, their wild, plaintive cry echoing through the groves of Ombu trees, almost as though it were a requiem sung over the tiny, crumpled body of Looja, lying among the leaves.

Chapter Eight

---◄ ❊ ►---

ZENKALI REVIVED

Kingy lay in his vast hammock, kicking himself to and fro with one leg and scowling ferociously. Near him sat Hannibal and Peter, his face criss-crossed with sticking plaster. They all clasped large glasses of 'Lèse-Majesté', but, in spite of this stimulation, none of them looked happy.

'Don't get me wrong, Peter,' said Kingy, taking a sip of his drink, 'don't for a moment think I am not grateful to you and Audrey for saving the valley and compromising that awful little runt, Looja. I am delighted. If only in Zenkali we had something like the V.C. or the Purple Heart, I would award you both one instantly, ephemeral though such thanks would be. I think I can do better than that, actually, but that's by the way. This whole valley thing has not solved our problem except by eliminating Looja. I still have, trumpeting at my palace door, Sir Osbert and Sir Lancelot, both diametrically opposed to each other and each with a fairly good case. That is why I called you both here this morning. I have Sir Lancelot and Sir Osbert coming at eleven to discuss things with me.'

'Good Lord,' said Hannibal.

'It's the only way, my dear Hannibal. Let them both have their say and, who knows, something may emerge.'

'I think Kingy's right,' said Peter, articulating with difficulty through his stitches. 'If nothing else, we can tell Uncle Osbert about Looja.'

'An excellent idea,' said Kingy, brightening, 'I hadn't

thought of that. By the way, did you get hold of Droom?'

'No, he's still in the forest somewhere. I left a message for him,' said Peter.

'It's amazing,' said Hannibal irritably, 'when we don't want him, the fellow haunts us and when we do want him, we can't find him.'

They relapsed into a gloomy silence.

Kingy drained his glass and struggled out of his hammock. 'Well, I see Malapi approaching so it looks as though my Nemesis is here. Let's go, gentlemen.'

Inside the great dining-room, Sir Lancelot and Sir Osbert sat on opposite sides of the great table, displaying the unconcern of two cats on a garden wall. They rose and gave cold, infinitesimal bows as Kingy, exuding false bonhomie, swept into the room.

'My dear Sir Lancelot, my dear Sir Osbert, please forgive my tardy arrival,' he boomed, his teeth flashing, 'affairs of State, you know, affairs of State. But there, I don't have to tell *you* gentlemen anything about that. Now, some refreshments – oh, surely, on a hot day like this? can't I tempt you? – we have, I think, nearly everything – ah, yes that's right, a whisky and water for you, Sir Osbert – and for you, Sir Lancelot? a gin and tonic – just so . . . Hannibal, Peter, there's a jug of that white drink you like so much . . . now then, are we all settled? Good, good.'

Kingy sat down and beamed around the table, as ebullient as a volcano, as irresistible as an avalanche.

'Now, Sir Lancelot, you got my letter? I sent a copy to Sir Osbert of course. Now, I should be delighted to hear your views.'

Kingy sat back, his face earnest and composed, his large chocolate fingers interlaced. Sir Osbert looked at Sir Lancelot as though only noticing him for the first time. There was a short silence. Then Sir Lancelot cleared his throat and gave them all a small, deprecating smile.

'Perhaps . . . maybe . . . if none of you have any objection, I might fire away first,' he suggested. 'My views will, I think, help us to formulate a *modus operandi*.'

Sir Lancelot ignored Sir Osbert's reverberating snort.

'I have read your letter with great care, your Majesty, and may I say, at the outset, that I do understand and sympathise with your somewhat unusual predicament. You had passed the idea of the airfield before the valley was discovered, hence the difficulty. Now, speaking for myself, as a conservationist, I deplore the whole idea of the airfield and the dam, but the decision as to whether or not to have it, of course, must be Zenkali's and Zenkali's alone.'

Here he shot a quick look at Sir Osbert, took a sip of his drink and continued.

'I think it only fair to make clear my own position and that of the organisation I represent. All over the world, man is damaging or eradicating the irreplaceable with ferocious rapidity; sometimes without understanding what we are doing, sometimes wilfully and deliberately, but always in the name of progress. We are, if I may use an analogy, cutting off the very branch on which we sit. Now my organisation is not obstructionist, as Sir Osbert believes. We merely plead caution. We are deeply concerned with animal life and its habitat, but what most people overlook is that that habitat may range from a tropical forest to the slum area of London. Now, the usual argument is, what use are these creatures to us, with our marvellous technology, our domination of nature, our ability to mould our own destinies as we are told we can? And the simple answer is that we don't know.'

Sir Osbert snorted again.

'Exactly,' he said, 'you don't know.'

Sir Lancelot looked at him.

'At least we confess our ignorance, Sir Osbert, we do not try to conceal it as you do.'

Sir Osbert reddened.

'All your arguments, all your obstruction, is based on ignorance, you say?' he snarled. 'How d'you expect to make progress like that? The world is growing, expanding, and you are constantly trying to hold it back.'

'If you are saying there is a choice between a dam and an airfield in Zenkali or the saving of Mockery Bird Valley, then I am certainly on the side of preserving the valley,' said Sir Lancelot, 'since – apart from its biological interest – we do not know how important it may be.'

'Important? Important?' said Sir Osbert. 'Do you expect us all to sit around, twiddling our thumbs, doing nothing, in case the valley is of importance? My dear sir, you are mad. This is the twentieth century. There is no place in it for these ecological luxuries . . .'

He broke off, for Hannibal was convulsed with laughter. Sir Osbert stared at him.

'I do apologise,' said Hannibal, with false contriteness, 'but that's one of the finest phrases I've heard in a long time – ecological luxuries . . . I like that. It has a ring of progress about it.'

'Yes,' said Sir Lancelot, drily, 'I fear though, that these . . . er . . . ecological luxuries Sir Osbert talks about affect us all, conservationists or progress planners.'

'I was not aware I had said anything humorous,' said Sir Osbert, tight-lipped.

'No, no, not humorous,' said Sir Lancelot, 'only sad.'

Kingy shifted his great bulk infinitesimally.

'While agreeing with you in principle, Sir Lancelot,' he said, 'I would like, if I may, to try and confine this discussion to our immediate problem. What are your views on the scheme we have come up with?' He looked intently from knight to knight.

'Preposterous,' said Sir Osbert, 'it would hold up the whole scheme interminably. I must make it plain that, representing Her Majesty's Government as I do, we cannot tolerate any shilly-shallying over a matter of such grave importance to the safety not only of the Commonwealth but of Zenkali itself.'

'I am flattered that you think the Russians are casting covetous eyes on such a humble island as Zenkali,' murmured Kingy.

'It's not just Zenkali, it's the whole Indian Ocean,' said

Sir Osbert irritably. 'What I don't seem able to get anyone here to realise is that, for all we know, the peace of the world is being put in jeopardy by a lot of damn trees and stupid birds.'

'I reminded you once before that the Mockery Bird is the personification of the Fangouan God,' said Kingy, frigidly; 'I do hope I won't have occasion to do so again.'

'Apologies,' gulped Sir Osbert.

'And you, Sir Lancelot?' enquired Kingy, removing his basilisk stare from the crushed Sir Osbert.

'Well, the difficulty as I see it is this. Even if you find out that the Mockery Bird can exist outside that tiny niche to which it has been adapted and even if you can do the same with the Ombu tree, you are preserving them, as it were, in a vacuum. Wherever possible, my organisation likes to preserve things *in situ* so I'm afraid we would, in principle, be opposed to the removal of the bird and the tree from the valley. Apart from anything else, I fear you would find the cost involved immense and I cannot conceive where you would get the funds. From your point of view, as a compromise, I can quite see its merits but I fear that my organisation would be opposed to it.'

'It's perfectly ridiculous that perhaps the whole future of the human race should be risked for the sake of a bird and a tree,' snapped Sir Osbert, having recovered from his reprimand.

'It is extraordinary to me that you cannot see that the whole future of the human race depends on conservation, not continual and rapacious exploitation,' said Sir Lancelot angrily, tried beyond endurance.

'Gentlemen, gentlemen,' said Kingy soothingly, 'I quite understand your frustration, but please don't let us lose our tempers. You have both put your point of view to me, and you have both come forward with valuable arguments. Now, I will if I may convey your feelings to the Special Council and, should they wish to question you both, would you be willing to outline your views once again to them?'

'Of course, with pleasure,' said Sir Lancelot.

'More delay,' said Sir Osbert, shrugging, 'but I suppose I must agree, although I should have thought the situation was sufficiently obvious to even . . .'

'Yes?' enquired Kingy, silkily.

'I was about to say that anyone can see how important the airfield is to Zenkali,' said Sir Osbert, hastily.

'And it must not be overlooked how important the Mockery Bird, and, to a lesser extent, the Ombu tree is to us,' said Kingy. 'You will both, I know, be shocked to learn that an attempt was made last night to enter the valley, destroy all the trees and kill all the birds.'

'Good God, no!' cried Sir Lancelot. 'What happened?'

Sir Osbert was silent.

'Fortunately, the plot was discovered and the miscreants apprehended,' said Kingy, smoothly. 'I hope in due course we can find out from them who was behind the attempt.'

Sir Osbert's face had gone a livid white, and then slowly turned red. He cleared his throat.

'Disgusting, disgraceful,' he said, with total lack of conviction, 'd'you know who the people involved were?'

'Unfortunately, a high official was the ring-leader,' said Kingy, sorrowfully, 'he will be deported, of course. But it is the people behind him we are really interested in.'

'Dashed difficult to get these chaps to talk,' said Sir Osbert, 'and even then you can't always take the word of a person like that.'

'Oh, I think he will talk,' said Kingy, 'but I mustn't bore you with all this rigmarole. I will be in touch as soon as there is any news. In the meantime, if there is anything either of you want, don't hesitate to ask. Hannibal or young Foxglove here will do their best to provide it.'

He ushered the two men to the door of the dining-room and handed them over to the major-domo. Then he came back to the table and sat down.

'Well?' he said to Hannibal. 'What do you think?'

'I must say, I warm to Sir Lancelot,' Hannibal admitted. 'He, at least, is an honest man while I doubt the integrity of Sir Osbert.'

'Agreed,' said Kingy. 'However, Looja is still unconscious so we cannot verify that point. There is nothing
really intelligent we can do until Droom reappears and
Looja regains consciousness. I suggest you two go home
and wait on events.'

Peter's head was aching savagely and the whole of the
left side of his face was stabbed with pain and felt
on fire. Hannibal took him by the arm as they left the
Palace.

'I've asked Audrey to lunch with us at my place,' he said.
'I should pack you off to bed but I selfishly feel I may
need you. I can, however, offer you four thousand aspirins,
as much drink as you think is good for you and a decent
meal.'

'Aspirins,' said Peter, 'and to just sit and let my mind go
blank.'

At Hannibal's Audrey fussed round Peter, fed him
aspirins, made him a cool drink and made him immerse
himself, all but his face, in Hannibal's swimming pool.
Then followed a quiet and delicious meal and at the end of
it, sitting on the verandah sipping coffee, Peter began to
feel almost human again. Presently, Hannibal disappeared
into town on some errand, and left the two of them on the
verandah.

'I can't imagine how you must feel, with your face and
everything, but during the last few days I've begun to get
so mentally buffeted that I can't think straight,' said
Audrey. 'I think it's mainly the contrast between our
peaceful existence pre-Mockery Bird and the turmoil
that's ensued since.'

'I know, my mind feels positively unhinged,' said Peter,
moodily. 'I sometimes wonder if it was worthwhile
discovering the bloody valley.'

'Oh, Peter, you can't say that.'

'Well, I don't know. What good's it done? A lot of moody
servicemen roaming around Dzamandzar like stray cats,
picking fights with each other because they can't go to
Mother Carey's. All the churches empty. Ginkas and

Fangouas at loggerheads. Kingy and Hannibal worried stiff. The island infested with awful people like Brewster and that strange bunch of animal lovers. It was such a peaceful place before we mucked it up.'

'Oh, rubbish, we didn't muck it up,' said Audrey, 'and the Fangouas are delighted to have their God back. And you should have seen Dr. F. when I told him the news about the Ombus. He burst into tears, poor man, and ran so fast to tell Stella I couldn't keep pace with him. I think the discovery has done more good than harm.'

'I suppose you're right,' said Peter, 'I only wish I could see the solution to our impasse.'

'The only reason we have this impasse is because Kingy, poor dear, wants to behave as democratically as possible,' said Audrey, 'we all know he could override the Special Council's decision on the dam, but if there is a milder way around it, he's going to try and find it.'

'After the meeting this morning, I'm afraid he's at the end of his tether,' Peter said, gloomily.

Tomba approached them on silent feet.

'Please, sah, Masa Foxglove, Masa Droom done come,' he said.

'Droom!' said Peter, sitting up. 'About time. Bring him here, Tomba, will you.'

'Yes, sah,' said Tomba.

Presently, Droom sidled on to the verandah, smiling his yellow-fanged smile. He was still wearing the same clothes as the last time Peter had seen him, and he did not appear to have bathed or shaved for several days. Over his puny shoulder he carried a large thin collecting case in a canvas covering, and the weight of it pulled his schoolboy body over to one side.

'Ah, Professor Droom, we've been expecting you,' said Peter, with what cordiality he could muster for this unsavoury little man. 'His Majesty and Mr. Oliphant are most anxious to have a talk with you.'

Droom bobbed.

'So they're willing to see me now, are they?' he asked.

'Like everyone else in this world they turn to science as a last resort instead of as a guide. Yes.'

'Do sit down and have a . . . have a lime juice,' said Peter, 'Hannibal won't be more than ten minutes.'

'Yes, a lime juice would be refreshing,' said Droom, seating himself and twining his hairy shanks round one another. His collecting box he kept on his lap and wrapped his arms protectively around it, as though it were a newborn and delicate baby.

'So, thus have the mighty fallen and the Philistine come to heel. Yes,' said Droom, sucking greedily and noisily at the lime juice that Peter poured for him.

'I don't quite follow you, Professor,' said Peter.

Droom held up a long, dirty finger.

'How many times, my dear Foxglove, have I craved audience with the King and Oliphant. Many, many times, you'll allow. Yes? How many times have they evaded me? Many, many times, you'll allow. Yet we men of science do not take offence at rejection by the masses. No. We realise, clear-thinking scientists that we are, that the world is governed by illiterates. Yes. You would scarcely credit it, Mr. Foxglove, but there is scarcely a politician in the world with the simplest grasp of biology. No. Most of them don't even understand how their own kidneys function, let alone anything more complex. No. Mention a word like ecology and they think you are referring to some obscure foreign statesman. Biology to them means the elementary sex instruction they received in secondary school. So is it to be wondered at, my dear Mr. Foxglove, that the last people our rulers ever consult are the appropriate scientists, until they have made a thorough mish-mash of a situation? Then they come crying to us, like a child with a broken toy, asking us to mend it.'

'There is a lot in what you say,' said Peter cautiously. Honesty compelled him to admit that basically he agreed wholeheartedly with Droom, but as the scientist was such an unpleasant person, it went against the grain.

'The situation here, as you may have noticed, is very

complex,' continued Droom, grinning his awful grin and nodding his head portentously.

'Yes, I had noticed,' said Peter drily.

'The discovery that you and Miss Damien made is of the utmost importance,' said Droom, slurping at his lime juice and dribbling it down his chin, 'I mean, of course, of importance to the future of Zenkali. Yes.'

'You mean because of the airfield?' asked Peter.

Droom's eyes became suddenly cunning.

'That and for other reasons,' he said.

'Yes, well, if you can throw any light on our predicament,' Peter started, when Droom interrupted.

'Light, Mr. Foxglove, light, you say? I can illuminate the whole thing for you. Yes,' he said, and gave a wild, shrill giggle. 'Yes. Our rulers have nothing to fear. I have solved their problem for them. In spite of the way I have been treated, ignored, ridiculed, I have laboured on, ceaselessly, tirelessly, night and day, pitting my not inconsiderable wits against the problem, filled with inspiration that amounts to little short of genius . . .'

'D'you mean to say you've solved the problem of Mockery Bird Valley?' said Peter, interrupting Droom's blithe self-analysis.

Droom put down his glass and cuddled his collecting box more closely in his arms.

'I have,' he said, in a whisper which did not conceal his excitement, 'I have, Mr. Foxglove. Here, in this box is the answer to the whole problem.'

Before Peter and Audrey could comment on this, Hannibal returned, stalking on to the verandah and sending his ridiculous sola topi flying down its length to land in a chair with a loud thump.

'Ah, Droom,' he said, smiling, 'my dear fellow, just the chap we want to see.'

'I am not at all surprised,' said Droom, bowing his cringing bow.

'Professor Droom was just explaining that he has solved

the problem of Mockery Bird Valley for us,' explained Peter.

Hannibal gave Droom a sharp look.

'Well, if you've done that you're without doubt the cleverest man in Zenkali,' he said sceptically.

Droom flushed with pleasure.

'Thank you, thank you. That is praise indeed. Yes,' he said.

'Well?' said Hannibal. 'Don't keep us in suspense. What's the answer?'

'The answer lies here, in my box,' said Droom. 'Is there perhaps a table on which I can display things and make a demonstration?'

'Come,' said Hannibal. He led the way into his vast living-room, pulled out a table piled high with books and documents and swept them all on to the floor.

'That big enough for you?' he asked.

'Admirable,' said Droom, and putting his box on to the table, he started to unpack it. He took out several little round tins, with perforations in the lid, a flat black box, a small plant press and a large packet of photographs. Audrey, Peter and Hannibal, standing on one side of the table, watched Droom arranging his paraphernalia like children watching a conjurer prepare a trick.

When he was ready, Droom clasped his hands behind his back, half closed his eyes, threw back his head and, projecting his shrill pedantic voice as though he were lecturing a hall full of students instead of three people the other side of the table, started on his discourse. Revolting though the man was, he had a certain mesmeric power and they listened to him attentively.

'You all know the importance of the Amela tree to the economy of Zenkali so I need not dwell on this. Yes. It is only fairly recently, however, that it was realised that the Amela tree could only be fertilised by the Amela moth, adapted perfectly for its task with its enormously long proboscis.'

Here he paused, opened the flat box and inside, carefully

set and pinned to the cork bottom, were a male and female Amela moth, their long proboscies stretched out in front of them.

'As soon as this discovery was made, it became essential to learn everything about the biology and life cycle of the insect since it should obviously be protected to preserve the Amela tree. Yes.'

He paused and looked at his feet for a moment, gathering his thoughts.

'So I was asked to come out to Zenkali and undertake the task which was one which my past experience and success fully qualified me for. But I know that, like the unravelling of any ecological problem, it would not be easy. No. Now, to begin with, what did we know about the moth? Practically nothing. We knew there was a slight sexual difference between male and female – you will observe the more yellow underwing of the male – and we knew what the adult insect fed on. But its life cycle was shrouded in mystery. And why? Because in the Lepidoptera the plant on which the adult feeds is not, of necessity, the one on which the larva feeds. In the case of the Amela moth, of course, not only were we ignorant of the larva's food plant but the larva itself had not been described. My first task, then, was to solve this problem. It was a simple, though tedious task, to catch several male and female moths, mate them and then, when the resulting eggs hatched – producing a tiny, black larva the size of a pin head – to try them on a wide variety of vegetation. I had no success. In spite of being offered an enormous range of food plants the larvae sickened and died. Yes.'

Droom opened another box. Inside were another pair of Amela moths, a small branch with a cluster of small white eggs encrusted upon it, and a tiny test tube full of spirit in which lolled several minute black caterpillars. Droom pulled at the plant press and opened it.

'Here,' he said, 'are samples of the four hundred and twenty plant species, both indigenous and introduced, which I tried to get the larvae to eat, without success. Yes.

Then, finally, I made my extraordinary discovery.'

He paused, rummaged through the press and produced and held up a large white card on which was mounted a most distinctive, arrow-shaped leaf.

'Here,' he said with great solemnity, 'is the leaf on which the Amela moth lives. It is the leaf of the Ombu tree.'

'Good Lord,' said Hannibal, his eyes narrowing, 'then that means . . .'

'Please, please,' remonstrated Droom, 'let me finish. Yes. Now it so happened that in my researches in the mountains I stumbled across that extraordinary valley shortly after Mr. Foxglove and Miss Damien had discovered it. It was there that I found the larvae of the Amela moth living on the leaves. Yes. But at the same moment of solving one mystery, another one made itself apparent. As you know, before the discovery of the valley, it was thought that there was only one Ombu tree in existence and, though this produced seed, these never germinated. This was a great puzzle to both myself and Dr. Fellugona. Yes. We decided that there must be some catalystic agent necessary to bring about germination, but, until the discovery of the valley I had no conception of what that might be . . . Now, however, I know.'

He paused. His hearers stared at him, silent and fascinated.

Droom fumbled in the collecting bag and produced a photograph which he held up silently.

'The Mockery Bird!' breathed Audrey. 'It's the Mockery Bird!'

'As you say, Miss Damien,' said Droom, inclining his head in majestic agreement, 'the Mockery Bird, yes.'

Hannibal pulled up a chair and sat down.

'Let me see if I have got this right,' he said, 'the Amela moth, on which the whole economy of the island depends because it fertilises the Amela tree, lays its eggs on the Ombu tree. The Ombu tree, in turn, cannot exist without the Mockery Bird?'

'Correct,' said Droom.

'Why?'

'Because,' Droom explained, 'the outer casing of the Ombu seed is exceptionally hard. It is necessary for the seed to be eaten and excreted by the bird before it can germinate.'

Hannibal gave a long, low whistle.

'So, in other words, flood the valley and the whole economy of the island is destroyed?' he said.

'Precisely,' said Droom.

'By God, Droom, you're a genius!' said Peter, leaping to his feet and shaking Droom's hand.

'This means that under no circumstances can we flood the valley and so we can't have the airfield,' crowed Hannibal. 'Oh, frabjous day!'

'Are you sure, Hannibal?' asked Audrey.

'Sure, absolutely sure,' he said, grinning wolfishly, 'it gives Kingy exactly what he wants. Come on, all of you, we're going to the Palace now to tell him. Come on, Professor, pack up your samples and bring 'em too, Kingy will want to see them.'

In a riot of barking dogs, Hannibal rushed them all out to Kingy Carts and they sped away to the Palace.

Kingy listened to Droom's exposition first with incredulity, then with dawning hope and finally with unalloyed joy.

'My very dear Professor Droom,' he said, 'not only I but the whole of Zenkali is more grateful to you than I can explain. We shall not forget our indebtedness to you, I can assure you.'

'Your Majesty is too kind,' said Droom, flushing with delight and corkscrewing his legs in an excess of pleasure.

'Peter, be good enough to pour out five large "Lèse-Majesté",' said Kingy, 'we must have a toast.'

While this was being done, Kingy lay back in his hammock, closed his eyes and lay deep in thought. He roused himself when handed his drink.

'A toast,' he said, solemnly, 'to the Mockery Bird.'

Kingy looked at Droom speculatively.

'Tell me, Professor,' he said, 'would it be possible to bring Ombu trees and Mockery Birds down to Dzamandzar?'

'From the valley? Yes, I see no reason why not,' said Droom, 'as far as I can ascertain the climate and soil are exactly the same. I would not advise you to try and move the whole lot, as they are too well integrated up in the valley, but there is no reason why certain specimens should not be removed. No. The bird is an omnivorous feeder. It just so happens it is particularly fond of the Ombu fruit. The Ombu is a tough sort of tree and is adapted, it would appear, to flourish in rather poor soil. With careful gleaning of the young trees, I see no reason why you should not have plantations of Ombus alongside the Amela plantation in the future. Yes.'

'Splendid, splendid,' said Kingy, looking at Hannibal with a mischievous glint in his eye, 'so we can have a parade after all.'

'Parade?' queried Hannibal.

'Yes,' said Kingy expansively, 'after all, we have here representatives of the armed forces, a wide selection of visitors of one sort or another. Most of them came here expecting a certain amount of pomp and ceremony, so let's give it to them. After all, it's a shame to waste all those marquees, all that bunting, all that careful planning of march-pasts and so on, that Peter so carefully arranged, to say nothing of my new uniform. So, we will have a giant celebration and we will bring down a pair of Mockery Birds and six Ombu trees to take part in the march-past. The Ombus can be planted in the Botanical Gardens and the Mockery Birds can come here to replace those awful, rowdy peacocks of mine. Don't you think that's a good idea?'

They all agreed, even Droom who, after his second 'Lèse-Majesté' was inclined to hiccough and giggle, agreed that the scheme showed merit.

'I will have to call a special meeting of Parliament to tell them,' said Kingy. 'Meanwhile, Peter, would you and

Audrey like to be in charge of the whole operation of the birds and trees?'

'Certainly,' said Peter, delightedly, 'I'd like nothing better.'

'I think we should confine it to one grand parade,' said Kingy, 'followed by a gigantic garden party here, at the Palace. Don't you think?'

'Agreed,' said Hannibal.

'Well, that's settled,' said Kingy, with immense satisfaction. 'Now, another drink, Professor Droom? Oh, surely, after all, it's not every day we can celebrate the work of a genius. That's right, Audrey, my dear, another for you? Splendid.'

For the next three days Audrey and Peter spent all their time up in Mockery Bird Valley. They chose and tagged half a dozen young Ombu trees and these were very carefully dug up by a team of Zenkalis and planted in large half-barrels of soil. This work was supervised by Doctor Fellugona, who proved to be more of a hindrance than a help since he was so frequently overcome with tears of joy and would then have to sit down to recover.

The Mockery Birds presented a slightly different problem. Peter constructed a large cage out of netting and into this he and Audrey lured, with the aid of titbits, a pair of Mockery Birds. The birds entered the cage without any hesitation, and did not appear to suffer in any way from their confinement. Indeed, their chief concern seemed to be that Audrey and Peter, who appeared to have a never-ending supply of delicious things to eat, would vanish forever. As soon as they left the cage, the Mockery Birds would be overcome with alarm and rush up and down, flapping their wings and uttering cries of distress at the disappearance of their food source. When the time came, bribing them to enter a smaller cage for the parade was simplicity itself.

Meanwhile Looja, having regained consciousness and discovering that he was being held on a number of charges, not the least of which was attempted murder, offered to bargain. Did they want to squash the idea of the airfield and dam? If so, he had written proof that Sir Osbert and Lord Hammer were deeply involved financially and both stood to gain an enormous amount of money if their scheme went through. Kingy, displaying a certain low cunning of his own, did not inform Looja that the airfield scheme was now impossible. Instead, he told him that in return for the documents compromising Sir Osbert and Lord Hammer and a full, signed confession of Looja's part in the whole business, he would merely banish Looja from Zenkali, and no charges would be brought against him. Looja seized on this and was on the next boat out of the island. Kingy then summoned both Sir Osbert and Lord Hammer to the Palace for a meeting.

'Looja, whom you both knew,' said Kingy in his most frigid voice, 'was a member of my cabinet. He has now been sacked and banished from Zenkali for a variety of reasons, one of the chief ones being that he was involved in a scheme to push forward the dam and airfield at whatever cost, and from which he stood to make a very large sum of money.'

There was a long and ominous silence, during which Sir Osbert changed colour and Lord Hammer, sweating slightly, built a variety of structures with his wallet, his spectacle case and his cigar case.

'In return for his banishment and in place of the very stiff prison sentence he most certainly would have received, he gave me certain documents that implicate you two . . . er . . . gentlemen.'

'Forgeries, blatant forgeries,' snarled Sir Osbert.

'They must be. You can't trust men like that,' fluted Lord Hammer.

'Nevertheless, they do raise certain doubts in my own mind and would, I feel sure, fill our government with grave misgivings. Fortunately, it will not be necessary for me to make these documents public,' said Kingy.

Sir Osbert took a deep breath of relief and Lord Hammer wiped his gleaming forehead.

'The reason is that Professor Droom has discovered that the continuance of Mockery Bird Valley is essential to the economy of the island and so in no way could we countenance the flooding of the area. However, these documents, together with Looja's signed confession, will stay on file and can be used at some future date, should it be necessary.'

'Things like that are better destroyed,' said Sir Osbert, 'might fall into the wrong hands.'

'Yes, indeed, most dangerous calumnies,' said Lord Hammer.

'They are in my hands,' said Kingy, gently, 'and so are quite safe, I assure you. But now, to other matters. I know the British Government has gone to a lot of trouble and expense sending out representatives of the armed forces and so on, and I would not like to feel that this was money, as it were, down the drain. Now, for us, the rediscovery of our God is a great event and well worth celebrating. Therefore, we are having, on Tuesday next, a grand parade, followed by a garden party here. I do hope, Sir Osbert, that I can count on the members of the armed forces here to take part in the celebrations?'

'Oh, yes . . . yes, of course,' said Sir Osbert, slightly dazed, 'only too glad to help.'

'Yes, indeed,' said Lord Hammer, 'anything we can do.'

'Good,' said Kingy, 'that is most kind of you. I will put young Foxglove in touch with you about the final arrangements, if I may.'

'By all means, by all means,' said Sir Osbert, 'only too glad to lend a hand on such an important occasion.'

'Indeed, yes, quite unique,' said Lord Hammer.

Peter and Audrey came back from Mockery Bird Valley to attend the meeting of Parliament at which Kingy was going to announce the decision about the dam and the airfield. Kingy and Hannibal had spent forty-eight hours cloistered together working out Kingy's speech. They had rewritten it six times and at three o'clock in the morning things were getting acrimonious. Kingy leant forward and grasped Hannibal's wrist in his large hand.

'Dear friend,' he said, softly, 'don't snarl at me like that. We both know that this is going to be the most important speech I shall ever make, because in it I have to state what I believe to be right for my people, and my country. To have you helping me in this, as you have helped me in all things, is an enormous privilege.'

Hannibal looked at him and smiled.

'You are far too generous to be a King,' he said. 'I am a bad-tempered fool. Take no notice of me.'

'My friend, I take notice of you because your counsel is always good. It is based on a love of Zenkali and a certain fondness of me, which flatters me greatly.'

'Well,' said Hannibal uncomfortably, 'don't let it get bruited about. Never do for people to get the idea I liked a wog.'

Kingy threw back his head and laughed.

'Oh, Hannibal,' he said, wiping his eyes, 'if I hadn't got you and the *Zenkali Voice* for amusement, my reign would be so dull.'

Finally, they hammered out the speech and, though the structure owed a lot to Hannibal, the sentiments embodied in it were entirely Kingy's.

Because of the occasion, everyone was wearing their most flamboyant robes. The crescent seats thus became as brilliant and multicoloured as a patchwork quilt. Kingy himself was wearing a scarlet and yellow robe of such brilliance that it dazzled the eye. He walked into the room slowly, bowing solemnly from left to right, looking like some newly emerged flamboyant butterfly. He reached the great throne and settled himself in it with care, arranging the folds of his robe to advantage. Then he took out his spectacles and settled them on his nose and carefully arranged the notes for his speech. He rose to his feet and stood silent for a moment, huge and majestic, his robes hanging from him like victorious banners.

'Friends,' he began in his deep, rolling voice, 'today I

bring you news that is not only astonishing but is of the utmost importance to you all and to the future of Zenkali. Today I wish to tell you we, on this island, live in an age of miracles. We are fortunate because to most people in this world miracles are past history, generally to be doubted.'

He paused, and you would not have thought that so many people packed into the great room could have been so silent.

'We will have to do without the airfield,' said Kingy, taking off his spectacles and using them like a baton to emphasise his points, 'but the reason that we will have to do without it is that, if we had gone ahead with it, we would have plunged Zenkali into economic chaos – all would have suffered, none would have escaped. Let me explain how we discovered this in time.'

He put his glasses on, consulted his notes, and then looked up.

'With the rediscovery of the Mockery Bird, we reinstated the god of the Fangouas. It has seldom happened that a people are allowed to rediscover a god thought to have vanished. But here we have a double miracle, for we have a god that has been working unseen and unsupported as the best gods should do, for the benefit of the whole of Zenkali, for Fangouas and Ginkas alike. To Professor Droom, whom you all know, goes the credit for a breath-taking discovery. You all know the importance of the Amela tree to Zenkali and, because of its activities, the Amela moth as well. Professor Droom has been working here trying to find out the life history of this important moth, for without the moth we lose the tree and unless we knew where the moth bred, it was impossible for us to protect it adequately. This place has been found.'

He paused again to allow his words to sink in.

Hannibal, watching him with respect and affection, realised how difficult this speech was for him. He had to explain without arrogance, to coerce with gentleness, and to try and depict the problem as simply and as colourfully as a child's alphabet.

'The home of the Amela moth, the place in which it lays its eggs, is none other than Mockery Bird Valley,' he said. Then, as a surprised ripple of whispers filled the room, he held up one huge hand for silence and continued, 'But that is not an end of the story. The Amela moths, when they hatch into caterpillars, feed on the Ombu tree.'

He took off his glasses and pointed them at the assembly.

'Professor Droom has tried to get the caterpillars to feed on four hundred and twenty different plants,' said Kingy, emphasising this by holding up his hands, fingers widespread. 'No less than four hundred and twenty choices of food were they given but nevertheless they sickened and died. It was not until the Professor entered Mockery Bird Valley and saw the caterpillars feeding in hundreds on the Ombu trees, that he realised the significance of this valley.'

Kingy took out a large, white silk handkerchief, patted his brow with it and then let it dangle from his fingers like a fly whisk and used it to underline his points.

'You are probably thinking to yourselves, what could be more extraordinary than the story as it stands? Here we were, dependent for our wealth and happiness on a moth, and this small creature, in its turn, was and is dependent on a tree that we thought had long vanished from our island. Now we have rediscovered the tree and at the same time, Professor Droom made the miraculous discovery that the Ombu tree is dependent upon no less than the Mockery Bird for its existence. That is why I say that we have a God that works. When the fruit and its seed are dropped from the tree, the Mockery Birds eat them. The seed passes through the bird and in the process is softened so that when it reappears, it can germinate.'

Kingy tucked his handkerchief away, took off his glasses and surveyed the assembly for a long moment.

'Is it not salutary to us all here to realise that our fortunes rest, firstly, on a moth?'

Here, he held out a huge chocolate-coloured hand that, so graceful was he, became a velvety dark moth with – as his hand turned – a delicate pink underside to the wing.

'Secondly on a tree.'

Here he spread his arms wide and became startlingly like an Ombu tree.

'And thirdly,' he thundered, holding out an admonishing finger, 'does it not make you all feel humble to realise that your fate is dependent on a bird's digestion?'

The members of the Assembly whispered and gesticulated to each other.

'So we are linked together like a chain,' said Kingy, interlacing his fingers and tugging at them by way of illustration; 'the Amela tree, the moth, the Ombu tree, the Mockery Bird and, finally, us. None of us can do without the other; without the help of these trees and these creatures all our hopes for the future of Zenkali wither and perish. We can do without an airfield. We cannot do without the help of Nature.'

Then he took off his glasses and, with enormous dignity, he strode out of the Assembly, leaving it in a turmoil of discussion and excitement.

The grand parade was a huge success. The *Zenkali Voice* stated: '*King to have God in Palace Garden*'. This remarkable headline set the seal on the whole affair.

The parade was led by Kingy in his huge ornate Kingy Cart, preceded by the band of the Loamshires playing the Zenkali National Anthem. This was based on a catchy tune from *Maid of the Mountains*, slightly amended by Kingy in his bath. It had stirring, pidgin English words invented by Hannibal, the first verse of which went:

> *Dis, na we, Dis na we, Zenkali, Zenkali,*
> *Dis na our own, our own countree.*
> *Zenkali, Zenkali.*

They were followed by two cleft stick bearers, carrying between them a banner reading 'Zenkali for Eve', owing to the fact that the lady employed to embroider it gave birth suddenly and unexpectedly and had, therefore, to down tools. After them, in a halo of pink dust, came a huge cart drawn by six specially groomed and glossy zebu. In it rode

Peter and Audrey with the large cage containing the Mockery Birds who were so enchanted to discover such a host of humans who might give them titbits that they ran up and down the cage shouting 'HA *ha* HA *ha*' and rattling their beaks together with machine-gun-like rapidity. All the Fangouas were enormously impressed with the vociferousness of the newly discovered god. After this came another beautifully-carved Kingy Cart, containing the Governor and Lady Emerald. The Governor was in full dress uniform, with plumed hat and sword.

The whole of Zenkali formed a multicoloured channel through which this procession ran. The lovely smell of massed, oiled and carefully dressed humanity was overpowering, combined as it was with the smell of flowers, zebu, curry, sunshine, and overall mellowness; the sort of ambrosial smell you get when you open a vintage keg of wine. Through this lane of bronze, chocolate, copper-coloured faces, lit, as though by lightning, by the flash of white teeth, and a forest of clapping pink palms, came the procession. The delight and happiness of the populace was almost tangible.

Hard on the heels of the Governor and Lady Emerald came a cart on which reposed six large barrels, donated by the owner and staff of Mother Carey's Chickens, containing a half-dozen baby Ombu trees, short and pot-bellied and waving twisted branches. Together with them in the cart rode Droom, looking more macabre than ever since he had donned a pin-stripe flannel suit, and Doctor Fellugona who sobbed for joy into a gigantic white handkerchief and constantly fondled the Ombus' trunks as if to reassure them. Behind them, tastefully interspersed with a glittering array of well drilled troops, came all the visiting dignitaries in Kingy carts. Sir Osbert and Lord Hammer, looking as though they had survived, with difficulty, the Black Hole of Calcutta. Sir Lancelot and the Hon. Alf, waving and smiling at the crowds as if all of them were in *Debrett*. The Press, who were in a regrettable state of intoxication, and the rest of the conservation contingent followed. The Swede looked as morose as only a Swede can look when surrounded by cheering, clapping, hysterically happy humanity; and the Swiss who, having got his watch repaired, kept referring to it, terrified that it might have stopped. Harp, who together with Jugg had obviously been at the Zenkali Nectar, had procured an enormous Stars and Stripes from somewhere and lay back in the Kingy cart enveloped in it, beaming and waving at the crowd. It was a happy, slightly uncontrolled procession in the best tradition of the Tropics. There was one tiny disturbing moment when the platform, so carefully designed and set up by Peter for the T.V. team, became inundated by excited Zenkalis who found that this added height gave them a new perspective on the parade. Immediately the rather slender edifice was swamped by some two hundred and fifty over-excited Zenkalis. Brewster, maddened beyond belief, tried to fend them off by hitting the first ones with his script, but he was soon lost underfoot.

'I am the B.B.C.,' he kept screaming, but this credential meant nothing to the Zenkalis. Blore and his extremely expensive camera were swept off the top of the platform and fell fifteen feet to the ground. Faint cries like 'you have no idea of the value of publicity' and 'we're B.B.C. *not* I.T.V.' went unheeded as the edifice that Peter had designed for two people foundered and crashed. The Zenkalis, of course, fell smooth and supple as eels. Most of them, however, landed on top of Brewster, who received a broken collar bone, numerous bruises and a black eye.

The crowd of Fangouas and Ginkas sang, shouted, played drums and pipes, and danced with the boneless elegance that can only be achieved by someone with a dark skin.

Gradually the procession reached the gates of the Palace, where the guards came smartly to attention and presented arms, as first the band, then Kingy and the rest of the entourage swept through. The crowd came to a halt, laughing, cheering and peering through the wrought-iron gates, their faces shining like a bank of aubergines in a basket.

Once everyone had been decanted into the brilliant, sunlit gardens of the Palace, the festive atmosphere accelerated.

The two over-excited Mockery Birds were now released and the first thing the male did was to dig its beak into Kingy's leg. (The next day the *Zenkali Voice* had the headline '*King pecked by God*'.) From then on, the party was a riotous success. Gallons of Lèse-Majesté were consumed, plates of venison and suckling-pig were devoured, and huge dishes of multicoloured vegetables. Kingy seemed to be everywhere, talking to everyone, and his great laugh rolled around his guests like friendly thunder.

Peter and Audrey had suddenly discovered that they were in love. So, hand in hand, they drifted through the crowd.

'You know,' said Peter, filling Audrey's glass for the fourth time, 'this is rather like swimming on a reef – you drift from place to place and odd bits of sea life are revealed.'

'Um,' said Audrey, 'let's swim on a bit.'

Hand in hand, daisy-chained together, they drifted on.

They discovered the unlikely combination of Harp and Jugg, lying side by side in deck chairs. Harp was just coming to the end of a spirited impression of a bull moose calling to its mate, which involved a lot of ululation and vibrating of the Adam's apple.

'Yes,' said Jugg, moodily as the last sonorous notes died away, 'we 'ad several of them once. But they all died. Tricky things, moose. Always dying on you. I'm trying to go in more for things that don't keep dying. Elephants are good, of course, but once you've seen one elephant, you've seen the lot, 'aven't you? You really need things with a bit of class to capture the public's imagination, like. But all these animals wot '*ave* got a bit of class go and die on you – finicky bloody things, I can tell you.'

'Manatee,' said Harp. 'Manatee is what you want. I

remember when I and my then wife, Mamie, went down to Florida and swam with the manatee. And Mamie, my then wife, said to me, Hiram, she said, they look almost human. Put a bikini on them and they'd look exactly like your mother, she said.'

'And wot did you say to 'er?' asked Jugg, astonished.

'I didn't say anything,' said Harp with dignity. 'I just divorced her.'

Audrey and Peter drifted on.

They came upon the Hon. Alf endeavouring to explain to Droom a long and complicated story that involved three dukes, a rajah and a princeling of sorts.

'And I always say that if you get the *right* people involved,' he bleated, 'your task in conservation is made immeasurably easier.'

'The right people to get involved are the scientists,' said Droom, 'without them all you other people are helpless.'

'There I beg leave to differ,' said the Hon. Alf, 'there I really do disagree. If you don't get the support of the right class of people your task is made more difficult.'

'Take my remarkable discovery here,' said Droom, not listening, 'without me where would Zenkali be? When my paper on the whole thing is published, it will create a scientific furore.'

'Yes, yes,' said the Hon. Alf, 'but you have not only saved the Mockery Bird and the Ombu tree but also the Amela and, as well, you have got the *King* involved.'

'That's of small imporvance,' said Droom, 'they can do what they like now with the birds and trees. The important thing is that I shall publish this paper which will vindicate me in scientific eyes. Do you realise, because there was a small error in my estimation of the density of tsetse flies per acre in my paper on the N'goro N'goro crater – a mistake due entirely to my assistant's imbecility, I might say – I have been pilloried by the academic world? Now I have paid them back in full measure. When my paper is published . . .'

Peter and Audrey drifted on.

Their next stop was the Governor and Lady Emerald, in incomprehensible communication with Carmen.

'What Hi say,' said Carmen, 'his that Hi'm glad all them birds and trees 'ave been vindicated, Hi really ham, and Hi tell you no word of a lie, Your Hexellencyness.'

'Extraordinary – most important – God and so forth – everyone to be commended – salt of the earth – ' said the Governor.

'And Hi'll confess to you, your Hexellency, that apart from all the political complications, Hi was 'aving trouble with my girls. Getting restive, they was, hin spite of believing in the cause. Well, you know 'ow hit his, hit's like not taking your dog out for a walk.'

'Noble body of women – backbone of Empire – extraordinary,' said the Governor.

Lady Emerald homed into the party by plugging her ear trumpet into her ear.

'You must come to lunch more often,' she said with considerable bonhomie, 'we don't see nearly enough of you and your charming daughters.'

'Well, ta,' said Carmen, going pink with delight, 'hif you're quite sure you want 'em hat Government House. Hi mean, Hi'll see they behave proper and that and they won't worry the gentlemen.'

'Salt of the earth,' said the Governor.

Audrey and Peter drifted on, collecting another drink en route. As they passed, they heard a scowling Captain Pappas holding forth to Lord Hammer.

'Yes,' Pappas was saying, 'so I've gots all these papers that bastard Looja gave me to keep safe for him. This was before I knew what he was doing, see.'

'I see,' said Lord Hammer, 'and what exactly are those papers?'

Pappas scowled even more ferociously.

'I dunno,' he said. 'I don'ts read people private papers. But now the bastard's left the island, what am I to do with them? Whats you think?'

He fixed his little black eyes on Lord Hammer, an expression of glowing innocence on his face.

'Perhaps,' said Lord Hammer, delicately, 'if we examined them *together* we might be able to reach a conclusion as to what should be done, don't you think?'

'Okey doke,' said Pappas, giving a wide, gold-toothed smile of patent untrustworthiness, 'I'll brings them round to you tomorrow, eh?'

'How has he got papers of Looja's?' whispered Audrey in amazement.

'He's a Greek,' said Peter, 'that is sufficient explanation.'

They next ran up against a gaggle of Swiss from the conservationist element, being given a long, slightly faulty, lecture on European history by the Admiral.

'And there we were at Jutland with you chaps on the right of us,' he said, his eyes watering with excitement, 'all spread out . . .'

'But we have no navy, sir,' said the Swiss in an agony of precision.

'No navy?' said the Admiral, aghast. 'You can't have no navy – everyone's got to have a navy.'

'But Switzerland is a small country,' the Swiss said, cupping his hands like one depicting a bird's nest. 'She is locked in by ze land.'

'Dangerous stuff, land,' said the Admiral. 'Take my advice and fight your way out.'

Audrey and Peter drifted on. Kingy, in an exquisite robe, beamed down on Sir Lancelot, who had got so carried away by the general air of conviviality that he had permitted an occasional smile to steal furtively across his face.

'I'm glad,' he said graciously, 'that I was able to bring you good tidings from the Duke of Penzance. He particularly asked to be remembered to you.'

'Dear Bertram,' said Kingy, his face smoothed of all expression, 'he was my fag at Eton, you know. They used to call him "bottoms up Bertram" for some reason I could never fathom.'

Sir Lancelot's flinch was almost imperceptible. He took a firmer hold on his glass and gazed about him.

'I'm so delighted that we have managed to solve this problem so satisfactorily,' he said.

'In Zenkali we generally manage our own affairs with some satisfaction to the island,' said Kingy; 'however, may I say, Sir Lancelot, that at no time did I consider you to be anything but constructive and sympathetic.'

'Thank you, thank you,' said Sir Lancelot, flushing with pleasure, 'I'm delighted to hear it, your Majesty. We conservationists get a fair amount of stick, one way and the other. It's very difficult to get people to understand that we are, in fact, trying to act in their best interests. People tend to think that we're just fussy animal lovers, who want to put animals before humanity. That is not the case at all, for the protection of Nature, the protection of the world *is* the protection of humanity.'

'I quite agree,' said Kingy, 'and I think what happened here underlines what you say. By not understanding the biological architecture of our island, we could have destroyed our economy and ourselves.'

'Indeed,' said Sir Lancelot, 'this situation here is a microcosm of what is happening all over the world but generally with much less happy results.'

'We are lucky in Zenkali that we have the power to make important decisions,' said Kingy, his eyes twinkling. 'I have always felt that power in most parts of the world was too diffused to be effective. Democracy is all very well in its way but occasionally you can get more done with a bit of benign dictatorship.'

'I suppose so,' said Sir Lancelot, doubtfully.

'And here,' said Kingy, 'is the happy couple who are responsible for it all.'

He threw his arms round the shoulders of Peter and Audrey.

'Audrey, my dear, you're looking particularly radiant today,' he said, 'can it be that you have decided to make an honest man of Foxglove here?'

'Yes,' said Audrey, smiling, 'I decided that what he needs most urgently is a nagging wife.'

'He should consider it a privilege to be nagged by someone as beautiful as you,' said Kingy, 'and I can tell you a secret: when the nuptials have been consummated, a very grateful island is going to give you an Amela plantation as a wedding gift.'

'Oh, Kingy,' said Audrey, 'that is generous of you.'

'No, not generous, far-sighted,' said Kingy, 'for I hope it will ensure that you make Zenkali your home always.'

'Would it be considered Lèse Majesté if I kissed you?' asked Audrey.

'It would be considered Lèse-Majesté if you didn't,' said Kingy, firmly.

'Peter, come on, let's go and tell Daddy,' said Audrey.

'Yes, and tell that father of yours that if he writes any more scurrilous stuff about me I'll run him off the island. "*King has god in Garden*" indeed. That sort of thing can ruin a king's reputation, I'll have you know,' said Kingy.

Under a giant of a Bougainvillaea, sizzling with insect life, they found Hannibal and the Rev sitting, swinging gently, in Kingy's hammock. Beside them, squatting on the grass, was Simon Damien.

'We have news for you, ancient and revered parent,' said Audrey, 'our gorgeous Kingy is going to give Peter and me an Amela plantation.'

'An Amela plantation, is it?' said Simon, 'I'm not having any daughter of mine bringing disgrace and ruination to her old father by blatantly living in sin on an Amela plantation under his very nose.'

'Who said anything about living in sin?' asked Audrey.

'D'you mean to say a daughter of mine has had the stupidity to allow that callow youth to talk her into wedlock? Holy Mother of God, that's almost worse than living in sin.'

'I'm all for a bit of sin,' said the Rev practically, 'after all, if there was no sin in the world, I'd be out of a job. But I hope you're both serious? Can I wed you?'

'Where else would they tie the knot?' asked Hannibal. 'I suppose this means that, not only have I lost the only girl I really loved but I'm stuck with you as my assistant for the next ninety years?'

'God willing,' said Peter.

'Well,' said Hannibal, 'now all this ridiculous fuss that you were responsible for has died down, you'll have some time on your hands, if that wretched girl lets you alone. So I have a task for you. I am thinking of bringing out a new and updated edition of my book.'

'What book?' asked Peter.

'*Zenkali, a Fragmentary Guide for the Casual Visitor,*' said Hannibal.

'Did you write that?' asked Peter, astonished.

'Who else on this benighted island would have the erudition and enormous command over the English language to achieve such a mammoth literary work?' asked Hannibal.

'Are you really going to update it?' asked Peter.

'Yes,' said Hannibal, 'if you'll help.'

'Of course, but you won't mind if we have our honeymoon first?'

'Honeymoon? You haven't even wedded the girl yet,' said Hannibal.

'Well, we've decided that we'll do it the other way round,' said Audrey, apologetically, 'we're going to have the honeymoon first and the wedding afterwards.'

'Oh, St. Paul and all the Apostles, that a daughter of mine should stand there proclaiming her sins to all the world,' said Simon, beating his brow, 'it's only because of the purity of me soul that I can endure the unendurable.'

'And where do you propose to go for this strange pre-nuptial assignation, may I ask?' said Hannibal.

'I know,' said the Rev, leaping out of the hammock, 'only place they could go, gosh darn it. The valley.'

EPILOGUE

'Can't you get any closer?' he asked.

'I can't, Peter,' she said, 'you've already managed to cram two bodies into a sleeping bag designed for one. How much closer do you want to get?'

'Much closer,' he said, contentedly.

The moonlight lit the strange fat, twisted shapes of the Ombu trees around them, and the thickets between were throbbing with fireflies.

'When did you decide you first loved me?' asked Peter, having made up his mind to be banal.

'When I first saw you,' said Audrey, in surprise. 'Why?'

Peter shifted himself cautiously on to one elbow and peered down at her face.

'When you first saw me?' he said, astounded. 'What d'you mean, when you first saw me?'

'When you walked into Hannibal's that morning. You looked so adorable – like – like a forlorn puppy.'

'Thank you,' said Peter, coldly, 'that's probably the most romantic thing that's ever been said to me.'

'But I mean a *nice* puppy,' Audrey protested, 'like the ones you see in the pet shop windows that you can't resist.'

'I see. All woolly and cuddly?'

'Yes, and sort of flopperty and helpless. And you know they'll wee on the floor and chew up your slippers, but you don't mind.'

'Have I, in your presence, ever shown any desire to wee

on the floor?' asked Peter, with interest. 'Or indeed to masticate any footwear you possess?'

'You know perfectly well what I mean,' said Audrey, 'don't be difficult.'

There was silence.

'You know what happens to those adorable puppies in pet shop windows when you buy them?' asked Peter.

'What?'

'They grow up to be wolves.'

'I've always wanted a wolf of my own,' said Audrey dreamily.

'Well, I didn't fall in love with you immediately,' said Peter, smugly; 'I admit I found you attractive, though.'

'If you call looking at me with all the lewd lechery of an Italian youth who's just attained puberty finding me attractive, I suppose you're right,' said Audrey.

'Now look here,' said Peter, indignantly, 'I did *not* look at you with lewd lechery.'

'You did. With your first look you not only stripped me but had me into the bed,' said Audrey, 'it was really a very nice sensation.'

'I don't agree with you,' said Peter, austerely, 'I have never looked at a woman like that in my life.'

'That's what I thought,' said Audrey, 'that's why I liked it.'

'I do not intend that we should have our first quarrel in a sleeping bag,' said Peter, 'there is not room to quarrel properly in a sleeping bag. One can't flounce.'

'There's scarcely room to do *anything* in a sleeping bag,' said Audrey, plaintively.

'Oh yes there is,' said Peter, 'I'll show you.'

There was a long silence, broken only by small noises of satisfaction.

'My own, very private wolf,' said Audrey at last.

'Moreover one who, I think you will admit, shows a certain agility in restricted circumstances,' said Peter.

'Marvellous agility,' Audrey agreed.

The moon moved slowly giving life to the Ombu trees,

making them move and seem to change position, to hunch in conspiratorial ancient groups. The fireflies, like tiny lantern bearers, illuminated their small world with green pulses of light. In the huge immensity of the sky, the stars glittered like sun-touched icicles and the moon slowly turned from marigold to mushroom white. In the depths of the Ombu trees a voice, sleepily as a first cock-crow, was lifted.

'Ha *ha*,' it called. 'Ha *ha*?'

Softly and interrogatively.

Another voice, as though to soothe, cried, 'Ha *ha* Ha *ha*.'

And then in a plaintive, sweet churning from the shadows of the trees, rose the cry on all sides 'Ha *ha* . . . Ha *ha* . . . Ha *ha*.'

'Listen,' said Peter, 'd'you know what that is?'

'What?' she asked.

'It's the Mockery Birds,' said Peter, 'having the last laugh.'

TAILPIECE

For those readers who are interested, may I say that
although this book has been written in a light-hearted vein,
all things described in it have happened or are happening in
different parts of the world.

In case anyone should think that the link between the
Amela tree and the Ombu tree, the Mockery Bird and the
Amela Moth is exaggerated, may I point out that there are
many more complicated associations in Nature. A lovely
one that was discovered recently is the case of a bird called
the Oropendola, which makes colonies of long, hanging
basket-like nests in trees in South America. In certain
areas, there is a fly which goes into the nest and lays its eggs
on the nestling Oropendolas. These then hatch into grubs
which start to devour the baby birds. However, there is a
wasp found in these areas which feeds avidly upon the fly,
its eggs and grubs that are laid on the baby birds. The adult
Oropendolas seem in some way to realise the benefit of the
wasp to their brood and so allow it access to their nests to
clean their babies. However, in a different area, where the
parasitic fly is not found, the Oropendolas do not tolerate
the wasp and will kill it if it goes anywhere near their
nesting sites.

The idea of the rediscovery of the Mockery Bird is based
on an incident that happened a few years ago in New
Zealand. There, in a remote valley – which I was lucky
enough to spend some time in – they rediscovered the
Takahe or Notornis, a bird which they had thought to be
long extinct; so there is hope that even today, while we are

with one hand destroying, with the other we may discover a population of tiny dinosaur lurking in a swamp.

The people in this book are, of course, imaginary but inevitably are an amalgam of characters I have met throughout my travels. The bad people in the book are, of course, modelled on bad people everywhere, some of whom I have met. If they recognise themselves, I hope it gives them pause for thought.

Finally, may I say this. If you have found the book amusing and if you appreciate the fact that the world and its wildlife is being steadily and ruthlessly decimated by what we call progress, I wonder if you would like to help us in the work that we are doing here at the Jersey Wildlife Preservation Trust? Here, we are endeavouring to build up colonies of almost extinct species, to save them, and to train people from different parts of the world in the arts of captive breeding, in order to help these animals that are being edged into oblivion by our unthinking rapaciousness. The fees for belonging to our Trust are modest but we can do with all the support that we can get in trying to help the wildlife of the world. We are pleading on behalf of these plants and creatures because they cannot plead for themselves and it is, after all, your world which we are asking you to help preserve. If you write to me at our headquarters:

Jersey Wildlife Preservation Trust,
Les Augres Manor
Trinity
Jersey. Channel Islands

we would be delighted to send you full details, and welcome you as a member.

We have many Mockery Birds and Ombu trees in the world that will be most grateful for your support. Indeed, without it they cannot exist.

G.D., Autumn 1981